Farm TO TROUBLE

A FARM *to* TABLE MYSTERY

AMANDA FLOWER

Poisoned Pen
PRESS

For Shiloh Seymour, who let me use her name

Published by Poisoned Pen Press, an imprint of Sourcebooks
P.O. Box 4410, Naperville, Illinois 60567-4410
(630) 961-3900
sourcebooks.com

Library of Congress Cataloging-in-Publication Data

Names: Flower, Amanda, author.
Title: Farm to trouble / Amanda Flower.
Description: Naperville, Illinois : Poisoned Pen Press, [2021] | Series: A
   farm to table mystery
Identifiers: LCCN 2020021116 (paperback) | (epub)
Subjects: GSAFD: Mystery fiction.
Classification: LCC PS3606.L683 F37 2021 (print) | DDC 813/.6--dc23
LC record available at https://lccn.loc.gov/2020021116

Printed and bound in Canada.
MBP 10 9 8 7 6 5 4 3 2

Chapter One

It smelled like home before I even saw it. I caught a whiff of freshly cut hay and plowed earth when I got off the highway and drove down the long country road to the small town of Cherry Glen, Michigan. Huckleberry, my pug, held his flat nose in the air as if he recognized it too. With the top down on my red convertible, the country breeze caressed his small ears. The wind was in my long blond hair—hair that remained blond due mostly to my ridiculously expensive stylist back in Los Angeles.

Just before I crossed the line that marked the town limits, an enormous billboard with a photo of wind turbines on it came into view. *"Support Cherry Glen Wind Farm"* ran along the top of it.

Huckleberry looked at me questioningly with his round brown eyes as we whizzed past pine trees and rolling farms. We weren't in California anymore, that was for sure. Huckleberry was a pug used to palm trees and traffic. He would get none of that in Cherry Glen. Although, like in California, there was plenty of sand. Beyond Traverse City, the closest city nearby, was the Sleeping Bear Dunes along the shores of Lake Michigan. There was more than enough sand there for a beach-starved pug even if the lake water was too cold to touch for nine months of the year.

I drove through the center of Cherry Glen. When I had grown up in this town, it was just a few mismatched buildings made of brick and weathered boards. Today, the downtown was quaint but bustling. Small businesses and shops lined the street. The two largest buildings held Fields Brewing Company, in an old grain warehouse, and Michigan Street Theater. The theater had been abandoned when I was a child. To my surprise, the marquee was lit and proclaimed the upcoming dates for Shakespeare's *The Tragedy of Julius Caesar*.

It was just after seven on a Friday evening in the middle of July. The sun wouldn't set for another two hours, and townspeople and tourists ambled up the new-looking sidewalk. Moms pushed babies and strollers, and school-age children ran in and out of the general store. The tourists, or fudgies as we called them growing up, were easy to pick out from their Michigan-mitten T-shirts and crisp shorts. We called them fudgies because most of them would travel up north to Mackinac Island and the U.P. in search of fudge before heading back down to wherever they came from. They stuck out from the farmers. The farmers wore their dusty jeans and work boots going about their day-to-day.

The town appeared to be thriving. It was nothing like the beaten-down, blue-collar hometown I remembered. Time had been kind to Cherry Glen. I hoped I would find the same at Bellamy Farm.

At the end of the street was the town hall, a modest brick building with a large Palladian window over the front door and a WWII Sherman tank sitting on its postage stamp-sized lawn. The tank had been a gift to the town from a collector who died before I was born. It was the only structure on Michigan Street that looked exactly the same.

I could distinctly remember climbing on the tank as a child with my father looking on. That was over twenty year ago, what felt like a lifetime, and it almost seemed like a memory from a movie I had seen rather than a moment in my own childhood. Despite the town's improvements, it still had the same down-home feel to it, and anyone walking along the sidewalk would take one look at me and know I didn't belong. Didn't matter that I had lived in Cherry Glen for the first twenty-three years of my life. I'd been gone for fifteen years. My capped teeth, blond highlights, red convertible, and portable dog belied that fact. Very few people would know the *new* me, as I cut most of my friends out of my life when I left to recover from what I had lost. In many ways, my father and the land were my remaining ties to this place.

Distracted by the tank, I was driving a little bit too fast. I had been on the road for countless hours and wanted to be over and done with this last leg of the trip.

That was my mistake. I should have slowed down going through the town. It was an afterthought I regretted immediately when I heard the sound of sirens behind me. I would have hoped at thirty-eight years old the sound of sirens behind me would no longer make me jump like a sixteen-year-old with a permit. Sadly, that was not the case.

I looked in my rearview mirror and saw a police officer on a motorcycle coming at me at a fast clip. I shared a look with a bewildered Huckleberry as I pulled to the side of the road. Speeding with California plates through Cherry Glen was a very bad idea.

I watched as the large man climbed off his motorcycle and hitched up his pants. He removed his helmet and laid it on the seat. He wasn't in a hurry to give me a ticket. He wanted me to sweat it out. If how damp my palms felt was any indication, his strategy worked. I wiped them on my skirt and reached for my small clutch next to Huckleberry on the passenger seat.

I had my license, registration, and insurance card out by the time the officer reached me. He was mostly bald but had tufts of hair springing sporadically out of his head. His hair was gray, but he had a wide, black mustache that was still dark, so I knew it had to be dyed. He looked familiar, but it had been fifteen years since I'd left Cherry Glen, so I couldn't quite place how I knew him.

"Well, well, look what the cat dragged in. Shiloh Bellamy. I didn't think we would ever see the likes of you around here again."

I grimaced.

"Remove your sunglasses, please."

"Oh, sorry," I said and took off my aviator glasses. I blinked in the bright sun as the police officer came back into focus. On his chest, a bright silver star read "Chief." Great. Not only did I get pulled over before I reached Bellamy Farm, but it was by the chief of police. What a terrific way to start my triumphant return home. It was time to negotiate, which, as a television producer who had spent most of my career trapped between a studio and directors and actors, I did best. "I am so sorry. I know I was going too fast through town. I wasn't thinking, not that that's any excuse. I'm just in a hurry to get to my father."

"I know all about Sully Bellamy not feeling well. I was the one who took him to the hospital after his last fall." He gave me a beady look when he said that, like it should have been me who took my father to the hospital. I bit the inside of my lip. He was probably right about that. I had wanted to be there, but meetings in New York kept me away.

"Thank you for doing that. My dad always speaks highly of his neighbors. I haven't been around as much as I would like, and I'm grateful to the community for rallying around him." I blinked back crocodile tears.

"You don't remember me, do you?" the chief asked.

I dropped the tears schtick and felt my face redden. This cop looked like he didn't do well with any funny business, so I simply waited.

He hooked his thumbs through his belt loops, and as he did, the gun on his hip shifted. "Chief Randy Killian, but everyone just calls me Chief Randy."

The name Killian immediately struck me—this was Quinn Killian's father. The Killians were a prominent family in the town. And the chief's son, Quinn, had been my fiancé Logan's best friend. I hadn't seen Quinn since Logan's funeral because I packed up the beat-up Jeep I owned at the time and left for California the next day.

I swallowed. I knew coming back to Cherry Glen would remind me of Logan and the guilt I carried over his death. I just didn't know it would be before I even reached my family farm.

"Nice to see you again, Chief Randy." I flashed him my thousand-watt smile—the one that made me believe spending three months' salary on it was worth it. "Again, I'm really sorry about speeding, but you know how my father is unwell, so you can understand my haste. I should have been here yesterday, but I got trapped tying up some loose ends and left later than expected..." I shouldn't be babbling to the police officer about my problems. What he said next proved that.

"You're still getting a ticket, missy. I don't abide by speeding in my town."

The smile clearly didn't work. Away from the bright lights of LA, my veneers were just another waste of money. I handed him my license.

Huckleberry and I sweated in the sun as Chief Randy took his good old time writing up my ticket. As I sat there, I remembered what summer in the Midwest was really like. Hot and humid with no ocean breeze to take the edge off. Huckleberry's tongue hung out as he stared at me. His face bore a look of betrayal, eyes narrowed and nose extra scrunched, as if he was wondering why I brought him to this steamy place. Then again, it could have been gas. You never knew with Huckleberry; he was a pug after all.

Chief Randy came back and handed me my ticket. "You go light on the pedal, all right?"

I nodded dutifully.

"Now, go see your pops. He needs you right now more than you even know." His black eyebrows, which were almost as impressive as his mustache, dipped down in concern.

I wondered what that meant. I knew my father needed me. He asked me to come back to Cherry Glen to help him with the family farm, and I was here, wasn't I? I'd left my career behind in California.

Chief Randy smacked the side of my car like he would a cow he wanted to move out to pasture and ambled back to his motorcycle. I waited for him to ride away before I pulled out onto the empty road.

I glanced at Huckleberry. "Huck, we aren't in LA anymore."

His eyes rolled into the back of his head, and his long tongue licked his flat nose.

Chapter Two

The drive to my family farm took twenty minutes. I could have gotten there faster since there was no traffic to speak of on the road, but I wasn't going to be caught speeding again by Chief Randy. I tried to push the speeding ticket out of my head and concentrate on what I had come to do: help my father and save the farm. For years, I'd been trying to talk my father into moving the farm in a new direction, but he wanted nothing to do with it. Though I'd mostly loved my LA life, I'd always wanted to come back to Bellamy and continue the family legacy—but my father's bullheadedness held me back. That is, until he hurt his back so badly that he had no choice but to ask for help. However, I knew my plans to overhaul my family's acreage into an organic farm-to-fork establishment was not what he had in mind.

Even so, I could see it all in my head. Fields of lavender, the cherry grove, community vegetable gardens that went on for acres, and even, someday, a café on the farm grounds. It was a lofty dream, but it was one that had come to me in the last few years as the grind of being a television producer in Hollywood had taken its toll. Fewer and fewer projects appealed to me the older I got, but my dreams of a revamped Bellamy Farm stood strong.

As paved streets turned into gravel and tar country roads, my car kicked up dust. Huckleberry sneezed and gave me another martyred glare. It seemed that I would have to do a lot to make things up to my pug.

As the farm came into view, I tapped the brakes. The steel archway over the entrance read *"Bellamy Farm,"* or at least it had. The *F* in Farm dangled below the other letters, and the *Y* was bent. The gravel driveway that led into the farm was overgrown; weeds and grass broke through the pebbles and small stones. This was a far cry from the Bellamy Farm I knew.

When I was growing up, the fence that separated the property from the county road had stood even and straight, and every summer, my father had me paint it white like the story from *The Adventures of Tom Sawyer* so that it shone in the afternoon sunshine. Now, the fence had fallen over, the posts uprooted and cracked. It seemed no one had painted that fence in a very long time. I turned into the driveway and slowed the car, continuing my assessment. If this was the state of affairs at the entrance, I was afraid to see what it looked like deeper in.

The farm itself was a mile from the road, and the closer I came to the house, the worse I felt as I saw the disarray of the unkempt pasture and weed-ridden fields. When I was young, in the midst of summer, the fields would have been bright green with soybeans, corn, cucumbers, and squash, and the pasture would be dotted with the cows and horses. Bellamy Farm had always, always thrived. However, it looked like most of the crops and animals were gone now, and what was left was unruly, fallow land.

Time may have been kind to the town of Cherry Glen, not so much my home. The farm was in much worse shape than my father had let on. This kind of condition didn't happen in the few weeks since he threw his back out. The farm had been falling into disrepair for years, and I had no idea.

I should have come back home earlier, but as much as I wanted to drop everything and run to the rescue months ago, that hadn't been possible. I couldn't just walk away from life and my job that quickly, and Cherry Glen held its own demons that I wasn't quite ready to face, no matter how much I wanted to. I had a house to sell and a position to pass on to another producer at the studio. Thankfully, my cousin Stacey was local in Cherry Glen and stepped up and had been helping my father. She had a farm of her own to care for that was an equal two hundred acres. I was sure she did the best she could. I knew better than anyone my father could pay very little for outside help.

I let out a breath. Maybe I was the one who could have done better. I thought I was helping by working in Hollywood— especially since Dad didn't want to hear my vision for what I thought Bellamy could be. I was the silent pocketbook, and Dad was the one charged with distributing those funds across our debts to keep the farm going. I sent money back home so he could pay down the handful of mortgages he had on the farm. Mortgages that went all the way back to my mother's cancer treatment. Mom got sick when I was just a toddler, and he had to use the farm as collateral to pay the piles of bills that were still rolling long after she died.

As an adult, I did what I could. Over the years, I had paid those mortgages off, but it didn't happen overnight. It took over a decade. And now I realized that while I was chipping away at the debt, the farm was falling apart. It had started to come into focus a few months back when I learned my father owed the government years of back taxes. When Dad had mailed the tax bill to me at my office in the studio as a last resort, explaining his injury and the trouble he was in, I read it and knew, despite our differing visions for the farm, it was time for me to finally come home. Now, the wreckage was staring me right in the face.

Other than the mortgages and the taxes, Dad always insisted he had all the other farm finances under control. I had taken his word for it, because even though I knew my ultimate dream was to run the farm my way, it was also painful for me to come back to Cherry Glen for brief visits. There were too many memories of Logan that underscored my decision to stay away. That was my mistake, and it had not been fair to my father or our family's legacy. Now I realized the effort I'd have to put in to care for my ailing father, save the farm, and face the memories that I had buried in my Tinseltown life for the last fifteen years. It would be no small feat.

To the shock of all my coworkers and horror of Briar Hart, my best friend, I cashed in my 401(k) and my savings, put my home on the market, and sold it for a pretty penny. Between it all, I had just enough to cover my father's taxes with a little bit left over. That little bit of money was all I had to bring the farm back to life. Seeing the current condition, I knew it wasn't nearly enough.

I shivered to think what Grandma Bellamy would say if she could see the farm today. Would she have been surprised, that of all the generations of people who have cared for the farm, I would be the one to save it? Or at least try to?

She died just a year before Logan; maybe it was a blessing she passed away, so she couldn't see the mess her legacy had become. I shook my head and tried to remove the sad memories from my mind.

As I continued up the long drive, my family home came into

view. It was a large blue farmhouse with peeling paint and missing shutters. The screen door of the house opened as I parked the convertible by the front walk. My father shuffled through the door on a walker. I expected to see Stacey follow him out, but instead, a tall, broad-shouldered man about my age was behind him with his hands out as if he was ready to catch my father if the need should arise. He had dark hair going gray at the temples and a strong jaw. The sleeves of his T-shirt hugged his muscular arms. He was older, but I immediately recognized Quinn Killian.

A wave of memories came flooding back into my mind. Not all of them were good. When we were teenagers, Quinn had always been the one with strong opinions about what Logan should do or where he should go. I wanted Logan to make up his own mind. Quinn wanted to tell Logan what was what. That had never sat well with me.

My father grudgingly let Quinn help him through the door. I wasn't sure if lawn was the right word for the knee-high grass and weeds around the house. Some of the weeds were so high they covered a portion of the front windows.

However, the condition of my father more than the house took my breath away. I knew he wasn't well, but I hadn't expected him to be so hunched over or look so tired. I had to remind myself he was almost eighty years old. My dad had been an older groom while my mother, many years his junior, had been a young bride. I supposed when they married, he thought she surely would have outlived him. It was a cruel twist of fate he had lived most of his life without her.

I hopped out of the car, and Huckleberry jumped out after me. "Dad!" I hurried over to him and kissed his cheek. "It's so good to see you."

He nodded. "Shiloh, you're finally home." His voice was hoarse.

I blinked tears out of my eyes as I gave him a hug. "I'm home. And I'm here to stay."

My father stood as straight as he could on his walker. "I am glad. I can use the help. I can't count on Quinn and Stacey all the time. They have their own lives to lead."

I nodded at Quinn. "Hi. I didn't expect to see you here."

"That's quite a greeting." He laughed. "I heard you met my father, and he gave you a speeding ticket coming into town."

I grimaced. "It's nice to know the Cherry Glen grapevine is alive and well."

He rubbed the day-old stubble on his cheek. "He texted me. So no traditional grapevine, I'm afraid. It will be in tomorrow's paper in the police blotter if that makes you feel better. A red convertible with California plates getting a ticket will be the talk over at Jessa's Place for at least a week."

I groaned. Jessa's Place was the local diner and an institution in Cherry Glen. I hoped he was just teasing me about being the talk of the town, but I doubted it.

Quinn nodded at Huckleberry. "And who do we have here?" He squatted in the grass, and the little pug ambled over to him. Quinn gave Huck his cheek, and Huckleberry slobbered up one side of his face and down the other. Quinn didn't even flinch.

My father cleared his throat. "Quinn lives in the next farm, the old Cumberlin place. He comes over now and again to check on things, and he's been taking care of the chores while I'm laid up." He glared at his walker. "I hate this metal contraption."

I winced. For the first time, the true enormity of my father's poor health hit me like a wave. "I thought Stacey was helping you."

"Oh," Dad said. "She is, but she's been so busy with the play these last few weeks that Quinn's stepped up."

"Play?" I remembered driving by the theater. "At the Michigan Street Theater? I saw it was set to reopen when I drove through town. I was amazed. That place closed down before I was born."

Dad puffed out his chest. "It's back all thanks to Stacey."

I raised my brow.

"She bought the theater and brought it back to life. *Julius Caesar* will be the opening performance," Dad said.

"Wow, I'm sure the town appreciates that. The theater has been an eyesore for so long." I couldn't help the sarcasm that dripped from my voice as I scanned the even bigger eyesore in front of me. The overgrown lawn, the fallow fields, and the shutters falling from the house. Stacey was supposed to be keeping an eye out for the farm, helping him out—was spending money on the theater more important than Bellamy Farm? And where was I even to begin fixing it? How did I tell my father something needed to be done without upsetting him?

"It has. Stacey has involved me in the play too. I will be playing the soothsayer." Dad seemed oblivious to my internal struggle, and then he added in a foreboding voice, "'Beware the Ides of March!'" He cleared his throat. "She is also using guns from my collection for the play. I was so thrilled when she asked."

"Your guns?" I pulled my mind away from the growing to-do list in my mind. My father was a lifelong collector of Michigan history, so much so he could have his own museum. He had a large collection of nineteenth century guns, coins, knives, and other artifacts. "*Julius Caesar* is set in ancient Rome. And wasn't he stabbed to death?"

"She moved the setting to Michigan's frontier era in the United States," Dad said excitedly. "My favorite time in history as you know."

"Ah." It wouldn't be the first time someone reinterpreted Shakespeare's work in a different time period. I glanced at Quinn. "Thanks for helping my father out."

"It's no trouble helping Sully. My daughter and I both enjoyed it. Hazel especially likes the barn cats and the chickens. I think she would move here if she could. There aren't any animals on our farm yet. I just haven't..." He gave me a sheepish look as if he realized he had said too much.

"How old is your daughter?" I asked, surprised.

"Eleven going on twenty-five."

I swallowed. "I appreciate everything you and your daughter have done for my dad and the farm, but I can take over the majority of the work now." Even as I said it, I wasn't completely sure that was true. I just knew I didn't want Quinn's help in the least. When Logan died, he had made it known in no uncertain terms that the accident that had killed him had been my fault. After all this time, that old hurt came roaring back, making it nearly impossible to look at him, let alone thank him for anything or ask him to continue helping out.

"Do you remember how to take care of the farm? You've been gone for what? Fifteen years?" Quinn's eyebrows raised in challenge.

I frowned slightly. Perhaps my designer jeans and silk blouse didn't give me the credibility I needed in rural Michigan, but I'd lived on a farm until I was twenty-three years old. It would be like riding a bike—or so I hoped. "I may have lived in California for a long while, but I'm a farm girl at heart."

Quinn held up his hands. "I know that. Your father brags about your big city life constantly. I'm looking forward to hearing more about it myself."

"Oh," I said, mollified.

"The more hands on the farm, the better," Dad said. "I can't say I have been doing the best job keeping it up these last several years."

I frowned and folded my arms. "I'm sure when I assess what's going on and make a list, I can get a handle on things."

Quinn cocked his head. "You still like to do everything your way, don't you?"

I turned to Quinn. "And what does that—"

My comment was interrupted when a large black pickup truck with polished tire rims and tinted windows lumbered down the driveway. It was not the standard farmer's pickup, more flash, less function. A man jumped out of the cab.

"This is it!" he declared. "I can see what you were talking about, Shiloh. With this much acreage, we have real potential here to make a go of an organic farm."

"What the—" My dad squared his shoulders in hostility at the arrival.

A groan rose in my throat. This was *not* how I wanted to tell my father about the new investor, but he had to understand we needed to borrow money. When all the mortgage firms and banks turned us down, I had to get creative, and an outside investor seemed to be the best answer. Unfortunately, it was also something Dad had never wanted to talk about, even when I broached the subject. In the end, he told me he trusted me to do what I thought would be best for the farm—something I had never heard out of his mouth before. Now, I was second-guessing my decision.

I hurried. "Jefferson! I didn't expect you here until later this week."

Jefferson Crocker matched the photo of him I'd seen: a tall, thin man in his early sixties who looked like he'd never done a day of manual labor in his life. His suit was as expensive as any studio executives in LA. He stood a stark contrast to Quinn and my father, who'd both clearly worked outside most of their lives with their plain clothes and skin weathered and creased by wind and sun.

Crocker grinned. "I knew you would be in town by now, and I couldn't wait to get here and check out my investment."

My father stared at me. "*His investment*?"

I licked my lips. "Yes. I told you we should find an outside investor to help save the farm. I—"

"You never told me it was Crocker you were considering. He's been trying to buy up every piece of property in Cherry Glen, and you go into business with *him*?" Dad's face flushed red.

I let out a breath. "I tried to tell you who I was considering, and you said it was my choice."

"You made the wrong choice," he said, his voice heavy with disappointment. "That rat has tried to yank my farm out from under me for years, and you just hand it over to him?"

"I—I didn't know that. If you would have talked to me about the farm and what I should do, I could have known that."

He glared at me. "Are you saying your stupidity is my fault? Crocker doesn't care about the legacy of this place. He will parcel it out and sell it off. That's what men like him do. Is that what you want to happen to the farm?"

"N-no," I stammered. "He said he wanted to help me save the farm."

"He lied to you!" Dad cried and then glared at Crocker. "You will be sorry you ever went into business with my daughter, mark my words."

I felt a migraine starting behind my eyes. "Dad, I tried to talk to you about this. It's the only way—"

"Quinn, let's go inside. I can't hear any more of this." My father awkwardly turned his walker around and shuffled back toward the house.

Crocker rocked back on his heels with his hands in his pockets. He didn't appear to be the least bit miffed by my father's poor reaction.

"Dad." I followed him. "Just let me explain. I told you, I want to make Bellamy Farm organic. It's the only way we can be different from the other farms in the area and survive. I told you that when I agreed to come back and help. You said that was okay."

He glared at me. "I said *you* could do it. I didn't say anything about that skinny pencil pusher being involved."

I winced, knowing Crocker must have heard my father's comment.

Quinn helped my father into the house. Dad wouldn't look at me as he maneuvered through the door. Quinn held the door for my father and, before following Dad inside, whispered, "Give him a little time to cool down."

I glared. Where did he get off telling me what to do? He hadn't changed a bit since we were kids.

I rubbed my forehead as I stumbled away from the house. Well, I had royally messed that up. Really, that couldn't have gone worse if I tried.

I turned back to Crocker, who was moseying around the farm as if he owned the place. He *could* own the place if I failed. If I didn't hit the revenue numbers I promised, he would have the chance to buy the farm out from under me per the contract. Now seeing the farm and the state it was in, I knew I was a fool.

Crocker had his hands in his pockets and walked over to me. "Looks like you need to get your father on board about this."

"I'll talk to him."

He nodded. "If you do this right, Shiloh, we will both benefit."

I lightly kicked a rock on the ground with the toe of my shoe.

"And remember, you reached out to me for this deal. When everyone else said no to you, I said yes."

I could feel my unease swell with each word. "You didn't give me much wiggle room in the contract. I didn't realize the exact state of the farm when I agreed. The timeline you gave me to make up my mind in twenty-four hours wasn't long enough." As I ran through the negotiations in my head, my panic grew. "I think my father was right and we should have waited to discuss this face-to-face," I argued.

He shrugged. "I didn't hold a gun to your head and make you sign that agreement. You made the choice."

I knew that, and it was the worst part.

He strolled back to this truck. "Let's talk more tomorrow. Meet me at seven at the farmers market. We can chat before all the stalls open and the place is overrun. I think you'll see the potential of what you can do with this place."

"I'll be there."

He smiled. "Remember, a deal is a deal. No takebacks."

I swallowed. "Right, no takebacks."

Chapter Three

The problems at Bellamy Farm weren't going to fix themselves, and I was up barely before the sun the next morning, climbing onto the barn roof to take inventory of the things I'd need to tackle. If I really had the nerve to do what I wanted with Bellamy Farm, my to-do list was extensive. Even so, I knew it was the right thing to do to bring the farm back and make it stand out in the market. I knew my father's traditional farm methods couldn't compete with the corporate farms. An organic farm, however, could stand on its own.

But it would take a lot. Organic farm certification was no joke. Every aspect of how the farm did business would have to be reassessed from the water to the electricity to the pest control.

The night before had not gone well. My father refused to speak to me. I told him how much it would cost to change the farm over to a sustainable and organic farm and what a good business decision that would be in the long run. He was having none of it. Dad had farmed this land his whole life in the same way his father did before him, with pesticides and fertilizers. It was the way he was taught, and he was loath to change his ways after seventy-some years.

Sleep had been elusive. I tossed and turned in my childhood bedroom, worried over my father's silent treatment and the niggling doubt that maybe he was right. Maybe I had made a mistake when I signed a deal with Crocker. As of yet, I hadn't taken any of Crocker's money, but I didn't think that would make much difference, since the contract was legally binding. In it, Crocker would give me money upfront to transform Bellamy Farm. Then he would take twenty percent of the profits from the farm over the next ten years. If the farm failed to make any profit in two years' time, Crocker would have the option to purchase it at a reduced rate. They were tough terms, but it was the only option I had. I could already hear the two-year clock ticking in my ear. I prayed I had made the right choice.

From my perch on the roof, I took in the scenery around me. Even as run-down and disheveled as the farm was, it was still lovely. The ground was green and lush, if overgrown. I knew that meant the soil was rich underneath and water was plentiful. With the bright sun hanging overhead, I already had most of what I needed. It reminded me of the times I worked with my father on the farm as a kid. I would squint at the sky, trying to gauge if the weatherman was right about coming rain. I never did that in California, since it rarely rained, and even when it did, my livelihood didn't depend on it. I guessed I would be squinting at the sky quite a lot in the days to come.

Much farther away, beyond the rolling plots of land, was the expansive blue of Lake Michigan. It went on seemingly forever, like it was an ocean in its own right. Sunlight danced on its surface, as it did when I was a child visiting the lakeside. Being back here was like returning to that simple time, reminding me again of how special Michigan was to me.

I couldn't lose this beautiful place that had been in my family for six generations.

From the top of the barn, I could see for miles. I spotted my cousin Stacey's house on her half of Bellamy Farm. When my grandfather died, he divided the vast four-hundred-acre farm between his two sons, my father and Stacey's father. Ever since then, the two farms worked independently of each other. I had never asked my father why this was the case. After Stacey's father died, she inherited his share. From what I could see from my perch, her portion was in much better shape. Beyond Stacey's property was the old Cumberlin place that was now Quinn Killian's home. Of all the people who I would want to live a stone's throw away from my doorstep, Quinn was at the bottom of the list.

Just below me, the chickens pecked at the ground near the barn, and two of the barn cats groomed themselves on an over-turned wheelbarrow by the barn door. Huckleberry watched all these foreign creatures with wide eyes and just a little bit of fear from his spot in the weeds. I would have thought the cats, at least, would be afraid of my dog, but they ignored him and continued their beauty treatments. My vague hopes of turning Huckleberry into a fierce and productive farm dog were quickly fading.

There were two nearby fields of soybeans on the farm. Dad told me they were the only crops Bellamy would have this season, and I guessed that was thanks to Quinn and Stacey. The fields would never have yielded enough to pay the tax debts, even if they produced one thousand bushels of soybeans. Other than those fields and the chickens, the rest of the two hundred acres lay fallow, only hinting at the farm's true potential. I could turn those unused acres and make them something more than even my grandparents imagined—if I was willing to give it my all.

And I was.

Standing on the roof, seeing everything that Bellamy Farm could be, I started to believe I'd made the right choice. The farm was near enough to Traverse City to attract tourists who would be intrigued by the organic farm-to-fork way of life as well as visitors stopping by picturesque Cherry Glen. In my head, in addition to the lavender fields and pick-your-own cherry trees, I saw beehives, and maple groves all grown organically, and using solar power to run the farmhouse and outbuildings. I had actually climbed onto the roof to judge where the best place for solar panels would be, and now my imagination was running wild. There was so much that could be done. I could even envision an organic café at the farm someday.

At first glance, though, there was much to repair: the shutters on the house, the fence at the road, the siding on the barn. Those were the things I could immediately start on. There were untold problems that may lie under the surface as well, and each and every one of them would cost money to mend or fix.

Most people didn't realize just how backbreaking and difficult traditional farming could be. Sure, farms sustained themselves for generations—just like my family's had—but there was not a lot of profit and very little margin for error. Weather, drought, pestilence, economy—so many factors could influence a crop's success. Expanding to include a "tourism" element would help overcome some of those unpredictabilities. And converting fully to an organic operation would secure a more sustainable future for the farm for generations to come. Whatever those generations may be. Since it was just me, what would become of the farm when I was gone? I shoved those thoughts to the back of my mind. I just had to get the farm through the next two years under this agreement with Crocker. Its long-term feasibility could wait.

Near the edge of Dad's property on a dirt road was a small cabin. It was the home where Grandma Bellamy had lived until she died, when I was a senior in college. How much I wished she were here today. She would have whipped the farm into shape in no time at all with her typical vim and vigor. She also would have scared the tax collectors away. I once saw her chase a corn whole-sale merchant who was giving her a bad price on her bushels all the way down the mile-long driveway with her broom. He never came back, and she sold the corn at top dollar to someone else. Gazing at her cabin, an idea sparked in the back of my mind. It could be the perfect home for Huckleberry and me.

My father's voice startled me from my thoughts. "Have you lost your marbles?" Dad stood with his walker at the foot of the ladder. "What on earth are you doing up there?" He sounded grumpy, but at least he was speaking to me. Huckleberry was at his feet, looking up with a matching dumbfounded expression.

I climbed down the ladder and jumped to the grass. "I was looking for the best place to put the solar panels. From the angle the barn sits, there is perfect solar gain. It wouldn't take much to harvest solar energy as soon as the panels are installed."

He grunted. "What happened to you? You went out to California and turned hippie on me?"

"Dad, I'm sorry. I've been trying to tell you for months about needing an investor. You told me you didn't want to hear about it and it was up to me to make a choice. Crocker was that choice."

He frowned. "And you made the wrong one. Crocker is a crock of—"

I nodded. "Dad, I want to save Bellamy Farm just as much as you do. You have to believe me that we can't do this without out-side funds."

Dad leaned heavily on his walker. "I know you do. You wouldn't have left your life behind in California if you didn't care. I know that was hard for you to do."

It was both the easiest and the most difficult decision I had ever made. Dad didn't know my whole life savings were now tied up in this farm. If we lost the farm, I lost everything too. And even though I had always dreamed of coming back and revamping Bellamy at some point in my life, my father's stubbornness had quashed those hopes many times over. I had grown accustomed to loving Cherry Glen from a distance, and even when Hollywood no longer held my interest, I still had a lot of security in my life there that I had to leave behind to return to the place that viewed me as a last resort. But it didn't matter. I left LA without a backward glance, both for my father and for this place I loved so much.

Even with the many risks in mind, however, I tried to focus on the potential reward ahead of me. It was true I'd left my steady job behind, but I also had the opportunity to build a better life here. Other than my friendship with Briar, all I had to show for my fifteen years working in television and movies was an addiction to coffee and better highlights.

Maybe in Michigan I would find what I never found in California. A life outside of my job. At the very least, I would be with my father again. Seeing him hunched over the walker reminded me how precious—and fleeting—our time together was.

"Are we okay, Dad? Really?"

He nodded. "But don't be doing any more deals without me. I want to be involved now. I want to know the details."

"I won't. Promise. I want you to be involved too. You may have given me the farm in name, but it's *our* farm at heart."

He smiled. It was the first genuine smile I had seen from him since I returned.

"I need to get going," I said. "I just wanted to get the lay of the land before my meeting. It helped me solidify some ideas."

He adjusted his hold on his walker. "What meeting?"

I wasn't sure he would want to hear the answer, but I told him anyway. "I'm meeting Crocker at the farmers market to discuss our agreement. Do you want to come with me?"

He shook his head. "I want nothing to do with that. I suppose you can't go back on your deal now, but be careful. Crocker is like a snake, and he's always ready to strike."

I shivered. What had I gotten myself into? I pushed the foreboding rising in me to the back of my mind. I kissed Dad on the cheek, scooped up Huckleberry, and headed to my car.

The farmers market was open on Wednesdays from three to eight p.m. and Saturday eight a.m. to two p.m. It was located in the parking lot where the old high school—*my* high school—had been. My father had sent me the local newspaper clipping when the building came down five or so years ago, but the town left the large parking lot for special events. The market was known for having interesting and organic vendors, and farmers and hand-crafters came from all over the county to sell there. It was also known for the cherries, which were the region's specialty. July was the height of cherry season, so the market would be busy later in the day.

When we got out of the car, I clicked Huckleberry's leash on his collar, and he looked at me like I was some kind of traitor. "Leash laws, buddy. I'm not sure what they are in town, but I'm not doing anything that might irritate the cops. I already have one speeding ticket that I will have to pay by the end of the month."

He grunted like only a pug could, and we made our way into the market.

It was early, but with the humid air, it would heat up fast. Around us, farmers and crafters set up for the day. Many of them placed their booths under white awnings or tents to fight the glare of the Midwestern sun. Some sellers had stands that looked like mini cottages with shutters around the sales window. I hoped to have a booth like that someday. Others who were selling produce simply opened the backs of their pickups and displayed corn, beans, and peppers directly from the truck bed. Regardless of the setup, stall owners bustled about, getting their wares reading for the incoming crowds. The market would open soon, and I felt invigorated seeing how vibrant and active it was already. Coming back to Michigan to take on this new venture had been the right choice. I hadn't felt this excited about something in years. As much as I loved being a producer, I had grown tired of documenting other people's lives and wanted to start participating in my own.

"Shiloh Bellamy!" a high-pitched voice cried. "As I live and breathe. What on earth are you doing here?" I turned to see a petite, Latina woman my age walking toward me, and it took me a moment to recognize her. I figured out what initially threw me off—my best childhood friend was very clearly pregnant.

"Kristy Garcia?" I smiled. "It's so great to see you!" I gave her a hug, taking care not to squeeze her belly.

Kristy placed a hand on her stomach. "Twins, if you're wondering, and it's Kristy Brown now. They'll be my first. My husband is absolutely terrified." She laughed. "But I couldn't be happier."

"Twins! Wow, congratulations!"

She grinned. "Thank you!"

"Do you have a booth here?" I asked.

She shook her head. "No, I manage the market. It's my baby." She patted her tummy. "Well, it was before these two."

Huckleberry spun in a circle and put his front paws on Kristy's leg.

"Huck, you need to ask first." I tugged on his leash.

She looked down at Huckleberry. "Who is this cutie?"

"Huckleberry. He's still acclimating to country living."

She laughed, squatted down, and patted the pug on the top of his head. She winced as she stood up, and I gave her my arm to help her make it the rest of the way.

After releasing me, she said, "Being pregnant with twins is not for sissies."

"I wouldn't think so," I said. "I'm glad you're in charge of the market. I'm actually interested in having a booth here too. I will need to talk to you when I'm ready to rent space."

"*You* want a booth? For what?"

"For my family farm," I said. "Produce, homemade goods, that sort of thing."

"Bellamy Farm hasn't had a booth at the farmers market in over a decade."

I nodded. "I know. I want to change that."

"Does that mean you're back in the Glen for good?"

"It does."

She nodded. "I'd heard you were, but I was afraid to even believe it. I never thought you would come back here after the accident."

The accident was Logan's death. He had been killed by a drunk driver one night while driving to Traverse City to see me. I shook the memory away and realized Kristy was still talking.

"You're a good daughter to take care of your father like that," Kristy said. "But it can't be easy to leave your life behind. Sully was very proud of his California producer daughter. He talks about you constantly to anyone who will listen."

I raised my eyebrows at this. This was the second time I had been told Dad talked about my LA life. He'd never said he was proud of me *to* me. I wondered what he thought about me leaving that career behind to farm. Did he like the idea or wish me away? I guessed now that I had hired Crocker, he probably wished I had never come back at all.

Something caught in my throat. I looked at my feet to cover my expression and then said, "I want to get the family farm back on track for Dad."

"Well, girl, you're a braver one than me to want to save a farm in this day and age." She gave me a hug. "I'm glad to see you back though. We must catch up."

"I'd love that," I said.

A vendor from a maple syrup booth waved frantically at Kristy.

"Oh, I have to go, Shi. The vendors are all so needy before the market opens." She rolled her eyes. "I'll catch up with you later."

I nodded and went back to looking for Crocker. I checked the time on my phone. He was ten minutes late. A small bead of worry began to grow in the back of my mind. I glanced down at Huckleberry. "Let's take a loop around the market. I'm sure he just got caught up in something and will be here soon."

Huckleberry snuffled in response.

As I made slow progress around the market with Huckleberry stopping and sniffing most everything along the way, many of the vendors waved or smiled at me, probably eyeing what they thought was a potential customer. The volume of the market rose as more vendors arrived, pulling up their cars through the wide aisles to unload their wares. Greetings were shouted, carts of produce squeaked by, and old trucks sputtered around the back of the stalls, clunky engines adding to the cacophony. As a car back-fired somewhere in the distance, a burst of laughter sounded from a close booth, and a trickle of early morning radio sounded in the air. It seemed that old Midwest friendliness was alive and well in Cherry Glen.

Huckleberry took it upon himself to inspect every booth and passerby. As we walked, he buried his nose in one of the many giant urns scattered around the parking lot that were bursting with summer flowers. I tugged on the leash, but he wouldn't come. Huckleberry loved flowers to the extreme. He also loved digging them up. I tugged again, and he still wouldn't move. Sighing, I bent over to physically remove the pug from the pot when I heard footsteps behind me. I glanced up just as a woman bumped into me and knocked me to the ground. She didn't pause and kept running. She didn't even apologize—so much for that Midwest friendliness!

The woman wore a ball cap that barely contained her black hair and turned back at me just long enough for me to see frightened dark eyes. I had never seen her before in my life. Then she was gone, swallowed into the hustle and bustle of the vendors prep-ping for the day.

I dusted myself and Huckleberry off. "That was rude," I told the pug.

He licked my cheek, which made me feel a bit better.

"Let's find Crocker and get out of here."

He snorted in reply, which for Huckleberry was pretty close to a bark.

Huckleberry and I walked toward a booth emblazoned with a Buzzin' Better Honey sign. The entire stall was shaped like a giant beehive complete with a metal weather vane waving back and forth on the very top. In the middle of the hive, a counter held jars of fresh honey, each with a different colored bow tied around the lids, lined up and ready to sell. I paused to take in the empty and elaborate setup before turning to scan for my investor.

I was at the very end of the large market and still no sign of Crocker. I grabbed my phone to text him and ask where he wanted to meet, meandering around the honey booth. As I turned the corner, Huckleberry gave a sound caught between a woof and a startled grunt. I pulled up short.

A man lay before me on the black pavement just on the other side of the booth, hidden from view. There was a red stain in the middle of his chest that was made more noticeable by his white button-down shirt. A shattered jar of honey lay at his feet, its pink bow stuck to the man's right shoe.

I'd found Jefferson Crocker, and he was dead.

Chapter Four

I braced my hands on my knees and closed my eyes and gulped air. When I opened my eyes again, Crocker was still dead.

Do something, my brain screamed at me.

What do I do? I looked around. *Do I take his pulse?*

I grimaced. He looked pretty dead. I mean, all the way dead. His blue eyes were open and unblinking. A terrible feeling bloomed in my stomach, equal parts sorrow and horror. With a giant dollop of dread, I scooped up Huckleberry and checked the pug to make sure that there wasn't any blood on him. Thank God there wasn't.

Don't touch the body, my mind told me. I had lived in the big city long enough to know not to leave physical evidence at a crime scene. Oh Lord, I stood in the middle of a crime scene!

"What are you doing at my honey booth?" a sharp voice asked.

I turned around to find a woman, with a nose not that different from Huckleberry's, glaring at me. She had her hands on her hips and stuck out her ample chest, reminding me of the bravado of the Big Bad Wolf. I wondered if that made me the house she wanted to blow down.

I couldn't speak. I opened and closed my mouth, but no words came out.

"I asked you a question." She shook her finger at me. "You had better not be trying to steal my honey." She moved around the side of the booth and screamed, "Oh my God! Look what you did!"

"I—I didn't," I cried back, because I had finally found my voice. "I didn't do that."

"And you broke a jar of my honey too." She glared at me. "You're paying for that!"

"I didn't—"

"Murder! Murder! She killed him!"

That was all she had to say to make half the farmers market come running.

"Shiloh, are you okay?" Kristy asked after she pushed her way through the crowd.

I shook my head.

"What the—" She stared at dead Crocker at my feet.

"It wasn't me," I whispered to her.

"You? Who would think it was you?"

"I would!" the bee booth woman said. "She killed that man. And my booth! My booth has been contaminated by all this. I might have to throw all my honey away! I'm ruined!"

I stepped back. "No, no, I was—I was just, I mean—I didn't kill anyone."

"You contaminated my booth," the woman said.

"I didn't do that either." I hugged Huckleberry to my chest, and the little pug kicked his feet, asking for relief. I loosened my grasp but still held him fast.

"Minnie, you need to back off," Kristy snapped. "Your booth will be fine. A man is dead. Put it into perspective."

Minnie jerked back as if she had been slapped.

"Coming through. Make room! Step aside. Police chief on the way," a deep male voice shouted.

Chief Randy slipped his fingers through the belt loops of his uniform trousers. "What kind of hullabaloo do you have going on at the farmers market this time, Kristy Brown? Please don't tell me I have to break up another fight about whose cherry preserves are better. Not again. I still have bruises from the last scuffle."

Minnie pointed at me. "She's a murderer. Arrest her right now!"

Chief Randy's mouth fell open. "Hold on there. Did you say *murderer?*"

"See for yourself." Minnie pointed to the other side of the beehive-shaped booth. Chief Randy and the small crowd that had gathered all moved as one.

"That's Jefferson Crocker," the chief said in a gasp. "He's dead. Shot in the chest!"

She pointed at me. "By her."

I frowned. What qualified a beekeeper to make such an accusation?

Chief Randy nervously tugged on his mustache, his voice ratcheting up as he took in the body. "We are going to need help," he stammered. "Someone call the coroner and the crime scene investigators. Someone call them."

"Isn't your job to call them, Chief?" Kristy asked.

"Right!" he yelped as if finally remembering, yanking his phone from the holster on his belt.

"And what are you going to do about her?" Minnie continued to point at me. "Why aren't you getting out your handcuffs and arresting this trespasser?"

"Trespasser?" I asked. "I grew up in this town."

"I've never seen you before, and I have been keeping bees in Cherry Glen for thirteen years." She spun around and looked at the chief again. "Do something!"

Chief Randy paled and turned to me. "Tell me what happened."

"I already told you what happened," Minnie interjected.

"I want to hear it from her, and if you don't like that, Minnie, you can step aside."

Minnie opened and closed her mouth for a moment.

"I didn't shoot him," I said, trying not to look at the dead man just a few feet away. "I didn't shoot anyone! I just came behind the booth because my dog was tugging me, and there he was." I hoisted Huckleberry up further in my arms as if the pug were all the evidence I needed.

Minnie narrowed her eyes.

I forged ahead before Minnie could make another accusation. "Huckleberry must have sensed that something was wrong, and I followed him. I have no idea who did this."

"So he's a detective pug? A snub-nosed Lassie, as it were?" Chief Randy nervously laughed at his own joke. No one else standing around the honey booth found it funny. I certainly didn't.

"Well, this is not the way I wanted to start my weekend. No sir." Chief Randy tapped on his phone screen and then bellowed on his phone. "We need some medics over here. We got a dead body at the farmers market. Oh, someone already called it in and they're on their way. Good, good." He paused. "No, I'm pretty sure he's dead." As he said this, it appeared to dawn on him that he might actually want to confirm that Crocker was, indeed, dead. Chief Randy stepped over to the body, squatted down, and pressed two fingers to Crocker's neck, just as I had seen in the countless true-crime television shows I had produced.

"Call the coroner too, and the county evidence team," he said to the dispatcher, any traces of humor completely gone. After he finished the call, Chief Randy turned back to the small crowd of vendors that hovered around us. "All right. Time to break this up. You all go back to your own booths. We need some space."

"How can we go back like nothing happened when there is a killer on the loose?" a short man at the front of the group asked. His bright-red T-shirt read "*Cherry Up!*"

Chief Randy slipped his thumbs through the loops in his duty belt. "No one said this was murder."

"Of course it's murder!" Minnie cried. "That's a gunshot wound to the chest. Anyone can see that."

"We don't know how the wound was inflicted," the chief said, but his expression seemed to contradict that.

Minnie looked like she wanted to say more but was cut off by the sound of sirens.

An ambulance pulled into the farmers market. Its arrival did much more to break up the spectators than Chief Randy's orders had.

The door opened, and a female EMT got out of the driver's seat. She looked vaguely familiar to me, but I couldn't place her. That was happening to me a lot since I returned to Cherry Glen. Everyone looked familiar but also a little bit different, making it impossible for my memory to pull up their faces and their names. It was funny because I went whole weeks in LA without seeing anyone I knew or even thought I knew when I was out and about. Here in Cherry Glen, it was the same faces over and over again.

I didn't have much time to place the EMT because Quinn climbed out of the other side of the ambulance. He had a medical bag in his hand. While the woman went around to the back of the vehicle, he walked over to us.

I stared at him. "I thought you were a farmer."

He gave me a lopsided smile. "I'm a lot of things, Shiloh Bellamy."

Annoying was one of them.

Chapter Five

Quinn turned his attention to his father. "What's up, Dad? We got a call about a body."

Chief Randy nodded. "I'm glad you're here, Son. I have a shooting victim here. You'll have to do your assessment, but he's a goner."

"Shooting victim!" Minnie said triumphantly. "See, I was right." She folded her arms as if the case was closed.

I had a feeling Minnie took great pleasure in being right all the time.

I, on the other hand, winced at the chief's words, and I was also perplexed. It seemed like no one standing around me was the least bit upset over Crocker's death. A man was dead, and not a single person said a word of regret over the loss of his life. I could have been mistaken, but it almost seemed like many of these merchants seemed to be relieved. In the crowd, I saw several of the crafters and farmers nodding and laughing together as if this were a completely normal day. Was this really the way to act when a man died? It also made me wonder what Crocker did in his life to cause this sort of reaction.

Quinn grimaced. "Was it a hunting accident?" He looked around. "We're at least a mile away from the closest woods."

"It was no accident," Chief Randy said, standing a little straighter. There was a gasp from the crowd. The chief glanced at Minnie as if waiting on her reaction.

Quinn frowned. "Who is it?"

"Jefferson Crocker. Take a look," Chief Randy said and stepped out of his son's line of sight.

Quinn glanced back at me. I knew he was thinking about Crocker's visit to Bellamy Farm yesterday. My heart sank. He knew I had a history with Crocker. Would he tell his father?

Quinn put his medical bag on the ground and pulled on gloves. He kneeled by the body and felt for a pulse. No one was surprised when he shook his head. "He's gone."

"We could tell that from here, Son," the police chief said gruffly. "I already checked for a pulse."

Quinn looked up at his father. "I still have to check. It's part of my job. Doc will have to make the determination as far as time and cause of death."

"Right, right." Chief Randy loomed over the body and his son, who was still kneeling on the ground. "What kind of firearm do you think did this?"

Quinn got to his feet. "The hole doesn't look like it came from a hunting rifle to me, but that's the doc's territory, not mine."

The female EMT pulled over a stretcher, and she looked in my direction with so much loathing in her eyes, I stumbled back and stepped on Kristy's foot. I forgot that she had been standing behind me all this time.

"Ouch," Kristy muttered. "Watch yourself, Shi."

"Sorry," I whispered. "Who is the EMT with Quinn? She just gave me the glare of death." I winced at my poor choice of words.

"Don't you remember her?" She chuckled.

I wrinkled my brow. "Should I?"

"Shi, that's Laurel Burger. Well, Laurel Anderson now. Or maybe back to Laurel Burger. She just got a divorce, but I don't know if she changed her name back."

My eyes widened. As soon as Kristy stirred my memory, all the harassment from Laurel Burger I had forgotten or had tried to forget over the years came back in a rush. Laurel had been my tormentor from kindergarten all the way through high school graduation. For whatever reason, Laurel hated me and made it her mission to make my life as difficult as possible. I was the nerdy, chubby girl from the farm with braces, glasses, and a backpack full of books. Laurel was the popular cheerleader from town. One of the best parts of high school graduation was leaving her behind.

I was thinner now—after a lot of hard work—wore contacts, and had a confidence that came from a successful career in Hollywood, but as far as I had come, after seeing Laurel, all those terrible insecurities came flooding back. The day grew worse by the second, and I'd yet to have my midmorning coffee.

"She still lives in Cherry Glen?" I asked, thinking wasn't finding a dead body enough for a bad morning? I had to see my archrival again too? "I thought she moved away after high school."

"She never moved very far away. Traverse City, I think. Then she came back after her divorce last year." She gave me a half smile. "Man, it would really tick her off if she knew you forgot who she was." Kristy smiled. "Not that she doesn't deserve it. I'm almost tempted to tell her, but then she would just try to make your life back in town worse. I hate to say it, but she hasn't changed much."

"Compared to some of the people I knew and worked with in LA, Laurel is nothing," I said with much more confidence than I felt.

A shiny silver SUV that looked like it was ready to drive right up the side of a big dune at Sleeping Bear pulled up behind the ambulance. The car—if I could call it that, since it wasn't that much smaller than the ambulance—door opened, and a tall, angular man stepped out. He wore cowboy boots and had the most impressive mustache I had ever seen, and I had the direct comparison with Chief Randy's mustache right in from me. He looked like he had just walked off the set of a western. I almost expected to hear the theme song to *Gunsmoke* usher him to the crime scene.

"Who's that?" I asked Kristy.

"The county coroner," she whispered back. "He must have been nearby to get here so quickly. He has a giant range to take care of."

Range seemed to fit in reference to the coroner. He definitely had a cowboy persona, which was a bit out of place. Among the Michigan farmers in work boots and camo T-shirts, he stood out like he had walked out of central casting for *Bonanza*.

"I was on the way to see my son's Little League game, Randy," the coroner said in a booming voice. "The wife is not happy she had to take him to the field. She hates baseball."

The chief walked over and met him. "Sorry to hear that, Doc, but we have a dead body here, and I don't think it was of natural causes either."

"That's what I was told. Is it true that it's Jefferson Crocker?"

"Come see for yourself."

The coroner walked around the booth and swore. I wanted to inch closer to them and overhear what they were saying, but Kristy grabbed my arm.

Kristy placed a hand on her belly. "So sorry about that. Standing in the hot sun like this makes me a tad dizzy."

I stared at her stomach. "Are you all right? All this must be so upsetting to you. Maybe you should go sit down?"

She smiled at me. "Yes, it's upsetting, but I'm fine. Just one of the little ones took this moment to kick me in the kidney." She moved her hand from her stomach to her back. "They are feisty babies. My husband says they take after me in that way." She touched my arm with her free hand. "Please don't look at me that way. I hate it when people treat me with kid gloves just because I'm pregnant."

"I'm sorry." The truth was I was concerned about Kristy, but I was also worried about myself too. What would become of the farm now that Crocker was dead? What would happen to the money he was going to invest? Or the contract I signed? Oh... wait. Could I get out of it? Did I even want to?

I closed my eyes for a moment. I should have taken my time with Crocker and waited until I was in Michigan to finalize everything. I had just been so afraid when he gave me twenty-four hours to make up my mind, I signed the contract faster than I normally would have. I never would have done that when it came to my work as a television producer. Maybe it'd been easier to say no because I knew I had the studio to back me up. When it came to making this decision about the future of the farm, I had been alone.

"He's been murdered all right," the coroner said after looking at the body. "Definitely no suicide, not like I have ever seen anyway. Not with a shot to the chest like that. The angle looks wrong. Plus, the head is a much more secure option if you want to take yourself out. That's my eyes-only assessment, but I'll take him back to my place and open him up. I don't see the exit wound, so the slug is still inside him. Should be able to pull it out without too much trouble."

I grimaced at his matter-of-fact description.

Chief Randy rocked on his heels. "Have you seen a gunshot wound like this before?"

"No, not exactly like this. Just at first glance, it seems to be at close range. The ones I have seen have been hunting accidents. Usually in those cases, the victim is shot when another hunter sees movement in the woods and thinks it's a deer. Before the hunter takes a second look, he fires. Usually happens at the beginning of the season when everyone is trigger-happy for a buck." The coroner shook his head. "No one is hunting now anyway. Everyone is on the lakes fishing. If my son didn't have a baseball game, I would have been out on my boat." He looked down to the spot where I knew Crocker lay dead on the pavement. "It's a real shame. Can't say that I care for his business tactics much, but he shouldn't have ended this way. No one should. What's the world coming to when we have a murder in Cherry Glen?"

"I agree, Doc," the police chief said. "We can't let things like this happen in our little town. I'll do whatever it takes to find the person responsible for killing Jefferson Crocker. I don't abide by murder in Cherry Glen."

I held onto Kristy's arm a little more tightly. This time, it wasn't to support her but to support me.

"Let's have the crime scene tech search the area, and then Quinn and Laurel can take the body to my office," the coroner said.

"Kristy," I said. "Maybe we should go."

"You can go," she said. "But I have to stay. This is a PR nightmare for the farmers market, and I have to ask Chief Randy how he plans to deal with it. I'm hoping he will let me keep the market open today... The honey booth is far enough away from the rest of the businesses I would think." Kristy left my side and went up to the police chief, who was still chatting with Doc.

I stood alone outside the circle of officials. Should I stay or go? No one had attempted to ask me any questions, and I was the one who'd found the body. Was I wrong in thinking that was unusual?

Laurel walked over to me. "Shiloh Bellamy. So this is what LA looks like."

Drat! I'd missed my window of escape.

She studied me. "You don't look like a California girl, or at least not one I would have pictured."

"It nice to see you, Laurel," I said, now wishing I had pretended to not know her just to get a reaction.

Her lips curled into a half smile. "That was almost a convincing lie. What are you doing back in Cherry Glen? Decided to pop in for a visit on your dear old dad?"

Before I could answer, Quinn joined us. "She's here to stay. She's helping Sully out with Bellamy Farm."

Laurel looked at me with renewed interest. "Really? I thought you were working as a runner on a TV talk show."

"I was a long time ago. Now, I *am* a television producer," I said. Not that there was anything wrong with working on a TV talk show. I was sure it was every brand-new producer's dream job, but the way Laurel made it sound…ugh, it was like we were still in high school, and she was trading insults at every opportunity.

"You're a producer. Really? Would you have worked on any shows that I know?"

"Most of my shows have been adapted from books," I said.

"I haven't read a book since college. It's a complete waste of time when everything you need to know is on the internet."

That was when I knew Laurel and I could never be friends.

"Then maybe not," I said. "I've also produced gardening and cooking shows."

"I don't do either of those things," she said, again in the dismissive tone, as if gardening and cooking were also a waste of time.

This did not surprise me.

"You were always a book nerd," Laurel added.

"I'll take that as a compliment." I cleared my throat. "I had better get back to Bellamy Farm and check on my father. He hasn't been well." I took two big steps back from them.

No one stopped me, so I turned around and was just about to hurry away when Chief Randy's voice rang out. "Where do you think you're going, Ms. Bellamy?"

My shoulders sagged. Busted.

Chapter Six

I turned back around with a glittering smile on my face, but from the chief's scowl, it had no effect. I wondered if I could get my money back from the LA expert who had promised me no one would be able to resist it. I was willing to bet he had never been to northwest Michigan.

I hugged Huckleberry to my chest. "I'm sorry, Chief Randy. Did you need me?"

"Do I need you?" He smoothed the corner of his mustache. "Yes, I do. We have a few questions for you. You were the one who first discovered the body."

There was no point in denying it. Heaven knew, Minnie would have outed me if I tried to tell another story. Not that I would lie to the police. And no matter what he might have done, I felt horrible for Crocker. Like Doc said, he didn't deserve an end like this.

Laurel looked at me with renewed interest when he said that, and Quinn frowned. I didn't know if he frowned because he felt sorry for me or because he felt sorry for my father for who his daughter was. I guessed the latter.

"And do you know the victim?" Chief Randy asked.

Out of the corner of my eye, I glanced at Quinn. He knew that

I knew Crocker. Was he going to tell his father that? He also knew the financial trouble I was in, but the last thing I wanted to do was get involved in a murder investigation. With Minnie already calling me a killer, I didn't want to further link myself and the Bellamy name to a crime I didn't commit.

"I—I—umm—I don't know him well." I bit my lip. Should I tell the chief about Crocker investing in the farm now? Would that threaten my fresh start somehow?

Quinn shifted his feet, and I waited for him to say something about the encounter at Bellamy Farm the day before. He said nothing.

I started to open my mouth to tell the chief about my business agreement with Crocker, but he said, "Tell me how you found him."

"Oh, umm, sure." I went on to tell him the story of how I found Crocker behind the honey booth. "I was there no more than ten seconds before Minnie came up and started yelling at me. I can understand why she was so upset. Her booth is her livelihood. I'm not sure how much time passed before Kristy arrived and called the police, and you know everything from that. In the short time I was alone with Crocker, I did nothing. I didn't breathe or move or touch a thing. I was in shock. Complete shock. I've never found a dead body before."

"Few people have," Chief Randy said. "I think that's all I have for you at the moment. You can go then, but I will have more questions for you after Doc takes a look at the body."

I knew I should tell him about the agreement with Crocker. "There is something—"

"Chief Randy!" A heavyset man called out and marched across the parking lot. His silver hair was thin on the top of his head, and he wore trousers and a white button-down shirt open at the collar.

The police chief spun around. "Mayor Loyal."

"Chief Randy, what do we have here?" the mayor wanted to know. "I have gotten ten phone calls that there is some kind of emergency at the farmers market. Then I call you for information about this, and you don't pick up your phone. I shouldn't have to come down here myself to tell you to do your job."

"Mr. Mayor, I can't be answering the phone when I am dealing with a gunshot victim."

"A what?" The mayor's face went slack.

Chief Randy nodded. "See for yourself. The crime scene techs are on the way to collect evidence, and Doc is here too." He paused. "The victim is Jefferson Crocker."

Beads of sweat appeared on the mayor's forehead.

"I want to see him," the mayor said.

Chief Randy nodded again. Before walking away from me, he said, "Don't you go back to LA." That came out as an order.

It wasn't like I was planning to return to California, but the option being closed was a little bit alarming. Did he think I was a suspect?

I thanked the chief, and with one more glance back at the honey booth, I walked away. I had crossed most of the large parking lot when I heard running feet behind me. I froze. This was it; the chief was coming to question me, and the whole town would quickly find out. I could already hear the rumors Minnie and Laurel would circulate through the Cherry Glen gossip mill—Shiloh Bellamy couldn't save her family without making a deal with the devil, and then that devil turned up dead.

I spun around and saw not the chief but his son running toward me. I couldn't help but notice with how much ease Quinn ran. He was probably one of those marathoner types, which I was so not.

"Is everything all right?" I asked. As soon as the words were out of my mouth, I knew it was the wrong question. Of course everything wasn't all right. A man had been murdered in the middle of the farmers market. I cleared my throat. "Do you need something from me?"

"Why are you hiding the fact that you know Crocker?" Quinn asked.

"I'm not hiding anything," I said. "I told the chief that I didn't know him well. That's true."

"You said nothing about Crocker being an investor in Bellamy Farm."

"I was planning to tell him, but we were interrupted by the mayor."

Quinn gave me a dubious look.

"I'm telling you the truth."

"Okay, then go tell him now."

I frowned. The chief was surrounded by the coroner and crime scene techs. I didn't want to get in the middle of all that again. He just said that I could leave.

"I'll tell him later. I have to get back to the farm. With Crocker dead, who knows how long that money will be tied up as his accounts get squared away or if the contract is even valid now. I may be back at square one with saving it. I need to find a new investor fast." Huckleberry was growing heavy in my arms, but I didn't dare set him on the ground for fear that he would run back to the crime scene. I just wanted to get out of there as quickly as possible.

"You should tell him now."

I folded my arms. Who was this guy, anyway, to tell me what was and wasn't unwise. "Why's that?"

"Because my father will find out and wonder why you didn't mention it. You are giving him a reason not to trust you. He may appear to be a bumbling country cop, but that is just part of his persona. Make no mistake; if this really does turn out to be a murder, he will stop at nothing to solve it." His green eyes bore into me. "That includes finding out any relationship you have with Crocker."

I shivered when he said that. "I don't have a relationship with him."

"You did if he was a business partner."

"We weren't business partners. We have an agreement that hasn't even happened yet. Why would I kill him before I even got the money?" I sighed. "Look, I don't mean to be that crass over a man's death. I didn't know him well, so I told your father the truth. I imagine he will learn about my connection to Crocker from you or from someone else soon enough. I will address that with him when it comes."

"You should tell him yourself," Quinn said.

"Maybe I will, but not right now. Look, I just got back into town, my farm and family's reputation is already in question, and the whole town knows Bellamy is failing. One rumor that we could be blamed could complicate everything I'm trying to build. I—I just need to get home to my father."

"You should tell the chief now. It will save you from looking like you're hiding something."

I scowled at him. "Or it could get the whole town talking when there's nothing to talk about. I told you, I will tell him. Now is not the right time."

He opened his mouth like he wasn't done arguing, but then snapped it shut again, stomping back to the honey booth.

Over Quinn's shoulder, Laurel glared at me. I had not expected for the people of Cherry Glen to run at me with open arms when I came home, but this welcome was less than desirable.

Chapter Seven

Huckleberry and I returned to my family farm, and I had an overwhelming sense of dread as my convertible bumped along the uneven driveway. It could have been the fact that I had just stumbled upon the dead body of my investor, or it could have been because more of the fence at the edge of the farm had fallen over since I arrived. Neither boded well for things to come.

Before I'd left my old life in LA, my worst fear was I would lose the family farm and let down my father and the memory of Grandma Bellamy too. Now, my worst fear was getting tangled in a murder investigation that could turn the whole town against me. How was I going to explain this to my father? He was already upset about Crocker's possible involvement in Bellamy Farm. How would he take Crocker's death?

I parked my convertible in a dead patch of grass beside the farmhouse. Resod the yard was another item I would have to add to my giant to-do list. Although fixing up the yard was quite a long way down from the top of that list. The very top would read *"Don't go to jail."*

I climbed out of the car, and Huckleberry jumped out beside

me. When he landed, he held up his paw to show me the dirt that
was on it.

"You're a farm dog now," I told him. "You will have to get used
to dirt on your paws."

He stared at me with the disbelieving expression that only a
pug could master. It was a mix of betrayal and bewilderment.

There was no sign of my father outside. I hoped he was in the
house resting.

I walked toward the old barn. It was giant, over eighty feet long
and forty feet wide. When I was a child, the barn held our herd of
dairy cows. Dad sold those years ago. Being a dairy farmer was one
of the hardest jobs around. No matter the weather, the cows had to
be milked twice a day. The only animals left now were a few chickens and barn cats. As if to prove my point, a ginger-colored cat
pranced by with a cricket in her mouth. She looked at Huckleberry
and swallowed the cricket in one bite.

Huckleberry whimpered and hid behind my leg. It seemed
to me that neither one of us was getting a warm reception in
Michigan.

It took all my weight to open the barn door—something else
I'd need to have fixed. The list grew by the second.

A blue pickup truck rolled up the driveway and came to a stop
behind my car. My cousin Stacey hopped out. She wore a tank
top, cutoff jean shorts, and sneakers. In her midforties, she looked
younger than I did in my thirties.

Though we had never been close, it didn't stop me from recog-
nizing Stacey was one of the prettiest women I had ever seen in real
life, and I had lived in LA. She could give any of those Hollywood
movie stars a run for their money. Not only was Stacey the beauty
of the town, she was also the star. She headlined every musical,

sang a solo in every choir, and was written up in the local paper more times that anyone could count.

Maybe farm work was a way to stay fit. Perhaps that was something I could be thankful for by coming back to Cherry Glen. The manual labor would get my body in shape better than any expensive LA trainer had. Even so, I knew I would never look like Stacey.

"There you are," she said. "Your dad said that you'd be getting in yesterday. I would have been here to meet you too, but I had a meeting in Traverse City." She flipped her long, dark hair over her shoulder. I almost asked what shampoo she used. Her eyes were the most startling color of blue. She really was leading lady material, which was exactly what she had wanted to be. At seventeen, she'd left Cherry Glen for the bright lights of the stage. She had the talent and the looks to make it. Everyone in Cherry Glen said so. But Cherry Glen was not New York, where she'd live for several years to try to make it on Broadway.

I could have guessed what happened. She never got her big break. I lived in California long enough to know some of the most talented and beautiful women and men were waiting tables and working in small boutiques all over the city while they waited for the callback that never came.

"It's good to see you," I said. "Thank you for all the help you have given Dad around the farm, especially after he hurt his back. I could never thank you enough."

"Not a problem at all. You and Uncle Sully are the only family I have. We have to stick together." She smiled her perfect smile, which I knew was thanks to genetics, not an LA smile doctor. Genes that skipped my side of the family.

I thanked her again. Stacey and my father were the only family that I had too. I was also relieved that Stacey was being so nice to me. When we were younger, she always viewed me as the annoying younger cousin, and since we didn't stay in touch after I left Cherry Glen, I wasn't sure if that impression had stuck.

"You thinned out while in California." She patted my upper arm. "But there are still a few places to work." She smiled as if that made up for the insult. "Don't worry about your flabby arms. A few months of throwing hay bales will put those to rights. I could show you how to do it."

Sheesh. I was starting to think that my whole idea that there was a Midwestern niceness was from rose-tinted memories from my youth. Between Minnie, Laurel, and Stacey, my welcome back to Michigan had been lukewarm at best.

I didn't say it, but little did she know that at the moment, I was in the best shape of my life, and it had taken years of discipline and work to get *here*. I bit my lip and gave her the benefit of the doubt. She hadn't seen me in person since I was an awkward, overweight teenager. She didn't know who I was today. Just like I didn't know who she was either.

"Can I help you with something? Were you looking for Dad?" I asked.

She nodded. "I came by to check on Uncle Sully and share the news."

"News? What news?"

Her eyes went wide. "You will not believe this, but Jefferson Crocker is dead." She waved her hand. "That means nothing to you, but in town, it's the biggest thing to happen in decades."

I bit the inside of my lip. "I already know. I was at the farmers market this morning."

"You were? Did you see anything? Everyone is town is saying he was shot."

"That's what I heard too." I looked at my feet so she couldn't see my expression.

"That's crazy that it happened at the farmers market." She took a breath. "I mean this is Cherry Glen. Nothing like that happens here. Ever."

I grimaced.

"I'm not surprised Crocker is dead," she said. "He had to be the most loathed man in the county. I can think of at least four people who would have wanted to shoot him themselves if they had the nerve and knew they could get away with it."

This was news to me, and I was just about to ask my cousin who those other people were when the back door of the farmhouse opened and my father shuffled out on his walker.

"Stacey!" he said with a giant smile on my face. "I'm so glad you're here. You're as pretty as a picture."

My father greeted my cousin like she was his long-lost child even though he saw her often. He had not greeted me like that when I came back to the farm after years away. I pushed the jealousy bubbling inside me back. My father had every right to greet his niece any way he wished. I couldn't discount that Stacey had been the one at his side when I had been away. Even so...

"Uncle Sully, you should be inside resting. It's too hot out here for you."

My father smiled at her. "Bah, you've taken such good care of me, Stacey, I'll be all right. Glad to have both my favorite girls back on the farm." He included me in his smile, and the green-eyed monster backed down just a tad.

"As you should be," Stacey said.

He smiled at her. "I didn't know you were stopping by today. Is there something you need for the play? You said you didn't need me at the theater until tomorrow."

"No, no, everything with the play is going swimmingly. I

couldn't be happier. I can't thank you enough for giving me the
idea to set the play in that important time in Michigan history. I
think it will be the perfect draw to bring everyone back to the theater after it was closed so long. I hope you've been practicing your
lines as the soothsayer."

He puffed out his chest and quoted, "'That I have, lady. If it will
please Caesar to be so good to Caesar as to hear me, I shall beseech
him to befriend himself.'"

Stacey smiled. "Perfect. At least I know you will be ready."

"I didn't know you had any interest in acting," I said to my father.

"I didn't know I would be so good at it until Stacey asked me to
audition. I think I took to it quite well. I might have found a new
hobby."

I opened my mouth to ask another question when Stacey said,
"You're a natural, Uncle Sully. But I just left the diner and came
here to tell you the news. I didn't know Shiloh had already heard,
or I would have let her be the one to tell you."

"What news?" Dad asked.

"Jefferson Crocker is dead. He was shot in the chest. Everyone
in town is saying it was murder."

My father's mouth fell open. "Crocker is dead." He looked to
me. "You knew this?"

"I just learned about it when I was at the farmers market."

"And why didn't you tell me this?"

"I just got home. Stacey pulled in two minutes after me. I didn't
have the chance."

Dad gripped the arms of his walker. "What does this mean for
the farm? Will we lose it now that he's dead?"

Stacey jerked back. "Why would you lose the farm if Crocker is
dead? He had nothing to do with Bellamy Farm."

"He had nothing to do with Bellamy Farm until my daughter decided to take his money." Dad's voice shook.

Stacey turned to me. "*What?*"

"I didn't take any of his money," I said. "I don't have anything of his."

"You were going to take it," Dad said.

"Why?" Stacey asked. "That's insane."

The knot in my stomach tightened. "We needed an investor in the farm." I didn't want to add because of my father's back taxes. "Crocker was the only one who showed interest…"

"Of course he wanted to invest in the farm. It was so he could take it over for his wind farm. You would have to be an idiot to think it was for any other reason," Stacey said.

I felt the blood drain from my face. "What are you talking about?"

"You honestly don't know? I thought you would have seen the giant billboard that Crocker put up when you came into town. It's technically the next town over, so Cherry Glen can do nothing to make it come down."

"What billboard?" I asked.

"About the Cherry Glen wind farm. Crocker wanted to put hundreds of those giant turbines in Cherry Glen to collect wind power coming off Lake Michigan to make electricity."

"Is that bad?" I asked. "Isn't wind power better than fossil fuels?"

"It depends who you ask," Stacey said. "And anyways, it's less about the wind farm and more about Crocker trying to buy up all of Cherry Glen for himself."

"Why didn't you tell me this yesterday when he was here?" I asked.

Dad frowned. "Would it have made a difference? You had already signed a contract with him to invest in the farm."

"Are you nuts?" Stacey interjected. "You shouldn't have done that. You have no idea what you're getting yourself into. He's a shrewd man. That contract would have been written to *his* best advantage. Trust me."

I scowled at her. "I know that now."

"I know why he went into business with you." She shook her head as if she could not believe how stupid I had been. "According to the study, your farm is in the perfect position to collect the best gusts."

"Was he going to pay you for the use of the land?" I asked my father.

"Yes," Dad said, "but I said no."

"Why?" I asked.

"I wasn't going to let that scoundrel make money off my land!" Dad shook with anger. "He had asked me countless times to build here and even offered more money than I could imagine to buy half the farm."

I bit down on my tongue hard. A wind farm on part of the farm could have solved all our financial problems. Why hadn't Crocker told me about this? Was it because he knew Dad would never agree to it?

"How much money?" I shouldn't have asked. I knew Dad would be offended by the question.

"It doesn't matter," Dad said. "I would never take it. Cherry Glen is my home, and I'm not selling any part of it to anyone. It's not the Bellamy way."

"But—"

"No but," Dad snapped.

I bit my lip to stop a retort. My father was ill and attached to the farm. How could I have expected him to make any other choice?

Huckleberry whimpered at my feet. I looked down at him. At least someone here was on my side. I'd thought Crocker had been on my side too. He was the only one I spoke to who seemed to like the idea of bringing Bellamy Farm back as an organic farm. I thought we shared a vision for the future of the farm, but had I been wrong?

My father turned his walker around and stormed back to the house.

"Dad, please," I called after him.

He didn't so much as look over his shoulder.

Stacey pointed her finger at me. "Listen to me, Shi. You made a huge mistake and one that will come back to haunt you. Choices like this always do."

Before I could respond, she hurried after my father to help him into the house, which left me wondering if what she said was a warning or a threat.

Chapter Eight

My Grandma Bellamy used to say to me when I was young, "Don't sit there feeling sorry for yourself, Shi. Hiding's not the answer. If you don't like how your life is going, it's up to you to do something about it."

I had dearly loved my grandmother. Being back in Cherry Glen, it seemed like everywhere I looked, I was reminded of her. The overgrown garden at the back of the house where we'd spend hours weeding and picking strawberries. The chicken coop off the barn where each morning, we'd gather eggs together. The mass of blackberry bushes that ran the length of the south pasture and how we'd pick them in the evening when the sun was low in the sky. If I closed my eyes, I could almost taste her blackberry cobbler.

Grandma Bellamy was present in my thoughts the next morning as the old saying of hers popped into my head. I covered my face with my pillow. Hiding seemed like a great idea at the moment. I didn't like how my life was going. My father was angry with me over the farm. My cousin was disgusted with me. Quinn was going to tell his father, the police chief, that I had a personal connection to a murdered man. Maybe he would use it as revenge to finally get back at me for Logan's death. I wondered why on earth I ever thought I could go home again. I should have listened to the adage that said you can't go home again.

I sighed heavily into my pillow. There was nothing I could do to make the contract go away without talking to Crocker's estate. I needed an attorney to walk me through the legal ramifications of being under contract with a murder victim. Was I able to get out of the contract now due to the unique circumstances? Did I even want to?

But it was Sunday and way too early to make the phone call I was dreading to my best friend, Briar, an entertainment lawyer back in LA.

I lowered the pillow and looked around my pink childhood bedroom that still had the white eyelet curtains on the window, although the light could barely peek through the dust-covered fabric. I let out a breath and tried to channel Grandma Bellamy. Even in the last years of her life, she was doing chores around the farm and checking items off her list.

I distinctly remembered one conversation we had when I was twenty-one. I had asked her to sit down and rest, just as the doctor had said.

She looked me right in the eye. "Shi, I will rest when I'm dead. Until then, there are pies to bake and stalls to muck. Now, why are you standing there doing nothing? You should be getting to work too."

Snapping out of my reverie, I threw the covers off, covering up Huckleberry, who was sleeping at the end of my bed, in the process. He snuffled and whimpered until I moved the blanket from his head. Like always, the pug looked at me with those big, brown eyes of his round with surprise.

"Huck, we have work to do. Do you think Grandma Bellamy

would be lying in bed when there are important things to take care of? No way. She'd get to work, and that's just what we are going to do."

He snuffled. I took that to mean he was on board.

When I got downstairs, I found a note taped to the front door in my father's wobbly scrawl. "Stacey took me to church. Running lines with cast after service. Don't expect me home for lunch."

Oh-kay, so he was still upset with me. There was nothing I could do about that right then, so I might as well help the farm.

Thirty minutes later, I went outside the farmhouse with a clip-board, paper, and pen. I walked around the farm and wrote down everything I could see that needed to be weeded, mended, painted, trimmed, mowed, or plowed. In no time at all, I was on the back of the piece of paper and then on to a second sheet.

As daunting as the list was, it made me feel better. Any prob-lem could be fixed with an orderly plan and hard work. That was another of my grandmother's beliefs. If you didn't know how to do something, figure it out. I wondered if I could apply that to Crocker's murder as well. I may not know how to solve a murder, but I would figure it out. And I had to if I was going to clear the suspicion that would soon surround my family as soon as word of our business deal got out.

There was an old tree stump just outside the chicken coop. The five or six chickens that my father had left pecked at the feed I had thrown on the ground for them. I sat on the stump and put a fresh piece of paper on the top of my clipboard. At the very top, I wrote "Suspects." Who knew I would ever be in this place where I would have to think of such a thing? I pushed through the worry, because I always felt better when I wrote things down. A list always made things more manageable. If I wrote it in a list, I could break a problem down in pieces that could be solved one by one. It was how I solved complicated problems on my production sets, and it would be how I solved this one too.

I decided to head to the cherry orchard, a fifteen-minute walk from the farmhouse, to let the movement help clear my head. Huckleberry toddled behind me the whole way. The orchard covered five acres of the farm, and when I reached the edge of it, my heart sank. This job was going to be even bigger than I feared. The trees that weren't dead were overgrown. Others had withered leaves and puny cherries dangling from the branches. Typically, the tree height for a cherry orchard was five to six feet so the fruit could be easily reached. Some of the trees in this orchard were over eight feet tall. I would have to hire an arborist to come out and assess it and decide which could be saved and which had to be removed. That would be another expense.

One of the trees had fallen on its side. It looked like it had been uprooted by a storm. I sat on the trunk with Huckleberry at my feet and, trying to concentrate on the murder to distract me from the state of the farm, wrote, "Crocker's friends and family?"

The people closest to the victim were always suspects. I knew that from television. Jefferson Crocker didn't seem like the kindest man in the world or missed by the general public of the Glen, but someone out there loved him. He must have a family. He didn't drop into Cherry Glen out of thin air, did he? Maybe he did something to hurt a member of his family before and it was a murder of revenge. Or maybe his heir, whoever that might be, wanted him out of the way for access to his money or real estate holdings. A man who could afford to offer me so much cash with so many zeros and still pursue the construction of a wind farm had to be well off.

There had to be others besides Crocker's friends and family. I wrinkled my brow, remembering my father saying Crocker was trying to buy up the town. It was very possible that someone or several someones didn't want to sell to him. I wrote "Someone in Cherry Glen" on the list.

I stared down at the piece of paper and sighed. My list was sparse at best. However, it was a place to start in my search for the real killer, because I knew I had to find out who did this. I also knew there had to be more suspects. Hadn't my cousin said she could think of four people off the top of her head who would have wanted Crocker dead? I wondered, after she cooled down over my mistake, if she would be willing to help me.

I heard a limb snap somewhere in the orchard. Huckleberry barked, which told me my mind wasn't playing tricks on me. I grabbed the pug and held him to my chest. "Hello? Is someone there?"

Another twig snapped. It sounded like a gunshot and came from my left. I spun around. "If someone is there, you'd better come out or I'm sending my attack dog after you!"

Huckleberry whimpered at me.

Through the trees, I saw movement. I shifted to get a better look, but all I could glimpse was a shadow flitting quickly through the orchard. When I fought my way through the cherry branches to the other row, the shadow was gone.

I shivered and told myself it was deer, but in the back of my mind, I knew there was a murderer on the loose in Cherry Glen.

Chapter Nine

Sunday night, I had trouble sleeping. I struggled because I never worked up the nerve to call Briar and tell her what was happening, and worries about the farm and the trespasser I had seen in the orchard during the day plagued me. The more I told myself it was a deer, the less I believed it. So I was up at five Monday morning, working on the barn. My goal was to clean it out and have room to store the new equipment I wanted to buy—assuming I could find the money.

Huckleberry, the barn cats, and the chickens looked on while I carried equipment out of the building and sorted it into piles to go to the dump or save for future use. Farmers weren't good at getting rid of things, and my father was no exception. Every broken piece of machinery was saved for decades just in case he could use a part from it. My hope was to organize the various pieces from the tractor, combine, and plow so the barn felt more open and usable.

The back door of the farmhouse opened, and my father came out. He was in his play costume: weathered trousers, a camping jacket, and a raccoon hat. I hoped it wasn't made with real raccoon but was too afraid to ask. The clothes hung loosely on him, and I saw his belt was cinched tightly around his waist to keep his trousers up. He leaned on his cane, which just barely supported him. He would have done much better with his walker, but I guessed it didn't go with the uniform.

"Dad, I didn't expect you up this early."

He eyed me. "Early? It's after seven. Any farmer worth his salt is up at five."

I grimaced. I didn't know that I made a very good farmer then. I was up early today because of stress, but if given the chance, I could easily sleep in until ten.

He shuffled to his old truck parked beside the barn. It was a red Ford with an extended cab, and he had owned it for as long as I could remember.

I followed him. "Are you going somewhere?"

He looked over his shoulder. "I promised Stacey I would help out with the play today. It's important that I'm there. I am a lead and the historical consultant."

That explained the uniform. "Is it a dress rehearsal today?"

"No, but I think it's important to wear the clothes you'll wear in the play during rehearsals. It keeps you in character." He paused. "Are you coming to the theater today?"

"I'm not sure. There's a lot to do…"

He frowned. "I think you should. You and Stacey didn't start out on the right foot, and she needs your support. *Julius Caesar* opens Friday night. It's important that this first performance goes well. The future of the Michigan Street Theater is riding on it. There's so much to do these last few days before the play. I'm sure she wouldn't turn down another volunteer."

I frowned. Stacey needed *my* support? What about her supporting me? I was the one trying to save our family legacy. I really didn't have time to volunteer at the play. Didn't my father see the state of the farm?

I bit my lip to stop myself from snapping back. "I can stop by the theater," I said, promising nothing more. "I would like to see the inside of the theater and you on the stage."

He opened the door to his truck and put his cane inside. "Good." Carefully, moving at a snail's pace, he climbed in. His movements were stilted, but I stopped myself from offering him any help. I knew my father well enough to know that it would not have been well-received. No matter what my intentions, he would find it insulting that I thought he couldn't do something himself. Which maybe explained his grumpiness given the whole farm situation and him needing my help. I wisely held back the questions on the tip of my tongue as to whether he should be driving at all.

Keeping a careful eye on him just in case I needed to jump into action, I went through my mental to-do list. Clean up and update the farm, find out the status of my contract with Crocker now that he's dead, and find a killer. There wasn't much time in there to volunteer at the theater. However, by the expression on my father's face, I knew there was a wrong answer in this case. "I'll drop in sometime today. Promise."

He nodded and slammed the door shut.

Huckleberry was at my feet, and I scooped him up while my father turned the truck around and drove down the long drive-way toward town. I watched him go with an ache in my heart. I had to make things right between my father and me, or I might as well pack my bags and head back to LA. I would be lying if I didn't admit that California was looking quite appealing at the moment.

I put the dog down and held the clipboard to my chest. "Huckleberry, I hate to say this, but we're going to have to go to Jessa's Place."

He looked up at me with those wide eyes.

"I know, I know," I said. "It's a terrible idea, but it's the best option we have to find out who would want to kill Jefferson Crocker."

He made a snuffling sound, which I took as assent.

"You will love it," I told him with more confidence than I felt. "I'm sure Jessa will spoil you. I, on the other hand, will not like it in the least." That, I was certain was true.

I went back into the house to get ready for the onslaught. Onslaught was no better way to describe a visit to Jessa's Place when you were the center of attention.

I had known when I returned to Michigan, I would be the talk of the sleepy town where I grew up, but I never knew it would be this bad, and I certainly didn't think it would include a dead body.

I tucked the convertible in the small gravel parking lot to the side of the diner between two pickup trucks with rifle racks. The term "gravel" was used loosely. Most of the small pebbles had been ground so far into the dust and dirt they could no longer be seen. My little convertible was out of place in the parking area dominated with trucks, minivans, and sedans that had been on Michigan's winter roads for two decades or more. I wrinkled my nose. Maybe I should start driving my father's truck with the hope I would blend in a little bit better.

I stepped out of the car, snapped on Huckleberry's leash, and asked him to hop out. We started toward the diner. As I remembered, Jessa had let dogs in the diner if they stayed by the front door.

"Hey, sugar," a man said to me as I walked toward the diner. "Looking good!"

I spun around. "Listen!" I prepared to deliver a tongue-lashing to the catcaller. My mouth fell open.

"I heard you were back in Cherry Glen." The large teddy bear of a man in the Cherry Glen High School T-shirt grinned from ear to ear. "Kristy told us. I said we should get the whole gang back together." He shook his head. "She didn't tell me how much you've changed. California has been good to you!"

"Wesley Sumner!" I cried. "I had no idea you still lived in the Glen." Next to Kristy, Wes had been my closest high school friend, but I hadn't seen or spoken to him since the day I left town. He had also been friends with Logan.

He laughed. "I was one of those who never got out. However, seeing how everyone seems to boomerang back to town, it seems to me I would be here one way or another by now."

Boomerang was the right word for it—or whiplash. I felt like I was in a constant state of memory whiplash since I came back to my hometown. "How have you been?" I asked.

"Can't complain," Wes said. "Amy and I have two boys now. They are both in high school."

Amy Mulligan had been his high school sweetheart, like Logan and I had been. Unlike Logan and me, they got married right out of high school.

"You have kids in high school?" I asked. "If that doesn't make me feel old, I don't know what will," I said.

He laughed. "As soon as my oldest entered ninth grade, I felt ancient. Now he's going into eleventh, and my youngest is going into ninth." He squatted down and scratched my pug between the ears. "Who's this?"

"This is Huckleberry."

He stood up. "My kids would love him. They keep asking for a dog. So far, we have resisted."

"I'm so happy to see you," I said. "Are you working on your family farm?"

A strange look crossed his face. "No. We had to sell the farm. Price of milk dropped too low to make a go of it. We just couldn't compete with all the factory farms out there lowering milk prices. We couldn't pay the bills. There wasn't much else we could do there after that. My pops never wanted to get into any other kind of farming. It was enough money for Mom and Dad to retire to a condo in Traverse City. Now, they play bocce every day of the week, and Mom's in a book club."

I nodded. It was the common story for a family farm. I supposed I should be happy we'd been able to hang on to the property. Unfortunately, the Sumner family hadn't been as lucky. I was relieved to hear it worked out for Wes's parents though. It didn't always go like that. Oftentimes, farmers were financially ruined by selling out.

"I'm sorry to hear about the farm. You had a beautiful piece of land."

He smiled. "Thanks. It was about ten years ago. It was for the best, but I will admit at the time, I was devastated. I always thought I would be a farmer and pass that legacy down to my kids. I never wanted to work in an office. It took me a little while to find something I liked as much."

"What are you doing now?" I asked.

"I work for the county park service. It doesn't pay much, but Amy is a teacher, and we get by. I love the work, and I have opportunities to collaborate with the National Park Service on several events a year. As sad as it was to let the farm go, I really found my passion in being a park ranger. I never would have found my true calling without it."

I smiled. "I'm glad to hear that."

"Have you seen anyone else from the old days?"

"Kristy and Laurel. Oh, and Quinn."

"Ah, how'd that go?" Wes leaned in like he was still in high school, waiting for a piece of juicy gossip.

"Fine," I said, hoping he wouldn't ask any more about it. I certainly hoped he wouldn't mention Logan. Quinn had been very vocal about how he felt about me after Logan's death. I was certain Wes knew that too.

He laughed and then nodded at the cinder block restaurant. "You heading into Jessa's?"

I nodded. "I'm hoping her coffee is as good as I remember."

"It is, but…" He rocked back on his heels. "I'm not sure you want to go in there."

I frowned. "Why not?"

"Well, there is the little issue of Jefferson Crocker's death."

"Ah, so you heard about that?" Just as I had expected, it was the talk of the town.

"Everyone who lives within thirty miles of the Glen has heard about it. I was just in Jessa's, and it's the main topic of conversation. Your name came up a few times."

I grimaced. "How did it come up?"

He winced. "There was a pretty vocal woman who said that you were the one who shot him. She told anyone who would listen."

"Was her name Minnie?" I asked.

"How'd you know?"

I shuffled back and forth on my feet. I hadn't seen or spoken to Wes since high school. He had been a close friend of mine when we were growing up. He, Kristy, a few other kids, and I would pal around together, but again, that was a long time ago. I didn't know anything about his life now, and he surely didn't know anything about mine. Even so, everything I could tell him about Minnie, she would have probably told him herself.

"She saw me right after I found Crocker's body and jumped to the conclusion I must have something to do with his death. She was also very upset he died so close to her honey booth."

He nodded. "She did mention the booth. She's still steamed about that. It seems the police confiscated the whole thing. I would stay out of her way if I were you. In her mind, you are public enemy number one."

I winced. From what I could tell about Minnie, I knew this to be true. "Is she still in the diner?" I would seriously rethink my bright idea of going in there if she was.

"No, she left a half hour ago. She said she had to make play rehearsal."

"Play rehearsal?" I squeaked. It couldn't possibly be the same play that my father was in, could it?

"Yep, she's in the production being put on by the Michigan Street Theater. I thought you would have known about it. Doesn't your cousin Stacey own that place?"

I nodded. Suddenly, stopping by the theater as my father requested felt like a terrible idea.

He cleared his throat. "If it makes you feel better, I know you didn't kill anyone," he said with confidence. "But if you did... Jefferson Crocker is not a bad choice, and I think most of the people in town would agree with that."

"Why is that?" My skin tingled. Maybe I would finally get some suspect names for my pathetic list.

"The man was a sleazeball. All he cared about was making more money. I think he must have had more money than God at this point, but for some reason, he wanted more and more, no matter what the cost. Trust me, if you ask anyone, they won't say they are sad he'd dead, not even his wife."

"He's married?" A wife would be an excellent suspect.

"Yes, but I think they were separated and have been for a long while. From what I heard, Crocker didn't want to get an official divorce because they didn't have a prenup. He would be stuck giving his wife half of everything. A selfish man like him wouldn't want to do that."

"What's her name?" I hoped my question sounded more casual to him than it did to my own ears.

"Shannon Crocker," he said. "I believe she's in your cousin's play too."

And now I had a real name to add to my list of suspects. I would say trapping a woman into a marriage she no longer wanted to avoid losing his fortune was a pretty good motive for murder. I hoped Chief Randy would put her on his list too. I didn't know how he could possibly ignore her, knowing that.

"I'm not kidding that no one misses Crocker. I was in Jessa's Place when I heard about the murder. A few people cheered," Wes said. "That is how deep their dislike of him runs."

I internally winced. As bad as Jefferson Crocker seemed to have been, I still couldn't fathom celebrating the fact that someone was dead. He might not have popular agendas, but he was still a person whose life was cut short by another person. Didn't that count for a little sympathy?

"I can see why his wife wouldn't be upset he was dead, but why would the rest of the town celebrate?"

"Because he owned Cherry Glen and reminded everyone in town of the fact as often as possible."

"How could he own a town?" I asked.

"By buying up all the real estate. Crocker had been doing it for years. A business failed or a house foreclosed, he bought. If someone else wanted the property that he wanted as well, Crocker would outbid the other person."

"When I arrived, I noticed that Cherry Glen had changed a lot. There are so many new businesses, and Michigan Street is barely recognizable."

He nodded. "That's because of Crocker. He had the money to build up the town."

"Is that a bad thing?"

"It depends who you ask. There are a lot of people who don't like the idea of one man owning so much of Cherry Glen." Wes folded his arms. "He bought the properties and rented them to the businesses. With all the changes in town over the last several years, he must have been making money hand over fist. He even bought the town hall. He owns it free and clear. Paid in cash, from what I heard. Don't tell me that doesn't give him an advantage when he's trying to push his agendas through the town council."

It seemed to me it would be a clear conflict of interest for him to own the town hall and still make requests from the town council, but I didn't know enough about rural Michigan policy to be sure.

"At least we no longer have to worry about his big agenda, the wind farm."

"The wind farm? My cousin mentioned that yesterday. She said there was a billboard coming into town about it too. I only vaguely remember seeing it."

He scowled. "I bet you can guess who put that up."

"Crocker?" I said.

"Right."

"Maybe I'm missing something, but what do people in Cherry Glen have against renewable energy? Doesn't everyone want that?"

"There is nothing against renewable energy. I'm a park ranger, and of course I want that, but the plan Crocker had was just wrong. He would put his wind farm on people's property without their permission. He said the town should claim eminent domain. He didn't care what impact it would have on the wildlife of the region or the parks either."

"Was the wind farm to be put on parkland too?" I asked.

He frowned. "You would be surprised what the government allows to happen in parks now if someone with enough money and influence asks for it." He scowled. "But no, in this case, the wind farm was to be all on private land only, so the parks had nothing to do with it or no means to stop it."

"I could see why the people who own the land would be upset, but why is the general public against it?"

"Birds."

"Birds?"

"Yes, birds. Wind farms kill thousands of birds every year while they migrate both in the spring and fall. Crocker is not taking that into consideration at all. I don't hate wind farms, but I believe that we have to be responsible about their placement."

I grimaced as I thought about it. "That's awful. I had no idea."

"Exactly, it is awful. We are only twenty miles from Lake

Michigan. Michigan, in general, is a major migration path for birds as they come from Central and South America to the northern United States and Canada every year. All the evidence proves that Cherry Glen would have been one of the worst places to put a wind farm because of migration patterns. Someone like Crocker cares more about making money than saving birds. He's not doing this because he's a good-doing environmentalist. He's doing it to make money."

Was I crazy to think Crocker might have been killed over birds?

"Was everyone in the town against it because of the birds?" I asked.

"Not everyone, but it wasn't a popular idea in general," he said.

"I would think there might have been enough public disapproval to stop it."

"Well, we'll never know now, will we? Anyway, most of the people just didn't like Crocker getting his way all the time. It was discouraging watching him buy up the town like he did. There are a number of conspiracy theories out there over what he was going to do with Cherry Glen when he bought up every last piece of it."

"He wanted all of it?" I asked.

"I don't know if he ever said that to anyone, but that's what most folks thought." He sighed. "If you're really interested in learning more about the wind farm, you should talk to Hedy."

"Hedy?" I asked.

"Hedy Strong. She's the driving force that has stopped Crocker from getting his way on this matter. She's a powerhouse and has raised thousands of dollars to cover the court costs to fight him. She's a hero to all the environmentalists in the region. There aren't many of us around here, but we are still a powerful and vocal group."

His cell phone rang, and he unclipped it from his belt. "It's the park. I had better get going. It was nice to see you, Shiloh. Maybe Amy and I can host a get-together. The kids are rarely home in the evenings. They are way busier than we ever were when we were their age."

"Sounds fun," I said, but as he walked away, I couldn't help but think my old friend just might be a new suspect in Jefferson Crocker's murder. Wes had always been passionate about animals. In fact, when we were in biology class together, he convinced me to help him free all the frogs from the lab one day after school. The great frog escape ended with a local pond being stocked with thirty new bullfrogs and a week's detention. So it didn't surprise me in the least that Wes would be so upset about the wind turbines.

"Oh, before I forget." He turned around and removed his wallet from his pocket, pulling out a bent business card. "If you want to talk to Hedy, that's the best way to get in contact with her. You might have to call a few times. If she's out birding, she will have her phone on silent so it doesn't scare the birds."

I took the card from his hand. "Grand Traverse County Birders. Hedy Strong, President." Below that, there was a phone number and a website. "Thank you," I said, because I did want to make contact with Hedy, but that had more to do with murder than with the birds. I realized it just might have to do with both.

Chapter Ten

As soon as I walked into the diner, all conversation stopped, and I didn't think it was because I had a pug in my arms. Huckleberry and I stood wide-eyed as we looked around the room for a friendly face. The only sound was the droning of an old television tethered to the wall. At this time of day, it was tuned to a game show. The host told the contestant she could be a millionaire if she just answered the next three questions correctly. The contestant looked as nervous as I felt.

Coming to Jessa's Place was a mistake. Why had I thought it smart to run right into the lion's den of gossip?

"Land sakes! Shiloh!" a woman called from the back of the diner. Jessa Yates hurried toward me. Although many years had gone by, I recognized her right away. Pink and purple highlights decorated the white ponytail secured at the nape of her neck with an orange bandanna. Jessa was into unicorn hair before it was trendy and even before it had a name. When I was a child, she had dyed it all sorts of different colors, determined by the time of year and the closest holiday. I'd been in awe of her boldness. As an adult, I admired her even more. She wove through the customers, saying, "Ope, sorry" as she went to reach me.

"Well, I can't believe what I'm seeing. It's Shiloh Bellamy all grown up!" Jessa cried and enveloped me in a giant hug before holding me at arm's length. "Shiloh Bellamy, you look good. You might be the closest thing this town has ever seen to a supermodel."

I blushed.

If any of the silent diners had missed my arrival when I stepped into the building, they certainly knew I was there now.

"That California sun agrees with you. I'm so envious of your tan. I would love to get a tan myself if I ever had a chance to get out of this diner, but you know how it is, business first." She backed up. "Who is this adorable little pooch?"

Huckleberry snuffled from being smushed in the hug. I set him on the floor. "This is Huckleberry. Is it okay if he stays up front here?"

"Of course it is." She pointed to the corner of the room beneath the television. "There is a water bowl there. I love dogs, and I can never say no to them." She reached into her apron pocket and came up with a dog biscuit. "There you go, Huckleberry honey. Go take a rest in the corner there while I speak to your mom."

The pug took the treat in his mouth and then looked up to me as if to ask if it was okay. I nodded. He trotted to the corner of the diner and plopped down.

"Now, you look to me like you could use some coffee," Jessa said.

"I could," I admitted, acutely aware of everyone in the diner watching us. The diner remained eerily quiet.

Jessa must have noticed too, because she said, "Hey, get back to eating, you nosey parkers."

Everyone, even the old, seasoned farmers who had come to

Jessa's every day for forty years, ducked their heads and dug into their breakfasts. They wouldn't risk upsetting the diner owner and being banned from Jessa's.

Jessa wrapped her arm around my shoulder. "Come with me. All our tables are full, but I can set you up at the lunch counter. That will be more fun anyway. We can chat."

When I didn't move, she tugged on my arm and pulled me through the tightly packed vinyl booths and faux wooden tables. At the lunch counter, she pointed to a stool, and I sat. The seats were covered with cracked purple vinyl, the same seat covers that had been there when I was a teenager. I took care to make sure my bare legs didn't touch the sharp edges for fear of getting cut. Wearing shorts had been another mistake I made that day. Even so, it was comforting to find one thing in Cherry Glen that had not changed.

"My, I don't think I have seen you since Logan Graham's funeral."

I folded my hands in my lap and squeezed them together.

"He was such a good kid, and the two of you were such a sweet couple. I really thought you were ones who were going to make it."

I had too. I cleared my throat. "Can I have a glass of water?"

"Of course, sugar. Can I get you some coffee too?" Jessa asked.

"Yes, please. Just with a little bit of cream," I said.

"You got it." She put a plain white mug in front of me that had been in the diner since President Kennedy was in office, perhaps even longer. Over sixty years ago, Jessa's father had opened the diner as a young man. When Jessa was born years later, he renamed it after his baby daughter.

Jessa filled the mug with coffee and slid it to me. "Can I get you anything to eat?" She set a glass of water next to the mug.

The diner smelled like bacon and fresh biscuits, like heaven and hell all at the same time. I had been on a strict diet in LA. I hadn't eaten bacon in over fifteen years and had told myself I would stick to that diet in Michigan. In theory, it shouldn't be harder to diet in my hometown than it had been in California, but in reality, it could easily all go out the window when presented with the blue plate special at Jessa's Place.

I shook my head. "Coffee is just fine." I took a sip as if to prove my point and burned my tongue in the process. I covered my mouth to hide my expression.

She tucked a pencil behind her ear. "If you're not here to eat, I would guess you were here for information."

My brow went up.

"Don't you look surprised, miss." She tapped her long pink nail on the counter. It was the same shade of pink as the dye in her hair. "I heard all about you finding Jefferson Crocker at the farmers market. Minnie Devani was in here this morning telling anyone who would listen that you killed him to close down her business. She had worked herself up good over it. I had to kick her out to keep the peace."

My shoulders sagged. "I didn't kill anyone, and I certainly wouldn't kill someone to destroy a business I had never even known existed." I winced. "I knew she had been here already though. I ran into Wes Sumner outside, and he mentioned her outburst."

"Outburst is one way to put it. I remember that you used to run with him and Kristy Garcia when you were young."

"Brown now," I said. "I saw her yesterday too. I can't believe she's having twins."

Jessa laughed. "I don't think she can believe it either, and her husband is walking around town in a constant state of shock over it. He teaches at the high school, so he has the whole summer off to wonder and worry about the babies. He shouldn't worry. Kristy is one of the most capable women I've ever met, but it does no good telling him that." She patted my hand. "And you should know I told Minnie it was a bunch of codswallop that you killed Crocker. You're not capable of it."

"Thanks, Jessa," I said and then lowered my voice. "Wes said not too many people would be upset over Crocker's death."

"I gather that he's right about that. Jefferson Crocker was not a popular man in Cherry Glen."

"I heard about the wind farm."

She rolled her eyes. "The wind farm is part of it, for some people. It is for Hedy Strong. She's a force to be reckoned with. But she and her bird people are as bad as Crocker and his developer types. They all have agendas if you ask me, and neither group takes the hardworking folks of Cherry Glen into account. They don't care if the impact of what they do affects people living here. One way or another, the only people who actually live and work in this town are the ones who are going to be hurt and the ones footing the bill. I have seen it too many times before. I don't know what will happen now. Maybe they will drop it. I can't see Shannon wanting to go through with it with public opinion so low."

"Crocker's wife, Shannon?"

She raised her brow at me. "How long have you been back in Cherry Glen? It sounds like you know quite a bit about what's happening around here."

"Wes filled me in."

She laughed. "That explains it. That man is the same chatterbox he was in high school. Have you seen your other old friends?" She raised her eyebrows. "What about Quinn?"

I was saved from answering because a customer from a table across the room waved his empty coffee mug in Jessa's direction.

She held up a finger to me. "Hold that thought, and we will get into it."

Get into it? Get into what?

Jessa filled the man's coffee, took three orders, called them back to the cook through the kitchen window behind the counter, lined her arms with six full plates, dispersed the plates to their tables with a smile, and was back standing in front of me in a matter of three minutes. She moved so quickly I got dizzy just watching her. No one would doubt Jessa's efficiency when it came to running the family diner. She had been working at the place ever since she could walk. My father would tell me stories about tiny Jessa seating customers and bringing them water when she was small. Clearly, no one cared about child labor laws at the time.

"What were we chatting about?" she asked.

The last thing I wanted to talk about was Quinn, so I quickly changed the subject. "You said Shannon Crocker wouldn't bother to go through with the wind farm."

She nodded. "That's right. She and Jefferson had no children, and now that he's dead, she stands to inherit more money than she can ever use. I can't see her wanting to pursue the wind farm when she's already set up for life. It would be a lot of work, and Hedy and her bird people are fighting it hard. The legal headache would be a nightmare for Shannon. I wouldn't say she's the most self-motivated woman I've ever met."

"How can I find Shannon?" I asked.

She studied me. "Why would you want to do that?"

"I—I—" It wasn't like I could say, "Because she might be a possible murder suspect." I didn't think it would endear me much to the people of Cherry Glen.

"Jessa, can I get a warm-up?" a man in a worn trucker hat asked from the end of the counter.

She slid down the counter and filled his coffee, grabbed plates from the window, and deftly delivered them to the right tables without missing a beat.

"Or maybe I'm wrong and Shannon will go through with it," Jessa said as she slid back in front of me. "She's a bit of a loose cannon. She's surprised us before."

I was relieved she dropped the question as to why I wanted to talk to Shannon, but now I was curious what she meant when she said Shannon was a loose cannon. Did that mean she was violent? But Jessa was called away again before I could ask.

When Jessa came back, she said, "It's hard to say how the town council will decide on the wind farm now that Crocker is dead. It was a shoo-in that Crocker would get his way. The council was to meet on Thursday evening and take the final vote, and the wind farm was bound to pass. It didn't matter what Hedy Strong and her crazy band of birders said about it."

"Was the town going to pass it because of tax revenue?" I could see how that would be appealing to a farming town. Property taxes for schools and other public services were constantly voted down because people owned so much land. A five percent hike on property tax on three hundred acres was a serious amount of money.

"Maybe," she mused. "But I would say it was more because they were in debt to Crocker. They are all protecting their own backsides."

"In debt how?"

A woman at a table waved at Jessa.

"Hold that thought, miss." She opened a glass-domed case that covered the most delicious-looking cinnamon rolls I had ever seen. With tongs, she removed the top one from the pile, set it on a plate, and slid it in front of me.

I stared at it. That one cinnamon roll could undo fifteen years of dieting.

Jessa shook her finger at me. "Don't you turn up your nose at that. You just found a dead body. If I ever saw a person who was in a desperate need of a cinnamon bun, it's you. I made them fresh this morning, and it's on the house. And I saw you staring at them any time I walked away from the counter."

I inwardly groaned. Had my longing for cinnamon gooey baked goodness been that obvious?

Also she had a point about the whole dead body thing. I pulled the plate closer and grabbed a fork from the glass Mason jar on the counter. I'd just have a taste.

Chapter Eleven

The bells over the diner's front door chimed, and Kristy walked in. Actually, waddled in would have been a more accurate description. She waved to a couple of people as she made her way across the room. I had to note no one stopped talking when she walked in the door like they had for me. That had been special treatment just for me.

She hoisted herself onto the stool next to me. "I've been looking for you."

"How did you find me? I forgot to give you my cell number yesterday."

"I know. Luckily, Wes shot me a text that you were here. I'm glad he did, because I went to Bellamy Farm looking for you. Girl, I haven't been back to your family farm since you left. It's a mess. You have your work cut out for you."

Before I could say anything in response, she pointed at the cinnamon roll. "Are you going to eat that?"

"No," I squeaked.

Kristy grabbed the plate and another fork from the jar and dug in. She moaned after her first bite. That only made me feel even worse for letting the treat go. I consoled myself with the reminder that I could zip up my jeans this morning.

"That is so good. I would take a bath in that icing if I could. Sugar heaven."

"Why were you looking for me?" I asked.

"I wanted to make sure you were all right." She studied me over another forkful of cinnamon goodness. "Are you all right?"

"I think so." I didn't sound convincing.

She frowned. "Wes told me what Minnie was saying too. Don't worry about her. Minnie is never happy. She's going to be horrid to live with as long as the police have her booth. She has texted me four times already this morning asking if she could get a refund back for the farmers market season since she has no honey to sell or booth to sell it in."

"What did you tell her?"

"Nothing yet. I'm going to let her sweat it for a bit. I'm seven months pregnant with twins in the middle of July. Everything hurts. I was finally able to fall asleep at five this morning, and I got awakened by her text less than an hour later. I'm not doing her any favors." She stabbed the cinnamon roll with gusto.

I didn't argue with a woman eating a cinnamon roll like it was her very last meal.

She licked her fork and set it on the now empty plate. "I had another reason to look for you too. Chief Randy was asking about you after you left the farmers market yesterday. He wanted to get my take on you now that you're back."

My stomach twisted into a knot. "What did you tell him?"

"I said the Shiloh Bellamy I knew would never hurt a soul. I said you were a quiet person who loved books more than anything."

I frowned. To my ears, it sounded like I was a crazy Unabomber type. I wasn't sure that was the perception I wanted Chief Randy to have of me.

"And I told him," she went on, "that you wouldn't have any reason to want to kill Jefferson Crocker. You've been in California. He didn't even live here when we were kids. You don't know him. You have no motive at all." She dropped her fork on her plate as if that was case closed.

Would Minnie get her way? Could people in Cherry Glen seriously think I could kill someone? What impact would that have on the farm if my reputation was ruined?

Kristy leaned closer to me. "I've never seen that happen before, but all the color drained from your face."

"I'm fine," I said and sipped my coffee.

"I know you're worried Minnie's jabber mouth, but I'm sure this will all blow over, Shi. You had no reason to kill Crocker. Chief Randy is just doing his job by asking."

The door to the diner opened again, and the mayor came inside. Kristy wrinkled her nose and whispered, "If anyone has a motive to take out Crocker, it's that man."

Mayor Loyal smiled at the people in the diner. He shook hands, patted people on their backs, and asked them about their work and children. I would have thought he was in the middle of a campaign.

"Is he running for office this year?"

She shook her head. "I think he has three more years on his term. Not that there will be any doubt he will win again. He's been the mayor for fifteen years."

That was interesting to hear. "He's acting like he's in the middle of an election."

"He's always in a race to win public approval, I guess." Kristy got up and walked around the counter to help herself to some of Jessa's coffee. She filled up my mug and two others sitting at the counter. "She won't mind. I do this all the time."

"Why do you say that about the mayor?" I asked.

"I'm sure I'm not the only one who thinks he has the biggest reason to want Crocker dead."

I lowered my voice, afraid someone would overhear. "What would his motive be?"

"Jefferson Crocker owns the town hall. He had the ability to make the town council do whatever he liked. A man as self-important as Mayor Loyal wouldn't want to be booted from his comfy office."

I opened my mouth to ask another question. Kristy gave me a slight shake of the head, and I snapped my mouth closed.

"Kristy!" The mayor called behind me. "It's so good to see you. I hope Saturday's shock doesn't take a toll on the little ones." He stared at her stomach and laughed. "I would say that the babies are looking well by the size of you."

Kristy's eyes narrowed. If I were the mayor, I wouldn't make any more comments about her size.

A woman in the next booth muttered to her friend, "Moron."

I had to agree with that.

"I know it must have quite upsetting to put the market on hold," the mayor went on. "But it couldn't be helped. When a prominent citizen dies in such a way, we have to stop and take note."

I frowned. I hadn't known that the farmers market had closed after I left.

"The farmers market will be back in business on Wednesday," Kristy said. "The chief has already told me that. Of course, we feel horrible over what happened, but it won't have any lasting impact on the market."

"That's good news." Mayor Loyal smiled at me. "Hello, who's your friend?" He held out his hand to me. "Mayor Fred Loyal. Are you visiting our charming little town? If you are, I suggest you take in the play this coming weekend. It will be quite the production if I do say so myself."

I removed my hand from his clammy grasp as soon as I thought it was polite but felt relieved that he didn't appear to recognize me from the murder scene on Saturday. I was proud of myself for not wiping my hand on my shorts, but goodness knew I wanted to.

"I'll be playing the lead, Julius Caesar. Stacey Bellamy, our director, told me I was perfect for the lead role."

I thought it was best not to make a comment on this. Or that Julius Caesar was the title character but that general literary consensus was Marcus Brutus was the lead of Shakespeare's tragedy.

"Mayor Loyal, Shiloh knows Stacey. This is Shiloh Bellamy, Sully's daughter."

He blinked. "Well, there you are. I didn't put two and two together that you were Sully's girl. It's been a stressful few days, and my memory is not what it used to be."

"Well, I moved away fifteen years ago," I said, nonplussed. I was thirty-eight and was often told I looked young for my age. I didn't believe the mayor thought the same. It made me wonder if all the people who had said that through the years had been lying. Or it could be the mayor was just a jerk. I'd put my money on the latter.

"Did you just arrive into town? Sully told me you were moving back. I think it's a great show of support for your elders that you've moved back. My son did the same. I couldn't be more proud of the boy."

Before I could ask who his son was, he went on to say, "Of course, Cherry Glen is a little different than you remember, I would wager. We are an up-and-coming town. The theater is a great improvement and the brewery too. We are really starting to attract tourists visiting Sleeping Bear Dunes and Traverse City. Why, I think in no time at all, people will be coming to quaint Cherry Glen to vacation and go to the dunes and the city for day trips. I'm proposing that we build an inn. It has to be country-simple yet state-of-the-art."

"Sounds impressive," I said.

"It's just one of the many improvements we plan to roll out."

"Who's going to pay for it?" Kristy asked. "I mean if Jefferson Crocker is dead, wasn't he bankrolling most of these *improvements*?"

The mayor tugged on his collar. "Yes, Crocker was an important part of revitalizing Cherry Glen, and I speak for all the city officials when I say we are deeply saddened at his passing. Even so, I believe that Jefferson Crocker would want us to continue on in the improvements and his good works."

Kristy picked up my coffee mug and drank from it. I thought that was comment enough from her.

The mayor tapped his chin. "Wait! I *do* know you!" He snapped his fingers as if a thought just came to him. "You're the one who found Jefferson. What a dreadful sight it was. You have had a quite a shock. I hope Jessa gave you one of her cinnamon rolls. There's nothing those rolls can't fix. She's given me quite a few over my years as mayor."

"I ate it for her," Kristy said with no apology in her voice.

I sighed. I could have really used that cinnamon roll right now.

"I hope you're not upset the police consider you a suspect." He smiled. "It's just part of the investigation."

I glanced around, and diners sitting at the tables around us had perked up when they heard that. I bet everyone in town was interested in this conversation. I would be surprised if a single person in Cherry Glen didn't know what happened and my involvement in it.

"That's ridiculous," Kristy said. "Why on earth would she be a suspect?"

The mayor cocked his head. "I was told Jefferson was an investor in her farm. If that doesn't make her a suspect"—he raised his eyebrows and turned toward me—"you are certainly a person of interest, right?"

Kristy's mouth fell open, and I jumped off my stool. It toppled over on the linoleum floor.

"I'm so sorry," I said, scooping up the stool. "It was so nice to see you both, but I need to get back to the farm." I forced a smile. "Farm work is never done."

I tossed a few bills on the counter for the coffee and for the cinnamon roll I didn't eat. Jessa told me not to pay her, but I wasn't going to look like I was running out of the diner without paying when I was already a murder suspect. I didn't want to look like a cheat too.

"Shi!" Kristy called after me, but I scooped up Huckleberry from the corner of the diner and was out the door before she could utter another word.

Chapter Twelve

On the sidewalk, I took a deep breath and clutched Huckleberry to my chest. I was in even more trouble than I feared. The police knew about Jefferson's contract with Bellamy Farm now, despite my trying to keep the rumor mill quiet. I was sure my family affairs were finally fodder for all Cherry Glen busy-bodies. Would it make a difference that I had not taken any money from him yet? It should. Why would we kill someone whose money would save our farm? Especially money we needed now, not whenever Crocker's massive estate may be settled in the future. However, I wasn't sure the police would see it that way. My father had been quite vocal in front of Quinn that he was upset with my decision. Quinn was the chief's son. It was pretty clear where his loyalties would fall.

A couple passed me as they went into the diner. They didn't give me a second look. They didn't know who I was, at least not yet. It wouldn't be long before everyone in Cherry Glen knew Shiloh Bellamy was back and had gotten mixed up in a murder investigation. If that rumor took hold, my dreams of turning the farm around were doomed.

Up the street stood Michigan Street Theater. I had forgotten it was so close to Jessa's Place. Where was the best place to go to learn more about Crocker and who might have wanted him dead?

Not to mention Crocker's wife was also in the play, so it was my best chance of finding her. If Jessa was right, I didn't think she would be that brokenhearted over her husband's death. Assuming she went to rehearsal so quickly after her estranged husband had died. That seemed unlikely, but it was the best plan I had. I crossed my fingers that Minnie wasn't at rehearsal.

Setting Huckleberry on the sidewalk, I clicked his leash on his collar. He looked up at me with concern.

"It's going to be okay, Huck," I said, even though I wasn't sure that was true. "Let's go." I tugged on his leash, but the pug wouldn't move. "What's gotten into you?"

He whimpered, and then I heard it. It was faint at first but got louder and louder until I spotted the approaching high school marching band. They stomped down Michigan Street in shorts and T-shirts while a band director walked backward in front of them. None of them seemed to be concerned with traffic. Cars pulled to either side of the road to let them pass. They blew into and banged on their instruments with gusto—playing the old high school fight song. It was clear they were already practicing for the coming football season. High school football in Cherry Glen was an obsession that bordered on religious at times. I knew because Logan had played all four years when we were in school. By the twelfth grade, he was big: six five and over two hundred and fifty pounds. He played defensive end and might have been able to play in college too, but he decided not to go. His whole life, all he wanted to do was work his family's farm. What he wanted and what I wanted had led to our last argument.

Watching the band approach, I felt that familiar guilt boil in my stomach.

Logan and I had been set to get married that summer, but I was starting to balk. After going to college in Traverse City and being exposed to more opportunities to write and work on short film productions through the university, I had gotten the bug to go to Hollywood and work on films. It was something I had been terrified to tell him. It had always seemed to be understood that after we married, I would help manage both his family farm as well as Bellamy. Like Logan would say: "Farming is in our blood. We can't run from it."

But I did want to run from it after Grandma Bellamy died from a sudden heart attack. I needed to escape from Cherry Glen. Everything there reminded me of her. I knew that meant leaving Logan too. I never for a moment wanted to break off my engagement. I loved him. He was the best man I had ever met and remained that to this day. But my university called me and said there was an internship for recent graduates in Hollywood to work in production. My professors encouraged me to apply. I never thought I would get it.

So when I found out I had won the internship, I was both elated and devastated. I knew Logan would not understand. If I took the internship, I would leave right after the wedding and be gone for two years. It wasn't ideal, but I truly believed we could manage it.

As I had expected, when I told him, the conversation had not gone well. We ended up in a huge fight. Although I never lived in Traverse City because I commuted from the farm to all my classes, I had several college friends who lived there. I left and went to see those friends in Traverse City. Six hours later, I learned he died in a car accident on the way to come see me.

The funeral had been massive. I only had a vague recollection of how many people were there, but it was easily the whole town and every farmer in the county. Logan had been beloved in the farming community and a hometown football star. He was the golden boy of Cherry Glen, and he was dead.

I thought in some ways Quinn had loved Logan just as much as I had. He showed up drunk at the funeral, forced his way to the front of the room when the pastor was giving the eulogy, and pointed at me in the front row where I sat next to Logan's parents. "It's your fault he's dead. He was never good enough for you. The life he'd planned was never good enough for you. Do you know he was driving back to Traverse City to talk to you? He loved you, and it cost him his life. You want to go to California now? Go! No one is stopping you!"

I sat there in shock, frozen in place.

After his funeral, I took the internship in LA and never looked back. Yet here I was in Cherry Glen again.

I let out a breath. Quinn had every right to think it was my fault his best friend was killed.

Huckleberry hid behind my legs as I watched the marching band go by. Even in the heat of the summer's day, I wrapped my arms around myself to fight off the chill that suddenly overcame me. I knew Huckleberry hid from the high school marching band because of the loud noise. I wanted to hide because it was such a flashback to a time in my life—a time I could not separate from memories of Logan, even if I tried.

The band passed, and although I could still hear them, when they disappeared in the distance, I let out a sigh of relief. I looked down at my pug, his face buried in my calf. Perhaps he thought if he couldn't see the band, they couldn't see him.

"Huck, it's okay. They're gone. I think this is a sign that taking you to any high school football games is out of the question."

He buried his head deeper in my leg.

Although I was cold a moment ago, I was now hot. The sun was beating down on my bare head. The heat was different here from in LA. The humidity was high. We were right in the middle of summer, the middle of the growing season, and Bellamy Farm had nothing to show for it. I hoped that next year, we would actually have cherries and other crops to harvest and take to market. The only way I was going to be able to do that would be to stay out of jail and on the good side of public opinion. I had always been a rule follower. It was almost impossible for me to imagine myself in the situation I was in.

Huckleberry and I walked along the new, even sidewalk that led to the theater, sidewalk that I guessed Crocker had a hand in installing. When I was young, the theater had been an eyesore. Today, with what I assumed a lot of hard work by my cousin, it was in much better shape. The marquee was new and shone brightly in the sunlight. The front doors were polished, and giant red all-weather mats had been placed in front of them. I wondered if the mats were there to cover the cracks in the sidewalk.

If it was locked, I would leave and go back to the farm, make a new list of suspects and how to get out of this mess, and maybe fix the blasted fence at the entrance of the farm that seemed to mock me.

I pulled the door handle, and it opened easily. There was another set of double glass doors in front of me, leading into the theater. Those were unlocked too. Tinny music played somewhere deep in the theater. A poster advertised the play that weekend. *The Tragedy of Julius Caesar* was produced and directed by Stacey Bellamy. Below her name, it read, "Set in the turbulent time of the Michigan Frontier."

To my right, the ticket booth stood. It was clean, and a roll of tickets sat on the counter. A cash register and laptop were just on the other side of the window.

A stack of playbills sat on the counter as well. I walked over to the window and picked up one of the playbills. On the back were the names, photos, and short biographies of all the actors. I saw my dad's picture and the mayor's. Shannon Crocker's was also there. Even in the black-and-white picture, I could see she was beautiful, with dark hair and long bangs that swept over her face. Below her photograph, it read, "Shannon Crocker as Calpurnia."

My footsteps and the click of Huckleberry's nails echoed on the clean but cracked parqueted floor. I could see all the hard work Stacey had put into the place. The theater was in the process of being saved by my cousin, but there were spots where it still showed its age. I guessed it had to be at least one hundred years old. All things considered, it held up very well.

There was a wide staircase leading to a second floor. It was covered with clean but threadbare red carpet. The theater setup was such that the main lobby was at ground level, and the entrance of the theater was on the second floor of the building. Inside the theater, the seating sat tiered, so the aisle was a long downward ramp that led to the stage and into the orchestra pit.

I hesitated before going up the steps and had to tug on Huckleberry's leash to convince him to come up behind me. I had promised both Stacey and my father I would come to visit the production, but now I regretted it. What if while I was there, the mayor arrived for rehearsal? I did not want to run into him so soon after fleeing Jessa's Place. My thoughts were so jumbled and con-fused over the murder, I didn't know what to do.

"Get a grip, Bellamy." I shook off my misgivings and marched up the steps before I could talk myself out of it. The stairs creaked under my weight. At the top of the stairs, there was a wide hallway. Across the hallway were three double doors. Each set of doors led into the theater.

Instead of opening the middle doors that would have me look-ing straight onto the stage, I went to the one on the left, hoping I would have a better chance of sneaking in and gathering my bear-ings before being seen.

I opened the door, wincing as its hinges screeched. I poked my head in, and when no one said anything to me, I picked up Huckleberry and slipped inside the vast room.

I found myself in an aisle, looking down at the stage. The end of the front rows butted up against the orchestra pit. There were five people on the stage in the bright lights. One was my father, sitting in his frontiersman costume on a folding chair, and there were three others who I assumed were actors all standing around Stacey. My cousin wore a headset and held a tablet in her hand. Not one of them turned their head in my direction. Perhaps the door noise wasn't as bad as I thought.

"We all need to give our very best," Stacey told the actors. The sound of her voice bounced off the ceiling and the walls. "This play must go on. Now, I know there's been a bit of a setback because Shannon had to withdraw from her part, but I can step in. This is Shakespeare. We have to live up to the bard."

My ears perked up when she said the name Shannon. She had to be talking about Crocker's wife. I wondered if I should leave now that I knew Shannon, who was the main reason I was there, was not at the theater.

"Now, I wanted you all here this morning because you are the lead actors in this production. We need to go over the script from the top. I'll read Shannon's part as Calpurnia and any bit parts that aren't present. I just want to test the flow with me in Shannon's part before Thursday's dress rehearsal. It's important we have chemistry onstage together."

Overhead, the theater ceiling had been painted to look like the night sky. A memory came back to me of breaking into the closed theater with my friends the last week of high school and staring up at that ceiling. We'd drunk cheap beer and talked about our hopes and dreams after graduation. I could almost taste the bitter beer in my mouth.

"Let's begin from act 1, scene 2," Stacey said, frowning. "No, that won't work. We have to wait for the mayor to arrive and play Julius Caesar." She scowled at her tablet. "Baker, where is your father?"

A man I hadn't seen until then stepped out of the shadows at the side of the stage. He held a tablet in his hands and was tapping on the screen. He wasn't in costume like my father or in casual clothing like the other actors at the rehearsal. He wore expensive-looking pants and a freshly pressed dress shirt. He was even wearing a tie. He was tan, and his blond hair was perfectly styled. He lifted his hand from the screen. "How should I know?"

Stacey put her hands on her hips. "He's your father, and you work in the same office."

The man placed the protective case over his tablet. "We work in the same building, *not* the same office."

Stacey opened her mouth like she was going to say something back.

"I can see that you are in the middle of rehearsal, and this is probably not a good time to talk to you about the building code," he said, walking down the steps from the stage. He turned and looked up at Stacey. "I'll be back later today. We have *a lot* to talk about if you think this building is going to be ready for Friday's opening night."

Stacey glared at him so hard he should have been vaporized on the spot, but that man in a tie just turned around and headed in my direction. "I'll give you a punch list. I'm not saying you won't be able to do it, but you are going to have work day and night to get it done. I'll be checking." He looked at his watch. "I have to head out to my next meeting. I'll be back later."

"I'm sure you will," Stacey said angrily.

I wouldn't for a second want to be the guy giving Stacey a punch list. However, he didn't appear to be the least bit phased by her anger and didn't glance in my direction as he pushed his way through the exit.

Stacey folded her arms. "I don't know what he is even talking about. We have done everything the town has asked to get the theater up and running."

"Calm yourself, Stacey. They are probably very tiny things on that list," Dad said.

She huffed. "I don't have time for him or his list." She clapped her hands. "Places, everyone. Let's do a scene without Caesar then."

"I could say one of my speeches as Brutus." One of the actors cleared his throat. "'Since Cassius first did whet me against Caesar, I have not slept. Between the acting of a dreadful thin and the first motion, all the interim is like a phantasma or a hideous dream—'"

"No." Stacey stopped him midspeech. "There's no need. I know you have your lines memorized."

Huckleberry looked up at me and barked as if he was asking what we were doing there. It was a soft bark, but in the theater's acoustics, it was amplified tenfold. I froze. Everyone on the stage looked in my direction.

"Huck," I muttered.

He whined.

"It's okay, buddy."

Stacey shielded her eyes from the stage lights. "Who would bring a dog into the theater?"

I didn't see how I could slink away now. I set Huckleberry on the carpet at my feet. I walked down the aisle and waved. "It's just me. Shiloh."

My pug toddled down the aisle behind me.

"Shiloh, I'm glad you came. I didn't expect you so early though," my father said.

"I drove into town on an errand, and I promised to stop by, so…" Huck put his nose to the floor and inhaled all the delicious new scents.

Stacey frowned. "And you brought your dog?"

"Huckleberry is always with me. I used to take him to work at the studio."

She pressed her lips together. "Okay, everyone, let's take a ten-minute break."

The younger actors didn't have to be told twice as they bolted from the stage. I had a feeling my cousin was a tough director.

"Shi, come up on the stage," Stacey said. It sounded more like an order than a request.

I edged around the empty orchestra pit to the steps to the left of the stage.

"The theater looks great, the best I've ever seen it," I said as the steps creaked under my weight.

Stacey pressed her lips together. "I don't know if that's a compliment, since it was abandoned when we were growing up."

"It was meant to be—a compliment, that is." I wondered how I could have so quickly have gotten on my cousin's bad side since returning to Michigan.

"They were going to bulldoze the place until Stacey stepped in and saved it," my father said with pride in his voice.

A knot tightened in my chest, and I told myself to relax. So what if my dad and Stacey were close? He spent much more time with her than he did with me. In many ways, I had been gone so long from Cherry Glen that I had become a stranger to my own father, and he was a stranger to me. Not for the first time, I wondered if Dad should have turned the farm over to my cousin and not to me. He was a traditional man, so I could see him thinking his own child should get the land, but was that really the right choice? I knew Stacey had inherited the other half of the farm from her own father. Maybe she should have been given the whole property. I surely had made a mess of everything I'd touched since coming back home.

She folded her arms. "Bulldozing the place was Crocker's idea. It took some quick thinking on my part to stop it. I'm quite pleased that this is one building he didn't own in town."

Ah, yet another reason my father and Stacey were so down on Crocker.

"Well," I said. "You did an amazing job, Stacey. I'm so impressed."

She smiled, and some of her iciness thawed. "This is just the beginning for the theater. I have big plans for it. Community events, movies, and more. This is a large facility, and the possibilities are endless, and I'm working on an agreement with the public schools to use the space for a discount as well. This theater is the crown jewel of the Glen."

"The crown jewel?" I asked.

She eyed me. "You have to have noticed how the Glen has changed. Did you see all the new businesses and shops on Michigan Street? The new brewery too? All this has happened in the last few years. Cherry Glen isn't a little farming hamlet any longer. It's a place where people want to visit, shop, and be entertained. The theater will provide that entertainment for them."

I didn't say it, but it seemed to me that Stacey was putting a lot of pressure on herself to revitalize Cherry Glen. What if the theater failed?

"I wish you all the luck then," I said. "I'm sure it will be great." Then I heard myself say, "If I can help you in any way, just let me know." As soon as they were out there, I wished I could reach out, pluck the words out of the air, and shove them back into my mouth.

Stacey cocked her head. "That's very kind of you, Shiloh. Perhaps we do have a job for you if you're up to it."

I inwardly groaned. There was no getting out of helping now, and I had so many things I needed to accomplish these first few days back in the Glen. That list didn't even include solving the murder.

"What's that?" I asked with a smile I hoped appeared sincere.

"We expect to have a full house. Since it's the first play in the theater for over forty years, we sold discount tickets just to get people in the door," Stacey said. "It was a gamble. It's always a gamble with discounts. It won't even pull in enough money to cover my overhead, but I hope everyone in town and from around the region will see what a gem Michigan Street Theater is."

I nodded and waited for her to tell me what she wanted me to do, because I knew it was something I most likely would not like.

"I could use someone to run the ticket booth opening night. The person I hired for the job had a family emergency and can't do it now. I've been trying to find a replacement, but no one seems willing to do it yet."

"What would be involved?" I asked.

"Not much. Most of the tickets were sold online, so it's just a matter of scanning the barcodes and being there if any issues come up."

I glanced at my father, who had a smile on his face as he looked at me expectantly. I really didn't have any other choice.

"Sure, I'd be happy to help. Just let me know when you want me to be here."

Stacey's eyes brightened. It was the first time she gave me a real smile since I'd been home. That was all the proof I needed that I made the right decision. Who needed sleep anyway, right? "Be here Thursday at nine in the morning at the ticket booth. I'll show you everything then." She started to turn away. She was trying to dismiss me.

I shifted my feet. "When I came in, I happened to hear you mention that Shannon had to drop out of the play. Would that be Shannon Crocker?"

Stacey frowned, and it seemed all the good will I garnered had evaporated in her eyes. "It is. She had to back out because of her husband's death. Of course, we understand that. This is a very difficult time for her."

"I'm sorry to hear that."

"Shannon is a sweet woman," my father said. "She shouldn't have been married to Crocker in the first place. He wasn't kind to her."

My eyes went wide. "Do you mean he was abusive?"

"No, not that I know of, but I know Shannon had wanted a divorce for a long time, and Crocker refused to give it to her. He was the one with the money, so he held all the cards. At least she won't have to bother with that any longer."

At least, I thought. Shannon was definitely on the very top of my list to speak to, but I had to find her first. By Stacey's expression, asking my cousin was a bad idea. That was fine. There were other ways to track down a person.

"I should get back to the farm," I said.

"What's the rush?" Stacey asked. "What can you do there without Crocker's money?"

I scooped up my pug. "Quite a lot." I glanced at my father. "It might take longer to bring the farm back than I thought, but I'm sure it can be done."

Dad scowled and was about to open his mouth and say something, but I was faster. "Good luck with the play." I skipped down the stage steps and for the door before they could stop me.

I had just reached the exit when the door opened, and Mayor Loyal stepped inside. "Julius Caesar has arrived!"

I pulled up short.

"Oh. Miss Bellamy, what are you doing here? I do want to speak to you about our conversation earlier at Jessa's Place."

"Oh, I'm so sorry. I have to go." I slipped around him, practically running through the theater's foyer and out the front door. Again, just like outside the diner, I doubled over on the sidewalk to catch my breath. I took big gulps of air. Running away from the mayor was becoming a habit I really needed to address.

I set Huckleberry on the sidewalk, and the pug appeared to be as bewildered as I felt. "Oh, Huck, I've made such a mess of everything. Let's go back to the farm and regroup."

He started down the sidewalk in the direction of my car. At least Huckleberry was on my team.

Chapter Thirteen

The next day, Stacey picked up my father for an early play rehearsal. Opening day was only a few days away, and Stacey had a lot riding on the play's success. When I was in LA and needed to decompress, I would go to the gym. At Bellamy Farm, I just needed to go outside. There was plenty to do to keep my body moving and my mind occupied.

Huckleberry followed me out into the summer sunshine and jumped into the dead grass. He looked up at me with those big pug eyes as if to ask what was next.

"It is a mess," I told the pug. "Grandma Bellamy would tell me to get on with it. That's what we are going to do."

I went into the barn to look for the lawn mower. The riding mower was buried under dozen of boxes, but I found a push mower in the corner. Maybe it would be insane to mow the massive yard with a push mower, but it would take my mind off everything falling apart around me. It was just what I needed at the moment.

The grass was impossibly long, and at first, the mower got caught every few feet. I pushed harder, and slowly the grass gave way. I looked behind me at the small patch I had mowed with a smile on my face.

Huckleberry trotted behind me for a few yards, but then he gave up and settled under the shade tree. I wished I could join him.

I didn't know how long I had been working in the yard when I heard the beep of a car horn. I looked up and saw a police car coming up the long drive. My heart sank, and I wiped sweat off my brow with the end of my T-shirt. There was no time to make myself more presentable.

Huckleberry got up and galloped over to me through the freshly cut lawn. As he did, I noticed I had mowed no more than two hundred feet, and the yard went on for acres.

The police car came to a rest next to mine, and I wasn't the least bit surprised when Chief Randy climbed out.

"Good day to you, Shiloh. It's a hot one."

I nodded. I assumed the fact that I was dripping in sweat was answer enough for that. "Can I help you with something?"

"I came by to speak to your father. He here?"

"Dad's at the theater for play rehearsal," I said. "I'm not sure how long it will last. He's been there most of the day."

"Oh right," Chief Randy said. "I should have looked there first. We are all very proud of Stacey for bringing the theater back in Cherry Glen. We need more people like her in our little town."

"Is there something I can help you with?" I asked.

"Well, maybe you can. I was wondering if I could get inside to take a small peek at Sully's gun collection?"

The feeling drained from my hands. I didn't know if I lost feeling because of the sense of overwhelming dread that fell on me or because I had been gripping the handle of the lawnmower so hard.

"Dad's not here. I can't show it to you without his permission. He's very protective of his collection."

"Oh, I know that." Chief Randy shifted his stance. "But I think you will want to let me inside. I'm here to look at his collection on official police business."

"What kind of police business?" I asked.

"I'm sorry, but I can't say. I just need to take a quick look at the collection, and I will be on my way."

"I'm sorry." I licked my lips. "I can't do that."

"You're going to say no to the police? Do you think that's a good idea considering the precarious position you are in? I'm telling you I need to get in there."

"I know that, but I don't have to let you inside without a warrant."

His mouth fell open, and he reminded me of the big-mouthed bass my father used to catch on the lake. I never liked those fish and refused to eat them when he fried them up.

"You're saying no to the police." Chief Randy folded his arms. "I'm sure that's not what you're saying."

Sweat dripped down the side of my face. "I'm saying this is my father's property that you would like to see, and it's up to him to show it to you. He should be home later today."

Chief Randy glared at me. "I knew you would be trouble as soon as I pulled you over the first day you returned. I can always tell when someone in my town is going to be trouble. And then there is your history..."

"My history?" I clenched my fists at my sides. "What do you mean by that?"

He rocked back on his heels. "Everyone knows you're the type to go against the grain. You weren't happy with what you had. You wanted more. At what cost?"

I closed my eyes for a moment. Was he talking about Crocker or

Logan here? He had to know the circumstances of Logan's death. He was Quinn's father after all, and Logan had been Quinn's best friend. Even so, I wasn't going to take the bait and ask him to clarify that. No matter what the chief's, Quinn's, or anyone in Cherry Glen's opinion was of me, I knew I wasn't responsible for Logan's death. It had taken years of therapy to come to that conclusion, but that didn't totally eliminate my guilt.

"I'm not trying to be trouble," I said as calmly as I could. "If that's all, I would like to get back to work. As you can see, I have a lot of work to do."

"It's not all."

I knew what was coming next. I hoped I was wrong, but if the mayor knew about my contract with Crocker, the police chief surely knew too.

"Why didn't you tell me you had business with Jefferson Crocker?"

"I—I didn't think it was important." That excuse sounded lame even to my own ears.

He folded his arms. "I would say it's mighty important since you were the one who found the body. By not telling me, it looks to me like you're hiding pertinent information. Now you won't let me see your father's gun collection. It all makes me wonder."

"I won't let you see my father's collection because it's my father's. It's not my place to let you inside. I'm sorry." I swallowed. I hoped that would put an end to it.

Chief Randy sucked on his teeth. "Very well. I will track your father down and ask him. I know Sully will be much more cooperative."

I didn't say anything to that.

"What about the contract with Crocker? Was that your father's idea?" He asked the question in a casual way, but I knew it was nothing close to a casual inquiry.

My throat had never been so dry. "No, it was mine."

"That's interesting," he said. "Since you were the last person to see him alive."

"What? How could that be?" I asked. "I saw him Friday evening. He left the farm around eight thirty."

"As far as we can put it together, your farm was his last stop before he died."

"But that can't be. He was at the farmers market on Saturday! I know the market hadn't opened yet, but there had to be dozens of people who saw him there."

He sucked on his teeth. "Well, so far, no one has come forward saying they saw him, and we've asked."

"Well, then one of them is lying!"

The chief held up his hands. "Easy there."

I closed my eyes and took a breath. "I'm sorry."

He changed his stance and studied me. "And how did Sully feel about you going into business with Crocker?"

"You will have to ask him," I said.

He folded his arms. "I don't have to."

I frowned. "Did you already speak to him?"

He shook his head. "Not yet, but I will. However, it just so happened he left a very strongly worded voicemail on Crocker's phone that said exactly what he thought of him and Crocker's involvement at Bellamy Farm."

The blood drained from my face.

"Ah, you didn't know about that, did you?" he murmured.

"I—I don't know what you're suggesting." The sweat on my body began to dry, and I suddenly felt cold.

"Just that Sully threatened a man, and now the man is dead."

"My father would never hurt anyone. Also, if you looked at the facts, you would see that was impossible. He uses a walker. He can barely get around as it is."

"He can drive though, right?"

"I don't know what that has to do with anything."

"The coroner said the victim was shot from above. Like the killer leaned out of a truck window and shot him. Even in his condition, Sully could do that, couldn't he?"

"You are saying my father is responsible for a drive-by shooting like a gang member?" I couldn't even believe I was having this conversation.

He shrugged.

"My father doesn't have a motive. I had just signed the contract. We needed that money to stay afloat. Dealing with Crocker was our fastest way to do that. It would be against my father's interest to do anything to him! There was nothing more to it than that." I licked my lips, trying to calm down. "I was supposed to meet him the morning I found him to talk about next steps in the agreement. We never had a chance to have that conversation."

"You do realize this makes you and your father look bad. You should have told me your connection to him right off."

"Maybe I should have," I admitted. "I was just so taken aback. It's not like finding a dead body has happened to me before." I closed my eyes for a moment, trying the push the image of Crocker lying on the ground to the back of my mind. It didn't work.

His expression softened just a tad. "No, I suppose not. I'm going to go find your father, and we will get this little issue cleared up quickly."

I wanted to ask him what exactly my father may have said on

that voicemail, but he was already walking back to his car. I waited a full five minutes after his car disappeared down the driveway, and then I ran to the house. Huckleberry sprinted after me as if he thought this was a game, but this was no game.

I went through the front door into the living room, down the hallway, and into the large farmhouse kitchen. My father said he had completely remodeled the kitchen for my mother. I was told she was a fabulous cook, but I can't remember eating anything she made me.

Behind me, Huckleberry's nails skidded across the tiled floor as he tried to stop his forward momentum. He couldn't slow down and bounced off the giant island in the middle of the room. He lay on his back and shook his head.

"Oh, Huckleberry, are you okay?"

The pug rolled over and snuffled. I took that to mean he was fine.

I went to the pantry in the back of the kitchen. The key was just where it had always been. It hung from a hook inside the pantry. I removed it and walked toward the spare room off the kitchen. Dad had built the room specifically for the purpose of organizing his collection of historic artifacts. I was afraid of what I would find or not find there. I tried to slide the key into the lock with shaky hands, but it didn't fit. I pushed it in again, and for a second time, the key would not go into the lock.

I held my hand and took a breath. "Breathe," I whispered to myself. I closed my eyes for a moment, and then jiggled the key into the lock. It finally went in, and with both hands, I turned the knob.

You would think a place that held so many old artifacts would be dusty, but it wasn't. My father may have let the farm go, but the same could not be said for his collection. Everything was in its place and polished to a high sheen.

Growing up, I had only been in the collection room a handful of times. It was my father's sacred place. It was where he spent most of his time when he wasn't toiling away out in the fields or in the barn. The moment I stepped into the room, I knew why Chief Randy wanted to see the collection.

In the middle of the pegboard that displayed nineteenth-century revolvers, there was an empty spot. Anyone looking inside the room would have seen the obvious void. It was perfectly shaped like a gun. And it wasn't the only one. There were other blank spots. Several actually.

I put a hand to my chest as if I were the one who had just been shot. I was about to turn around and leave the room when a shadow filled the door. I was trapped.

Chapter Fourteen

I grabbed the first thing I could reach from the table behind me. It was a paperweight shaped like President Abraham Lincoln's head.

"Are you going to knock me over the head with Honest Abe?" Quinn asked.

I lowered the paperweight. "What are you doing here?"

"I stopped by to talk to you and Sully."

I set Lincoln on the table where I found him. I hoped I put him in the same spot. If I didn't, my father would notice. "You can't just barge into someone's house like that."

"I didn't barge in. I knocked, but no one answered. Sully doesn't mind if I come in the house unannounced."

I folded my arms. "He's not the only one living here anymore."

"You're right." He hung his head. "I should have thought about that. I'm sorry for scaring you, and I'm grateful you didn't clock me with a paperweight."

Huckleberry poked his head into the room between Quinn's legs.

"Some guard dog you are," I muttered. "Aren't you supposed to bark when an intruder is about?"

"I don't think pugs have been known to be guard dogs." Quinn's mouth quirked into a smile.

"Let's get out of this room. Dad wouldn't like us in here."

Quinn took one step back into the kitchen and then froze. "Is there a revolver missing on that pegboard?"

I put my hand on his chest and forcibly pushed him out of the room. My palm felt hot where I touched him, and I shook my hand as if to cool it before closing and locking the door behind me.

He stared at me. "Does your hand hurt?"

Uh, awkward. "I'm fine," I said. So many times, I'd come across one of those cliché moments in a script where all of a sudden, two characters connect and there's heat or electricity or some such nonsense. That flutter of heat in my hand just now, I'd chalk that up to static.

I was about to pocket the room key when he said, "You don't have to hide where the key goes from me. I know Sully hangs it from the hook on the pantry door."

"You're an EMT, not a detective," I said and replaced the key on the hook in the pantry.

"Technically, I'm a firefighter. Budgets are tight in town, so they merged the departments, let go of the regular EMTs, and the firefighters had to cross-train."

"Does that mean Laurel is a firefighter too?" I didn't know if I liked that idea. If she was responsible for rescuing me from an inferno, I bet she'd let me burn.

"She is. She's actually very good at it. She's fearless."

I would have expected nothing less from her. "What are you doing here anyway?"

"I came to tell Sully my father was on his way here to look at his collection."

"You just missed your dad."

"He was here? Did he take that revolver with him?" Quinn asked. "Was that what he was after?"

I shook my head. "No, I didn't let him inside."

His eyes went wide. "You didn't let him in?"

"He didn't have a warrant." I crossed my arms. "Also, Dad's not here. He's at play rehearsal. This is his collection, and it should be my father's decision who sees it."

He rubbed the back of his neck. "Don't you see how that makes you look bad to my father? He will think you and Sully are hiding something. You're already in hot water."

"Oh, I know." I frowned at him. "Chief Randy and the whole town seem to know about the contract I had with Crocker."

He held up his hands in surrender. "Don't look at me like that. I didn't tell anyone."

I wanted to believe him.

"But you came straight here after my dad left to see what he was looking for. I guess that empty space where a revolver had been was it."

"He might have moved it somewhere else for cleaning. It doesn't mean anything."

"Sure, it doesn't." He shook his head. "Or it could be the murder weapon."

I felt sick.

"Jefferson Crocker was shot with an old revolver. Doc found the round in his sternum. He said that it looked like it was nine-teenth century. Of course, everyone in Cherry Glen knows about Sully's collection. It's not a great leap to think the gun came from here."

"So it's not *proven* that it was the murder weapon," I said.

"Then why are you acting guilty by not letting my dad into the house. We both know Sully was not keen on the deal you signed with Crocker, and he can be hotheaded. Maybe showing the police some transparency will help since he's a prime suspect."

I glared at him. "Are you saying you think my eightysomething father who shuffles around on a walker killed a man? Are you insane?"

He held up his hands. "I'm just telling you how it looks. I know Sully. We've become close since I moved back to Cherry Glen. He's my friend. I don't think he would do this, but it doesn't look good. No matter how much my father might like him, as the police chief, he has to look at the facts, and they are damning where your dad is concerned."

I gritted my teeth. There went Quinn Killian pointing blame again where it wasn't due, and this time, he wasn't even drunk.

"Dad, you are taking forever," a high voice said, and a moment later, a young girl stepped into the kitchen. She wore shorts and a T-shirt that was three sizes too big for her. Her long, dark hair was pulled back into a ponytail on the top of her head, and she wore a teal cat-ear headband.

Quinn frowned. "Hazel, I told you to wait outside."

She flapped her loose sleeves around like they were wings. "I *was* waiting outside, but it's hot."

Huckleberry ran over to her and put his paws on her bare legs. He wagged his stubby curl of a tail. Hazel knelt in front of the dog and scratched him between the ears. Huckleberry closed his eyes in doggie bliss.

The girl looked up at me. "You look like you fell into a pond. I looked like that when I fell into a pond once. It was so gross. I felt like I would never get clean."

Blood rushed to my face as I realized what I must look like for the first time since Quinn stepped into the kitchen. I guessed her assessment of me looking like I had fallen into a pond was being polite. "I was mowing the lawn. It was a bit harder than I thought it would be."

Quinn's mouth fell open. "With that push mower out there? What are you, Amish? You're lucky you didn't pass out from heat stroke."

"I couldn't get to the riding lawn mower. It was too buried under stuff," I said. "And I'm certain it was out of gas anyway. I had to do something. Have you seen this place? The farm is falling apart," I snapped.

Hazel's eyebrows went up.

My stomach dropped. "I'm sorry. I shouldn't have let my frustration out like that. The farm will be fine. It will just take a little bit of time and hard work."

"You're Sully's daughter from California," Hazel said. "Dad said you were here and you were very pretty." She cocked her head as if she wasn't sure about her father's statement.

Quinn's face turned bright red. "Hazel, why don't you go outside and find something to do?"

She put her hands on her hips. "Dad, I'm eleven years old. You can't treat me like a child anymore."

Quinn grimaced. "Eleven years old is still a child."

"I'm practically a teenager."

"Lord, give me strength," he muttered.

If I hadn't been so worried about the missing revolver, I would have enjoyed their little father-daughter back-and-forth. It reminded me so much of growing up alone with my own father on the farm.

Hazel held out her hand to me. "I'm Hazel Quinn. My dad and I live in the next farm over. My mom died."

"Hazel!" Quinn cried.

She eyed him. "It's true, and it's just easier if we get that out of the way. People always ask, and it's less awkward this way to tell them she's dead straight off. That way, they won't ask those questions like 'how's your mom' and 'what does your mom do for a living.' When I answer that she's dead, people squirm and tell me I'm young to have lost my mother. Like I don't already know that." She rolled her eyes.

"So much less awkward," Quinn grumbled.

I shook her small hand. "I think you're right that it makes it less awkward," I said. "I get it better than most. My mom died when I was young too, and it was just easier to tell people."

Hazel glanced at her father. "See."

He held up his hands. "I can't argue with both of you."

Chapter Fifteen

"W hy don't we go outside," I said. "Huckleberry could use some fresh air."

Hazel scooped up the dog and carried him out of the kitchen.

Quinn glanced at me. "She's been begging me for a dog. I've been putting it off because we aren't home enough. I'm on twenty-four-hour shifts at the fire department, and she's with my mom when I'm there."

"Is that why you moved back to Cherry Glen?"

He nodded. "After Logan died, I left too." He cleared his throat. "I moved to Detroit, met Hazel's mom, and got married. I was a fireman in Detroit for a long time, but a few years after my wife died, it got harder and harder to find child care. Dad told me about the job opening here in Cherry Glen's department. It seemed like a good move for us. Although I think it was a big adjustment for Hazel to move from the city to the country. Detroit and Cherry Glen aren't much alike, even though they are in the same state."

I nodded. "I don't know if it's appropriate to say now or not, but I'm sorry about Hazel's mom. I kind of know what she's going through since I had a similar situation. If she ever needs to talk to someone about it…" Why was I offering to counsel his daughter?

He most likely thought I'd killed a man. I shifted from foot to foot.

He glanced at me. "It's been six years, but thank you. It's still nice to hear that. I might take you up on it too. Raising a tween girl alone is a lot harder than I thought. My parents try to help as much as they can, but I get the sense they also think I'm failing at it a lot of the time."

"I'm sure that's not true," I said.

He laughed. "You don't know my mother."

I nodded. I'm sure I had seen his mother when we were younger, but I couldn't say I remembered that much about her.

We followed Hazel out of the house and found her chasing Huckleberry around the yard. The pug's grin ran ear to ear, and his long pink tongue hung out the side of his mouth. He was having the time of his life.

I smiled. "No matter what she says, she's still a kid, and now she's a kid having fun."

"I wish I could keep her this way," he said wistfully. "She's growing up too fast."

"I think every parent has said that a few times."

He nodded. "Now I get it."

Huckleberry spun around and began chasing Hazel. The girl yelped in glee and ran. I had been a girl just like her once, running around the farm with my grandmother looking on. Logan would have been there. When we were young, my grandmother watched him on most summer days. We dashed through the cherry orchard, jumped off the hayloft, and stole cookies from the kitchen. That was when I started to fall in love with him. He was so easygoing and happy. He was always willing to go along with my adventurous ideas.

Until those ideas included leaving Cherry Glen.

Quinn spoke, shaking me from my memory. "Anyway, you're going to want to talk to your dad about that revolver. I would suggest you do it before my father gets a chance." He clapped his hands. "Okay, Hazel, it's time to go."

"What?" the girl asked as she pushed her dark hair out of her face. "I was just starting to have fun."

"I have to take you to Grandma's so I can go to work." He gestured for her to get moving.

She scowled at him and didn't budge. "All I ever do is go to Grandma's. It's so boring over there, and she makes me eat canned peaches. What is with Grandma and canned peaches? They look and taste like slime. I don't believe her when she says they will make me sweet." She folded her arms. "Maybe I don't want to be sweet. Maybe I want to be tough."

"Please don't let your grandmother hear you say that." Quinn looked pained.

"You can come by and play with Huckleberry any time," I said to Hazel. "He hasn't had a good workout like that in a long time."

"Are you serious? That would be great. Dad said we could get a dog when we moved out to the country, but we've been here for a year, and we don't have one yet. I don't think it's unreasonable to want a pet. I need someone to hang out with. At this point, I would take a turtle."

"Honey," Quinn said. "I know I told you that, but Grandma can't take care of a dog and you. I'm away at work too much of the time. Maybe when you're a bit older—"

"I know. You've only told me that a hundred times. What's the excuse for the turtle?" Hazel said and walked to their truck.

Quinn winced. "I'm sorry you had to see that. Things are better when she's at school and has after-school things going on too. This is our first full summer here—we moved here right before the school year—and I didn't realize how hard it would be for her."

"She sounds bored. I mean, I'm sure you already know." I looked down at my shoes that were grass-stained from my attempt at mowing the lawn earlier. "I know what it's like to be her age and wish you had your mom. If it hadn't been for my farm chores and my grandmother, I don't know what I would do on long summer days. Dad was always so caught up in his collection or the farm itself." I blushed, not knowing why I was telling him all this. He didn't care. The only reason he had spent any time with me when I was younger was because I was Logan's girlfriend and then fiancée. "Anyway, what I mean is she is welcome here any time. I may be working on the farm, but I wouldn't mind the company."

He studied me. "Honestly, Hazel would probably love the farm work. She likes to help anywhere that isn't home."

I smiled. "Sounds like a normal kid to me."

He nodded and walked toward his truck. I called Huckleberry, and after getting one more scratch from Hazel, he scampered to me. I scooped him up in my arms and watched Quinn's truck bounce down the driveway. I sighed. At the root of it, Quinn and I had both loved Logan so much that we had always been a little jealous of each other, even if we tried to keep it from Logan. I knew Logan would have wanted us to be friends, but too much had happened.

I looked down at Huckleberry. "At least you made a new friend today, and I'm happy for that."

He made a snuffling sound and stared down the driveway as if begging Hazel to come back.

I slid my phone from my pocket and tried to call my dad. I

needed to warn him about the chief wanting to see his collection. It went right to voicemail. I was certain he'd turned the phone off during play rehearsal, and that was if he had remembered to charge it the night before at all.

I had to get into town and warn him myself. I was fearful about what he might say to the police that could put him in even more hot water.

I put the lawn mower away and headed back to the house to get cleaned up. I needed to ask my father about the missing revolver.

As Huckleberry and I drove back into town, I tried not to think about the fact that I was probably already too late. Surely, the police chief had found my father and asked him if he could see the collection. At least Chief Randy didn't know the revolver was missing. Quinn did of course. Would he tell his father about the missing gun?

I parked behind the theater, clipped Huckleberry's leash on his collar, and got out of the car. We went up to the door. The back door of the theater was locked. When we walked around to the front, we found that door to be locked too.

My shoulders sagged, and I called my dad again. Again, it went directly to voicemail. Now I was worried.

"Huck, what are we going to do?" I asked.

The pug looked up at me.

"Does your dog usually answer your questions?" a male voice asked.

I turned around and found the man in the tie I had seen at play rehearsal yesterday. He was handsome on closer inspection, with steel-gray eyes and tousled dark-blond hair. His tie had a geometric pattern of falling blocks that I couldn't stare at for too long without getting a headache.

"Umm, no…" I said.

He smiled. "That's good to know. Is the theater closed?"

"It is. I was hoping to catch the end of the rehearsal," I said.

"Are you involved in the play?" he asked.

I shook my head. "My father is though."

"Who's your father?"

I frowned. I didn't know if I wanted to be that forthcoming with a virtual stranger, let alone the mayor's son.

He held up his hand. "I didn't mean anything by it."

I shook my head. "I'm sorry. I just need to talk to my father. I thought he'd be here."

"Looks like we are both out of luck. I'm here to check on the process for the building. I'm Baker Loyal, the city inspector."

"The mayor's son." I nodded, confirming what I had already gleaned from my overheard conversation at the theater.

He grinned. "You got it. He's in the play too, which was why I asked about your dad. I'm sure I know him. I have been in and out of the theater countless times throughout Stacey's restoration. I might even know the building better than she does."

"Is there something wrong with the building?" I remembered him threatening my cousin with another punch list of things to fix before opening night.

"No, but everything needs to be up to code if she thinks she's going to open this place to the public in a few days. She's made great strides. I saw the inside right after she bought the building. It's unbelievable how much she's accomplished in such a short time, but I'm a stickler for these things. Cherry Glen has come a long way in the last few years, and to do that, the city has held a very high standard on any projects, especially in the historic downtown area."

"Stacey's my cousin." I held out my hand this time. "I'm Shiloh."

He shook my hand. "You must be Sully's daughter then. He's a great guy. I've seen some of their play rehearsals, and he really gets into his part."

I smiled. "Thanks. He's always loved plays and movies."

My father had never been one to tell anyone, let alone his daughter, what he was feeling. It seemed the only time when I was a child he would share anything with me was in the evenings; I would sit with him in the living room watching television with him. He especially liked anything with cowboys. When I was young, it was the only time I could remember my father smiling, and I wanted him to smile so much. I didn't need my fancy LA therapist to tell me those memories were the reason I majored in production in college and why I ended up in Hollywood. I just wanted to make him proud of me for something he cared about.

I let out a breath. "I think for him, this is kind of a dream come true. He was more into westerns than Shakespeare though. I'm not the least bit surprised he was able to convince Stacey to make it a frontier version of *The Tragedy of Julius Caesar*."

"Do you want to get a cup of coffee?" Baker asked with a charming smile.

I stared at him. "I—I really need to find my dad. There is some… Anyway, I need to talk to him about our farm."

He nodded. "I'll take a rain check then."

I frowned.

He started to walk away and then turned. "If you see your cousin, tell her I'm looking for her, okay? Opening night won't happen if the building is not up to code."

Chapter Sixteen

I kicked myself for coming to town at all. If my father wasn't at the theater, he was mostly likely back at the farm. I should have stayed home and waited for him. As Huckleberry and I walked back around the side of the theater, I called Stacey, but the call went to voicemail too. What was with people not answering their phones in Cherry Glen? I shot her a text asking if she knew where Dad was. A text came back. "He's home."

Huckleberry and I sped back to Bellamy Farm. I knew I was at risk of getting another speeding ticket, but I didn't care. The Cherry Glen police could just add that to my list of mistakes.

I wasn't the least bit surprised when I spotted three police cars parked on my freshly yet badly cut grass. My cousin's pickup truck was there too.

I climbed out of my car, and Huckleberry jumped onto the grass. He looked up at me as if asking what he should do next. I didn't have an answer for that. I didn't know what I should do next. The police were already here; was there any point going inside and asking what they were doing?

Stacey came out the front door of the large farmhouse and slammed it behind her. She saw me and glared.

I looked down at the pug. "I think we're in trouble."

Stacey stomped over to us. "Where have you been? Your father's house is being searched by the police, and you are off on a joy ride in that ridiculous car."

"Did they say why they were searching house?" I asked, even though I already knew.

"For a gun. For the gun that killed Jefferson Crocker."

I winced. "Did they have a warrant?" I asked.

"I don't know. I don't see why it matters. No one would believe Uncle Sully could have hurt anyone. The man can't even stand upright without support."

I bit my lip. This would not be a good time to tell her that the coroner thought Crocker had been shot from a truck.

"How long have they been here?" I asked.

"I'm not sure. They were here when Uncle Sully and I arrived. The police called me at the theater because they couldn't get ahold of him. He, of course, was with me at rehearsal. We canceled the rest of rehearsal and came right here. We expected you to be here." She glared at me. "Where were you?"

"I went into town to look for Dad. I went to the theater."

"When you didn't see us there, why didn't you call me?" She frowned at me.

"I tried, and when you didn't answer, I sent you a text."

"Well, it came too late," she huffed, but she cooled down a bit. I was grateful for that; I couldn't deal with the police and an angry cousin at the same time.

The front door opened, and Chief Randy walked out. He stood outside the door and waited for my father. He was there to offer a hand if need be.

I liked him a little bit better for that kind gesture.

Leaving Stacey standing in the middle of the semi-mowed front lawn, I walked over to my father. "Dad, is everything all right?"

He looked at me. "No."

He was standing next to the police chief in his front yard, and this wasn't a social call. Of course it wasn't okay.

"Miss Bellamy," Chief Randy said as he placed one hand on the hilt of his gun in his duty belt. "I'm going to have to ask you down to the station. We have a few questions for you that need to be cleared up. Your father has been very cooperative, and I hope you will too."

The blood drained from my face. "Can't you ask me those questions here?"

"I'm afraid not." He glanced at Dad. "I think it's best if I get your stories separately." He smiled. "Just to make sure everything checks out. You understand, don't you?"

I swallowed. "Am I in trouble?"

"Oh no. Not at all." He smiled and stopped just short of twirling his mustache.

He doth protest too much, methinks. Stacey wasn't the only Bellamy who knew her Shakespeare.

"Did you find what you were looking for?" I asked.

"The revolver was never here. It was at the theater being used as a prop for the play. I hadn't realized it was missing from the theater," Dad said. "It's a very valuable piece."

I let out a breath. "It was already outside the house. It couldn't have been stolen from here then. I don't understand what any of this has to do with us."

The chief stood up a little straighter. "Miss Bellamy, we can discuss this more at the station."

"I don't know why you need my daughter to go with you. I told you all you need to know," my father said.

Chief Randy glanced at him. "She just might have something different to say…"

I glanced at my father, who paled at the chief's words.

What was it that Dad was afraid I would say?

"Can I at least drive myself there?" I asked the chief.

The police chief considered this.

"If I don't, you will have to give me a ride back to the farm."

"Fine. I don't have a problem with that." He turned to my father. "I hate to say this, but don't leave town, Sully." He turned to me. "Let's go, Miss Bellamy. It's time for a little chat."

My heart sank like a stone as I walked back to my car.

Chapter Seventeen

A s much as I didn't want to, I left Huckleberry back at the farm with my father and cousin. I knew Chief Randy wouldn't want him at the station for my interrogation—or whatever less threatening word he called it. Oh, chat. Yeah right. The chief of police doesn't invite you to the station for a chat like you were grabbing a cup of coffee with a friend.

The police station was inside the town's municipal building, which also housed town hall. It stood all the way at the end of Michigan Street, the same street with the theater, Jessa's Place, the general store, and the giant brewery that dominated half a block. Tourists went in and out of the brewery. There was a young police officer standing just outside it, as if a reminder to them not to drink and drive. A very good reminder, but it also told me that Chief Randy, for all his bumbling facade, ran a very tight ship in his town. It would do me well to remember that during the questioning. I needed to pay attention and not say anything that might put me or my family in a bad light. That was much easier said than done.

I knew I had a right to an attorney with me anytime I spoke with the police. Should I request one? Not that I knew any attorneys in town. Besides, Chief Randy's head might pop off his shoulders if I refused to chat without legal representation present. Was it best just to get this over with?

The building itself was like most of the structures in the downtown area. It was constructed of red brick and had small windows. There was a cornerstone in the side of the building, and it read 1889. I believed before it became the municipal building that housed the police, fire department, and town offices, it was a federal bank that worked with the farmers in the area. It was the tallest building in Cherry Glen, standing four stories high. It would have been miniature in LA, but here it appeared massive and foreboding. With its rough brick and small windows, it reminded me of a prison. I shivered as I realized this must be the building that Crocker owned, since it included the mayor's office.

Even though I grew up in Cherry Glen, I had never been in the police station. I was a good girl. I never got in trouble in all my growing up years, or at least I never got caught. In fact, it was not uncommon for my teachers to tell my father they wished they had a whole classroom of Shilohs. No, I definitely wasn't the type of kid who would see the inside of the police station...until now. Also at thirty-eight, I doubted anyone would consider me a kid.

I left my car in a small parking lot behind the building. There was a door in the back of the building, but I decided to walk around to the front. To my surprise, there was no one there to escort me to where I was supposed to go. I would have thought an officer would have been posted in the parking lot to make sure I appeared or that Chief Randy would have been standing there himself with a pair of handcuffs.

I took a deep breath to calm myself and went through the glass doors into the main lobby. The floor was gray marble, and intricately designed plated tin covered the ceiling. Wood paneling covered the walls. I could imagine the bankers who walked around this building in the 1940s wearing gray suits and smoking cigarettes.

There was a desk in the corner of the room, and an elderly woman smiled at me from the desk. "You much be Shiloh Bellamy. We've been waiting for you. The police chief is eager for a chat." She stood up. "Follow me, and I will take you to him."

She was no more than five feet tall and wore a long skirt and heavy wool sweater despite it being the middle of summer. Her hair was styled in soft curls on the top of her head. I looked around. She was acting like she was a hostess who was escorting me to my dinner table.

"I feel for you, sugar," the woman said. "Your family seems to have gotten into a pickle. I'm sure it will all get sorted out. But the chief is just doing his job. You understand, don't you? Sometimes when we bring people in, they can be so disagreeable."

"Do you work for the police department?" I asked.

She shook her head. "I'm the receptionist for the town offices. I do a little bit of everything. I even answer 911 calls when the department is in a pinch. My, that's thrilling, but I've never gotten a call over a dead body." She unlocked a door with one of the keys that hung from the key ring on her belt. The key ring reminded me of something the housekeeper in *Downton Abbey* would carry.

"And you are?" I asked.

She held the door for me. "Oh dear me! Where are my manners! I just assumed you knew who I was. Everyone in Cherry Glen does. I'm Connie Baskins. I've been working for the Glen, well, just forever. Our current mayor would have been in diapers when I began this job. I don't have any plans to retire. What's the point? What would I do if I retired? Working keeps me young."

We were in a different part of the building now, and it looked much different from the old and ornate front room. I walked on linoleum flooring, and the walls were painted a sickly yellow color. There was another door, and Connie unlocked this one too.

"Go in and have a seat. I'll tell the chief you're here."

I stepped into the room, and before I could say so much as thank you, she closed the door behind me, and I heard the key in the lock. For the briefest moment, I felt panicked. I was locked in. Also, Connie seemed nice enough, but I didn't completely trust the woman would tell the chief I was even here.

I closed my eyes for a moment, took another deep breath, and opened them again. Scanning my surroundings, I found myself in a windowless room. The flooring and walls matched the sickly yellow in the hallway. There was a filing cabinet in the corner, a small desk in one corner, and a metal folding table in the middle. There were four folding chairs around the table. It looked like I was in someone's sparse but neat office. I found that comforting. If I was in someone's office and not an interrogation room, the police must not think of me as too much of a threat—or at least that was what I told myself.

I was just starting to wonder how long I would be left alone in the room when the door opened and Chief Randy stepped inside, carrying a shoebox. "Shiloh, thanks for coming down." He said this like he had given me any other choice. We both knew he hadn't. He sat in the closest folding chair at the table and gestured for me to sit across from him.

I sat and folded my hands on the top of the metal table. I had never been questioned by the police before. I didn't know what to do with my hands. Should I keep them where the chief could see them?

I tried to think back to my time writing for soap operas when I first moved to LA. Guilty parties usually had a tell. Wandering eyes. Twitchy movements. Or sometimes they were just too calm and poised. Should I let all my nerves show? Put on a brave face? Which of these would endear me more to the chief?

"You are wound tighter than my wife at Christmas. She's always a nervous wreck around the holidays. Kind of takes the enjoyment out of it if you ask me."

I dropped my hands onto my lap. "You said you need to talk to me about Crocker's death? I will say for the hundredth time, I had nothing to do with it."

"And I've heard you say it every time."

His comment didn't give me the impression he believed me, even if he had heard me.

He set the shoebox in the middle of the table and lifted the lid. Reaching inside, he came up with an old-looking revolver in a labeled evidence bag. He pushed the box aside and set the revolver in the middle of the table. "Can you tell me what that is?"

"A gun."

He smiled. "Yes, I know that, but do you recognize it?"

"It looks like one of my father's old revolvers, but you will have to ask him if it actually is. I haven't seen his collection in a long time."

"I did show it to Sully, and he confirmed it was his revolver."

I nodded. I didn't know what else he wanted me to say.

When I didn't speak, he added, "We found this under the honey booth after it was moved."

He didn't have to say near the body. It was understood.

"The coroner removed a bullet from Crocker's body, and it matched this gun. It was a very easy match. How did the revolver get to the farmers market, and how was Crocker shot?" he asked in a casual way.

"I—I don't know."

"I asked your father the same questions."

"And what did he say?"

"He said he didn't know either."

"Then it must be true." My father was a lot of things. He could be cranky, distant, and standoffish to most people, even his own daughter, but I've never known him to lie. In fact, I wished he had at times when I was growing up. Like when I messed up a solo in a school concert. He told me honestly where I went wrong. It had crushed me at the time. However, it was proof to me now that he wasn't lying about the gun.

"I'm not sure why I'm here," I said. "You already found out what you needed to know about the gun from my dad."

"Not everything." The police chief tapped his fingers on the tabletop, and a vibration moved through the thin metal. "In the play, they would not use real bullets like the one found in the victim. They were blanks at the theater. How could real bullets get into this gun?"

"I don't know."

"Your father told me he had some unspent bullets for most of the guns, including this one. However, he said he did not take those to the theater. There were five missing from his collection room. Lucky for us, your father keeps very detailed records of his collection."

"He always has," I said. Sitting at that table, memories of my father puttering away in his collection room flood my mind. There were so many times I wanted to ask him something or I needed a ride somewhere but was afraid to interrupt him in the room. In most cases, I went to Grandma Bellamy instead. "Your father had always been interested in frontier life and history," she had told me once. "But after your mother died, it became his obsession. He collected more artifacts as a way to bury his own pain. I have told him many times before that money would have been better spent on updating the farm. He won't hear of it. Just remember, Shiloh, I have a security policy for you."

I never found out what that security policy was when my grandmother died.

"Are you listening to me?" the police chief asked in an irritated voice.

I jumped, not knowing how long he had been trying to get my attention. "I'm sorry. Can you repeat the question?"

"When was the last time you were in your father's collection room?"

"I went in there today after you left the house."

"Before that?" he asked.

I shook my head. "It'd been years."

He frowned as if he didn't like my answer. That was just too bad, and besides, I didn't like his question.

He set a folder on the table, opened it, and slid it across the table to me. "What's this?"

I peered at the piece of paper on top. I immediately recognized it as my agreement with Crocker. I should have expected that he'd already have a copy of it. "It's my contract with Crocker. How'd you get that?" I asked.

"Crocker's business attorney was happy to turn over all documents that might be pertinent to the case. He and Crocker's widow are very eager to find out who might have done this."

"Dad can't be the only suspect," I said. "You have to have his estranged wife, Shannon Crocker, down as a suspect as well. I have heard from several people that she was trying to divorce Crocker, but he wouldn't agree with the divorce because they didn't have a prenup. He was trapping her in a loveless marriage."

"I don't think you should be worrying about the other suspects," Chief Randy said. "The only suspect you should be worried about is yourself."

"Me?" I choked on the word, and my palms broke out into a sweat.

"Now, please tell me about the contract."

He had it right in front of him. I didn't know how telling him the gist of it would do me any harm.

"Crocker agreed to invest one hundred thousand dollars in the farm over the next year so that I could update it to be a certified organic farm. I had two years to spend the money and show progress."

"How were you going to show that?"

"In the contract, it states there was a certain revenue number the farm would have to hit. It was a modest number, or at least it seemed to be a modest number before I saw the state the farm was in. I would be putting my money in too. I'm fully invested in saving the farm."

"So he gave you one hundred thousand dollars."

"No! Not at all. He hasn't given me any money yet. The day he died, we were supposed to meet and discuss how I could make withdrawals from the loan he was going to set up. I don't even have access to that account. I don't even know if he created it yet. So, you see, it was actually *against* my best interests that Crocker was murdered. Now I have no idea what's going to happen with that money. I don't even know if the contract is still valid!"

"Unless you recognized the futility of the contract and knew you'd default and lose everything, in which case getting rid of Crocker would be a solid recourse. If no one was going to enforce the terms, the contract is rendered basically void. And even if the new executor of his estate stumbles upon it, it could be months until the red tape is cleared to even collect what you would owe," he speculated. Chief Randy rocked back in his chair as he thought this over.

"What? No! We weren't trying to get rid of Crocker or get out of anything!" My voice rose in panic. I took a steadying breath. "Do I wish I had never signed that contract? After all this, yes. Do I hope nothing comes of it now? Absolutely. I don't want anything from Crocker anymore, but that doesn't mean we killed him!"

Chief Randy took in my outburst with a stony expression. "Do you have an attorney, Shiloh?"

"Not in Michigan."

"You might want to get one," he said. "I don't think this will be the last time we are bringing you in on this case. The next time might just be in handcuffs."

My hands were ice cold.

Chapter Eighteen

I stumbled out of the room and rubbed my hands together. I couldn't get them warm. This wasn't the first time this had happened. Any time I was especially stressed, the blood drained from my hands. A therapist back in California I saw to help me deal with Logan's death told me once it was my body preparing for fight or flight. All the blood was rushing through me to my internal organs to protect them. I took this to be a bad sign.

What the therapist hadn't known was I was always a flight risk, not a fight risk. I felt the urge to run away from the police station, away from Bellamy Farm, away from all of it. It was what I had done when Logan died and Quinn made a scene at his funeral. Here I was, wanting to do it again. I pressed my hands at my sides and whispered "Stay" to myself like I would to Huckleberry.

I thought the chief would escort me out of the building, but when we stepped into the hallway, he pointed to the door at the end of the hall I had come through with Connie. "You can go out just that way there."

I nodded and shuffled down the corridor, back into the old great room of the building. Just being out of that circa 1950s space with the bland colors, it was easier for me to breathe. Connie wasn't at her desk. The security around this place seemed more than a little lax. Even though Chief Randy thought I killed a man, he didn't see me as a threat to anyone else. If he did, he had a funny way of showing it.

The front door of the building opened, and Quinn walked inside. Of course it would be him. He seemed to pop up everywhere I went. "Are you following me?"

"I work here," he said. "Cherry Glen is a small town. The police and the fire department are in the same building."

"Oh, right. I knew that." I kept walking toward the door.

"Shiloh." His voice was soft. "Are you all right?"

Tears came to my eyes. "Of course I'm not all right. Your father and the rest of this town think either I killed a man or my father did, all to save the farm. It's very likely one of us could be arrested for something we didn't do, and the money I invested in the farm to save it will have been wasted. The farm has been in our family for six generations. I will be the generation that ruined it."

Quinn opened his mouth like he wanted to say something.

"I'm sorry. I shouldn't have dropped all this on you. It's not your problem at all." I hurried out the door and around the building to my car. I was both relieved and strangely disappointed that he didn't follow me out.

On the drive back to Bellamy Farm, I wondered what I could do. One thing I needed, both for my father and maybe even for myself, was an attorney. Briar could help me with that, as much as I dreaded calling her and hearing how right she was to think it was a bad idea for me to leave California.

This wasn't a conversation I could have while driving. At the end of Michigan Street, I pulled off onto a little side street, and the elementary school came into view. I turned into the parking lot.

The school was closed for the summer, and a group of children played on the playground. I wished I could say their happy cries lifted my spirits.

I took my phone from my pocket and made the call I was dreading.

"For goodness' sake, I have been texting you nonstop for days. I thought you were dead. I thought you were dead and I would have to go to Michigan to find you. Do you have any idea how hard that would have been for me? I am not a Midwest girl. I don't even own a trucker hat," my friend Briar Hart cried into my ear.

"Everyone living in Michigan doesn't wear trucker hats. In fact, I think Hollywood has a lot to answer for by giving off that impression," I said.

"Well, that's a relief. I'm glad I don't have to worry about the hat, but I'm still worried about you. What is the deal with you going dark on me? Don't you for one second blame it on the phone connection. We are in the middle of the twenty-first century. I don't believe bad reception stories anymore for anyone, not even on the North Pole."

"It's been hectic since I got here," I said. "I've only been here a few days."

"Maybe you have only been in Michigan a few days, but you drove across the country with that gassy pug in the front seat of your car—anything could have happened to you! I deserved an update." She huffed. "I haven't heard a peep from you since you texted me that you got there."

"You're right. I'm sorry," I said.

"And the farm is okay?" Her voice was less irritated now and more concerned.

"It—" What could I say? Nothing was okay. The farm. Me. Nothing.

"No, it's not. I can tell from your voice. You can never hide anything from me, Shiloh Bellamy. Something bad has happened. I
told you this would happen. I told you that moving to the middle
of nowhere Michigan was the dumbest idea you have ever had,
and I remember the time when you tried that weird electric belt
thing to trim your waist. Do you still have scars from the burns on
your stomach?"

I knew I shouldn't have told Briar about my exercise belt. I
had just wanted to find something to trim my waistline a little
bit faster. The infomercial had said it was perfectly safe. Who
knew I would have that kind of skin that would react poorly to
electroshock?

I met Briar when we I first moved to LA. We were both book
nerds and hit it off at a local bookstore. I wanted to be a producer,
and she wanted to be a big shot entertainment attorney. Both of us
achieved those dreams; however, Briar was still living hers, while I
was a murder suspect back in my hometown.

"Tell me what happened and how I can get you out of it.
Hopefully, I can do that remotely, because trucker hat require-
ment or not, I am not keen on the idea of venturing into the wild
Midwest." She took a breath. "But for you, I'm willing to do it."

I took a breath and watched the children play in the playground.
I didn't even know how I was going to explain the situation. "I got
to my family farm, and remember I told you I found an investor?"

"And I told you you should wait until you met him in person
before going into business. I think it's best to see the people you're
going into business with whenever possible."

I sighed, wishing I had listened to her.

"But that's water under the bridge now. Go on, tell me."

"Well, I'm in a bit of a—"

"Jasmine, you need to retype this. It's a mess." She paused. "I'm sorry. I swear to heaven these interns are going to kill me. They were raised learning to type, but spelling is a challenge."

I took a breath. Maybe it would be better if I just came out with it. "I found a dead body. It was the investor in my farm. He was murdered, and the police think my father or I did it. I was advised to find an attorney. You're the only attorney I know very well, and I was calling to get your help." I winced and waited for the onslaught of outrage, swearing, and shouts. Nothing came.

There was silence. Dead silence. I had known Briar a long time; I had never known her to be silent. As the silence grew, I looked at my phone to see if I had lost the connection. The numbers were still running to show how long I had been on the call. It hadn't been dropped.

"Bri?" I asked.

There was another beat, and then she said, "I'm just processing. Give me a second."

"Okay." I shifted in my car seat. Briar's reaction to my sticky situation was worse than if she had started yelling at me. In fact, I think I would have preferred the yelling, cursing and all.

Just when I was going to ask her again if she was still there, she said, "Do you want me to fly out there?" There was no humor in her voice, no jokes about trucker hats or her less than stellar impression of the Midwestern accent.

Tear sprang to my eyes. "No," I swallowed. "You can't leave your family right now."

"Yes, I can for you, Shi. Cam would understand and stay with the baby. He's on paternity leave. I'm sure my mother-in-law would be willing to come in to help. She's been chomping at the bit to reorganize our pantry. The woman cannot be stopped."

Cam was Briar's husband. They had been married for five
years and had just adopted their first child a month before I left
California. Briar's mother-in-law, Darla, was a professional orga-
nizer for the Hollywood elite. I could easily see her eyeing their
pantry. If Briar came to Cherry Glen to rescue me, it was very likely
all her closets would be redone by the time she returned home.

Now that I thought about it, if I had the ability to stay out of
prison, I might hire Darla to come to the farm and help with a plan
of attack for the massive to-do list I had created. She'd make short
work of it. However, the truth was, I couldn't afford her even when
I had a six-figure salary back in LA.

"No," I said. "The baby is still small, and Cam needs you. I'm
not taking you away from her right now. I just need help finding an
attorney. I don't know who to trust. There is one lawyer in town,
but he works for Crocker, the man who was killed. I have a feeling
he wouldn't be a great deal of help to me."

"Serious conflict of interest. Let me make some calls. I'm sure
there is someone there who hung up his shingle as an attorney in
the back and beyond. What's the biggest city close by? Detroit?"

"No, Detroit is actually pretty far away on the other side of
Michigan. The closest is Traverse City," I said. "It's about thirty
minutes away."

"Okay." I heard her clicking on the keyboard. "I got it," Briar
said triumphantly.

"What? What is it?" I was preparing myself for her to tell me
there wasn't an attorney within one hundred miles of me who
would take my case.

"Leif Jansen," she said.

"Who?"

"Leif Jansen is in Traverse City. What do you know? I seem to recall he was from around there. I thought it was Wisconsin. I get all those flyover states mixed up."

"Who's Leif Jansen?" I asked.

"He's an old friend of mine from law school. He was one of the smartest guys in our class. He was a good guy too, if a little on the overly cautious side. I don't honestly know if he will take your case, but it's worth a shot. At the very least, he would know other attorneys in the area. Unless he changed his number, I should still have his cell number. Let me give him a buzz, and I will call you back."

"Okay, and, Briar?"

"Yeah?" she asked. I could tell by the sound of her voice she was already distracted and ready to move on to the next task. Briar was always in a hurry—you either had to keep up or hold on for dear life.

"Thank you," I said. "I really mean that. I'm so grateful for you. You've been a really great friend to me, and I should tell you that more."

"Okay, okay, you're going to make me cry, and that will ruin my reputation in the firm. Damn these glass walls between the offices to give the workplace a more open feel. A woman can't cry in peace. Ever since we got the baby, I have been a puddle, and I used to pride myself on being rock-hard." She took a breath. "I'll call you back as soon as possible."

She ended the call before I could say goodbye.

Chapter Nineteen

Briar said she would call me right back, but I knew it might take her some time to get ahold of her old friend Leif. I couldn't sit in the parking lot forever, and I didn't want to go back to the farm just yet.

I made another call to another old friend. It seemed to me I was realizing I couldn't handle this on my own. Kristy picked up on the first ring and told me to meet her at the brewery.

It was late afternoon, and early diners at the brewery were beginning to go into the building. The front door was heavy and I thought original to when the building was a granary. I stepped inside and was surprised at the dim lighting. To my left behind a glass wall were giant steel fermenters that had to be twenty feet tall. To my right was the dining room and bar.

"Shi!" Kristy called and waved at me from the bar. She was sitting on the edge of one of the metal stools and looked like she was about to slide right off. A glass of water was next to her on the bar.

I smiled at the hostess and hurried over to her. "Thanks for meeting me."

She patted the empty stool beside her. "Have a seat. You are probably wondering why I asked you to come to a brewery when I'm pregnant."

The thought had crossed my mind, but I didn't say that.

She smiled. "That handsome guy there is my husband, Kent. He's a teacher and tends bar here in the summers to make a little extra money, and boy, do we need that right now."

At the end of the bar, a tall man with dark, curly hair filled two steins from the tap.

"I usually come here when he's working for an early dinner before the rush so we can talk. We both work a lot, and it's hard to make the time, you know?"

I nodded, but I wasn't sure if I really knew. The last serious relationship I had been in had been with Logan, and I had been so young.

Kent set the two steins in front of customers and came down the bar to us. He smiled at me, and his whole face lit up. "You are the famous Shiloh. Kristy has told me so many stories about you."

"It's so nice to meet you," I said, returning his grin. "And congrats on the upcoming little ones."

"Ah, thanks! Twins, can you believe it?" He gazed lovingly at his wife. "So, what will you have?"

"Diet Coke?" I asked. "I think with everything going on, having a beer is a bad idea right now."

Kent snapped his fingers at me. "You got it."

Kristy watched him go and sighed. "He's such a hard worker. Just a really fantastic guy."

"That's great, Kristy. I'm really happy for you," I said, smiling as I set my phone on the counter next to me, face up. I didn't want to miss the call back from Briar.

"Did you leave anyone special behind in California?"

"I have friends there, but I know that's not what you mean. I wasn't seeing anyone when I left. There's really been no one since…"

"Oh wow, you haven't dated since Logan died?" She grabbed my hand and squeezed it tight.

"I have, just not seriously. LA is a grind, and there's just not been much time for dating." I closed my eyes for a moment, and Logan's cheerful face and mischievous brown eyes filled my head. He had been gone so long now, and I wondered if it had not been for the few pictures I'd kept, would I have forgotten what he looked like?

"There hasn't been much time, or you've used that as an excuse not to get close to anyone?" she asked as she lifted her water glass to me.

It was super annoying that Kristy still had the ability to see through me. Thankfully, I was saved from saying anything because Kent returned with my Diet Coke.

He set it in front of me. "I'd love to chat, but a party of eight just came in, and they all want cocktails. I'm the only bartender here until six when it really starts to pick up." He smiled. "I'm glad I finally got to meet the famous Shiloh Bellamy."

"Or infamous," Kristy said.

I nearly snorted my drink.

"I'm glad I can still make you shoot liquid out of your nose." She handed me a napkin.

I patted my nose with it. "No one would think I was infamous."

She cocked her head. "Maybe not back in high school days," she agreed. "You always were the teacher's pet. But now might be different."

I grimaced. "Are people talking about me when it comes to the murder?"

Kristy touched her glass of water but did not pick it up. "I've heard rumors…"

I wanted to bang my head on the bar. "How bad?"

"Pretty bad. Chief Randy doesn't seem to have any qualms about telling anyone who will ask that you and Sully are suspects. In a town the size of Cherry Glen, just about everyone is asking."

"Great." I tapped my phone to see if I missed a call. Nothing.

"You've been poking at that phone ever since you got here. Do you need some kind of social media fix?"

"No, I'm waiting for a call from a friend." I sighed. "Who is also an attorney."

"Oh boy. Are the rumors right? Spill."

"Well, you remember when we were in the diner and the mayor said Crocker was an investor in Bellamy Farm…"

She stared at me expectantly.

I leaned in close and told her the rest about Dad being against the Crocker investment but it being too late and the murder weapon being my father's gun.

Kristy put one hand on her cheek and the other on her round stomach. "I can see why you want to talk to an attorney."

I nodded. "My friend Briar is an attorney in LA, but she has a friend who's a lawyer in Traverse City. She's trying to see if her friend will take my case."

She patted my arm. "I'm sure the attorney will clear up this mess in no time."

"I'm not as sure. If the chief has already made up his mind like you said…" Tears came to my eyes.

"Oh no, we need emergency care here." She slapped the bar and waved at her husband.

Kent stood in front of us a second later. "What's up? I have four more cocktails to make."

Kristy slapped the bar. "We need a cherry tower."

His eyes went wide. "Are you sure?"

She pointed at me. "Do you see her face?"

I waved my hands in the air. "No, no, I don't need a cherry tower."

Kristy shook her finger at me. "You're not in your right mind. Of course you do."

Kent nodded. "I'm on it."

"Kristy…"

"Hush." She patted my arm. "These are desperate times."

I sighed. She was right about that.

A minute later, Kent came back from the kitchen with the cherry tower. It was a dessert distinct to Cherry Glen, and I hadn't eaten one in well over a decade. It was served in a tall and narrow sundae glass. The bottom was pie crust, followed by four kinds of cherries—this time of year all grown in Cherry Glen—vanilla and cherry ice cream, whipped cream, and of course topped with a cherry. It was over nine inches tall.

"I can't eat that," I said.

"Sure you can," Kristy said. "You need energy right now to get through what you're facing."

"Energy maybe, but energy in that form is going to have me crashing in thirty minutes." I pushed the spoon away.

"But what a way to go," she said with a smile. "If you go to prison, don't you want to go with this taste in your mouth? It will bring you happy memories on that hard cot."

"Not helping," I said.

"I'm just trying to paint a picture for you."

"No need. The picture is seared into my head."

She moved the cherry tower a little bit closer to me. "You need it."

I gave her a look. "I'll take one bite." I picked up the spoon.

The cherry ice cream was as good as I remembered. I stopped myself from moaning—or at least I tried to.

Kristy laughed, telling me I hadn't been quiet at all. I put my spoon down before I ate the entire sundae.

Kristy picked up a spoon of her own. "So if the attorney isn't enough, what are you going to do to help your family stay out of prison?"

I shivered when she put it so matter-of-fact like that. "I need to find out who the real killer is."

Ice cream dripped from her spoon to the bar. "I was afraid you would say that."

"I have to find the killer myself. I have a feeling that Chief Randy already sees this case as closed. I can't be arrested. I did nothing wrong. And my father can't either. I need to clear my family's name."

She picked up a napkin and cleaned up the ice cream drips on the bar. "Shi, this isn't some movie or television show that you wrote. This is real life. It's dangerous. Need I remind you what the scene by the honey booth looked like? Someone shot him in the chest!"

A couple sitting a few seats down the bar from us stared at Kristy, openmouthed.

I smiled at them. "She's just talking about one of those television true crime shows."

"I'm not—"

"Kristy," I said, spinning back in her direction. "I have to do this, and I need your help."

She stared at me. "Help? If you haven't noticed, I'm super pregnant. I'm not hunting down a killer in this condition. Have you seen my stomach?"

"And I would never ask you to, but I saw someone just before I found Crocker's body. Since you run the farmers market, I thought you'd be able to tell me who it was."

She picked up her spoon again and dug into the cherry tower. "All right, go."

I described the young woman who had been running through the farmers market that morning and knocked me over.

She wrinkled her brow.

"Do you know who that woman was?" I watched her closely.

"I—I might, but I have to check before I tell you."

"Why can't you tell me now?"

"I might be wrong, and I don't want to involve this person if I'm wrong."

"They could be the killer." I set my spoon on the bar. I had lost my appetite.

"I doubt it if I'm right."

"Kristy, my life is on the line, and this person could have the answer."

"I know that, but yours might not be the only life on the line."

I opened and closed my mouth.

"Just trust me, Shiloh. Please?" She waved her spoon at me. "Give me some time. I'll text you as soon as I know more, I promise."

I didn't think I had any other choice.

Kristy and I finished the cherry tower, and I told her I had better get back to the farm. Call me a coward, but when I returned home, I wasn't ready to talk to my father about the conversation I had with the chief. I collected Huckleberry, my father's old toolbox from the barn, and a shovel and set to work on the broken fence near the farm entrance. From what I could see, the task was daunting. Every last pole was leaning in one direction or the other. Huckleberry lay in the middle of the driveway with his head on his paws as if to tell me I was on my own on this one.

I walked up to the first pole and pushed it. It didn't budge. I pulled it to the same effect. I grabbed the shovel and dug around. When the dirt was loose, it moved a third of an inch, but it was all the encouragement I needed to keep digging.

I had just started to make some progress when my phone buzzed in my pocket. I leaned my back against the pole so I wouldn't lose the ground I'd made.

Sweat trickled down both sides of my face as I answered the phone.

"This is Leif Jansen. May I speak to Shiloh Bellamy?"

"This is Shiloh. I guess you've spoken to Briar if you're calling me."

"I did." His voice was clipped and distant like an attorney I would see on a courtroom drama on television. "She told me about your situation, and I said I would give you a call myself. From what Briar said, we need to act quickly."

Something about his quick assertiveness made the reality of the situation crash down on me all the harder.

"Let's cut to the chase," he said. "Tell me what you know."

I bit the inside of my cheek, feeling hesitant to open up to a man I didn't know. However, I reminded myself Briar trusted him, and I trusted Briar. That would have to be enough. I quickly told him about Crocker's murder and why the police suspected my father, and maybe me.

"It doesn't look good for your dad," Leif said.

"But I told you he's on a walker."

"Can he still drive his truck?"

"Yes, but—"

"Then he could have killed him, especially if the shot from the chest came from above."

I frowned at the phone. This attorney Briar found wasn't making me feel any better.

"Listen, it's always been my method with my clients not to sugarcoat anything. My advice is to cooperate with the police as much as possible. If you or your father is arrested, call me. I'll come down."

"Why would I be arrested?" I yelped.

"You might be seen as an accessory," he said, completely matter-of-fact. "Or you might have tried to get out of the contract with Crocker to save your tenuous relationship with your father. Crocker says no, and you shoot him in anger. It happens," he said, as if it were an everyday occurrence.

Maybe it was in his world, but it wasn't in mine. I felt sick.

"Or," he went on, "you could be seen as an accessory for covering up your father's crimes. In either case, it's jail time. The length varies though between murder and accessory."

"I didn't kill anyone."

"I'm not saying you did," he said. "It's my job to defend my clients, not to make judgments. From what I can tell, your father has the best motive, means, and opportunity, but I wouldn't say you personally were in the clear. In any case, the police will be keeping an eye on you too."

I had to swallow down an irritated sigh. I'd kind of figured that one out all on my own.

Chapter Twenty

My calendar on my phone reminded me I had a meeting the next morning in Traverse City to tour a farm-to-table café and see what the business included. I almost canceled because a café like that at Bellamy Farm was so far out of my reach at the moment, it seemed like the meeting would be a waste of time. However, I realized with everything going on, I could use the distraction, so I kept the appointment and headed out of Cherry Glen as soon as I woke up the next day.

After an interesting meeting with the farm-to-table owners, I exited with a bag of fresh produce and a host of ideas the restaurateurs graciously shared with me. As I took in the still, quiet streets, I was distracted by the fact that I wouldn't be able to open a café at Bellamy Farm for a very long time, at least not without the assistance of Crocker's money. That was assuming, of course, neither my father nor I were thrown into prison. I sighed and continued down the street.

Traverse City sat on the edge of Lake Michigan. It had a vibrant downtown area that on the weekend was full of foot traffic. Visitors and locals alike went in and out of the many specialty shops. So early on a Wednesday morning, the shops were open, but the street was relatively quiet.

I continued in the direction of the public parking lot where I had left my car when a woman strolling down the sidewalk caught my eye. She carried five shopping bags, swinging them back and forth. She wore a brightly colored summer dress, and a pair of oversized sunglasses sat on the top of her head. I blinked. It was Shannon Crocker. I recognized her from her photograph in the theater's playbill for *The Tragedy of Julius Caesar*, and she did not look the picture of a grieving widow.

Shannon hurried down the street and stopped in front of a dress boutique. She went inside. I hesitated for a moment and then followed her.

The boutique was clean and bright. All the clothes were perfectly folded or hung from wooden hangers spaced precisely one half inch away from one another. The floor was polished concrete and gave the room a hip industrial feel when it otherwise would be too stark. I was in Michigan, but I could have been in any of the high-end shops in LA at that moment.

Three women browsed the clothing racks and spoke softly to one another like they were inside the church of textiles. I flipped a tag over on a blouse and whistled under my breath. They were LA prices too. I guessed this boutique set prices for the thousands of visitors who vacationed in the Traverse City area each year, not for the local residents or college students. When I was going to college in town, I couldn't afford these prices. I couldn't afford them now.

A tiny shopping clerk in impractical shoes followed Shannon around the store. The new widow plucked items off the racks and handed them to the clerk, who stumbled under the weight of the garments. It looked to me like someone was on a shopping spree because she had come into a lot of money.

"I'll start with these," Shannon said to the clerk. She floated back toward the dressing rooms.

"Can I help you?" another clerk asked me. Her tone told me just how much she did not want to help me or any other person on the planet.

I smiled and grabbed a blouse that was most certainly not my size. "I'd like to try this on."

She looked at the size, then at me, and back again. Shaking her head, she said, "Follow me."

There were six doors leading into the private changing rooms. Shannon's clerk stood outside one of those doors, biting her fingernails. My clerk unlocked one of the dressing rooms. "There you go." She turned to the other salesclerk. "Annie, we need you on the register. I'll watch the dressing room."

Annie dropped her hand from her mouth and bolted down the hallway. She seemed more than eager to escape.

"Do you need anything else?" the older clerk asked me.

I shook my head.

She shrugged and walked down the hallway too. So much for keeping an eye on the dressing rooms.

A hand tossed a floral blouse over the side of the door Annie had been watching. "Can you get this for me in a smaller size?"

I picked it up and looked down the hallway. What should I do? Get the shirt and come back pretending I was the clerk?

Apparently, I took too long, because Shannon said, "Can't you hear me?"

Before I could answer, she flung the door open. She was wearing a black-and-white-striped jumpsuit that on me would have looked like a prison uniform. Considering the situation I was in, it wasn't too far from the mark.

"Who are you? Where's the girl I was working with?" Shannon looked around the room.

"She was called away to the register."

Shannon sniffed. "I came in here with the intent to spend money. You would think the staff would pay a little more attention to me." She eyed me. "Do you work here?"

"No." I held up the too small blouse in my hand. "I was going to try this on."

"That top is too small for you. You should get a large." She said large as if it were equal to a death sentence.

I hung the blouse on the rack in the corner.

Shannon walked over to the three-way mirror and examined her body. "I have to cut back on the sugar. I've put on a few pounds."

Her figure looked perfect to me, so I didn't know if she was fishing for compliments or if she seriously had a low opinion of herself.

"That jumpsuit looks great on you," I said. Since I wanted information from her, I thought it would be best to throw a compliment her way.

She turned. "Hmm, it shows every imperfection."

I didn't see any imperfections.

She walked back to her changing room.

"Can I talk to you for a moment?" I asked.

She stared at me. "Do I know you?"

I shook my head. "But I'm from Cherry Glen. You're Shannon Crocker, right?"

She narrowed her eyes. "How do you know that? Who are you?"

"My name is Shiloh Bellamy from Bellamy Farm. I knew your husband."

"Bellamy. You're the people who killed my husband." She pressed her red lips into a thin line.

I let out a breath and was so grateful no one was close by to hear her say that. "I didn't kill your husband, but I would like to speak to you about his death." I glanced behind me to see if any of the salesclerks or customers were headed for the dressing rooms. So far, the coast was clear.

She shrugged as if that wasn't important. "Just to show you what a small world it is, I went to high school with your mother in Bellaire."

Bellaire was another small town near Cherry Glen. "I—I didn't know that."

She shrugged again. "We were high school friends. Didn't see her much after she married your father. Everyone was shocked when she married a *farmer* old enough to be her father." She said farmer like it was some kind of curse, or maybe she thought marrying an older man was the curse.

I stared at her. I didn't know what to say. A comment about it being a small world seemed out of place.

"How did you find me?" she asked.

"I was in Traverse City for an appointment and spotted you. It was completely by chance, but I thought this might be a good time to talk."

"You thought catching me in the dressing room was a good time to talk?"

I had to admit it didn't sound so good when she put it that way. "I'm sorry. I can see why this would be a bad time. I just didn't know when I'd run into you again. And I didn't kill your husband. I didn't kill anyone. I swear."

"It was you or Sully. It makes no difference to me. Had it been you, I was going to thank you. Jefferson was the worst kind of man. He was selfish beyond belief."

"Because he wouldn't give you a divorce?" I said.

She folded her arms. "How do you know?"

"Several people in town told me."

"I can't wait to get out of there. All anyone in Cherry Glen can do is gossip."

"Why didn't you move before if you hate it so much?"

"And give up the giant house I can live in for free?" She laughed and plucked the blouse I had hung up on the rack, holding it against her body in front of the three-way mirror. "No, thank you. Now I can sell it and not have to share any of the profit with Jefferson. My patience has paid off. Good things come to those who wait." She hung the blouse back on the rack.

Her patience with her divorce brought her good things? Or the murder brought her good things?

She continued, "I know everyone in the Glen is talking about me. Maybe some of them even think I killed him."

"Did you?" I was surprised at myself for just asking her like that, but she opened the door for the question.

She eyed me. "No, I wasn't even in town when that happened. I was visiting my sister in Madison. I flew home that morning and found the police on my doorstep that afternoon. They told me what happened and that they already had a suspect in mind. Your father."

My heart sank. Now I knew why the police weren't taking a close look at the ex-wife; she had an airtight alibi. There couldn't be a more airtight alibi than being on an airplane, a location where your identity was checked multiple times before you even boarded.

"Do you know anyone else who would want to kill your husband?" I asked.

She laughed. "How much time do you have? Half of Cherry Glen is celebrating his death right now. However, as much as I hated Jefferson, I don't think anyone hated him more than Hedy Strong. She's a complete bird nut. In her mind, they are more important than people. She would probably push a man out into traffic to save a bird."

I shivered and thought of the business card Wes gave me. It seemed to me I needed to give Hedy a call, and soon. "Are you going to go through with the wind farm?"

"My, you do know a lot about all this. I'm impressed. From what I heard, you just moved to Cherry Glen." She paused. "As for the wind farm, that was Jefferson's project. I have no interest in it. He's been fighting for it for the last five years. I'm not going to waste the rest of my life fighting those bird lovers. I have enough money now to buy whatever I want for the rest of my life. I'm not so greedy that I would want more than that."

"Did Hedy know you weren't interested in the wind farm?" I asked.

"Of course she did. She tried to corner me so many times on the topic. She thought by talking to me about it, she could reach Jefferson. I told her we were separated, but she tried anyway. The woman was desperate to save her birds. Absolutely desperate."

Hedy Strong just went up several notches on my suspect list.

Chapter Twenty-One

T he drive back to Bellamy Farm from Traverse City was uneventful. My brain was swirling with thoughts of the murder, but I couldn't pin any of them down.

Grandma Bellamy's voice filled my head again. "Work. If you're stuck on something, do something about it. Sitting around worrying and moping doesn't make it any better. If you can't fix that problem, there are plenty of other problems in your power to fix. Fix those."

I had once come home from school to find her in the middle of the barn, rebuilding a tractor engine. I'd asked her why she hadn't asked my dad to do it for her. She peered down her pert nose at me. "Why should I let him have all the fun?"

I parked my car by the barn and was happy when Huckleberry came running out of the building to greet me. I scooped him up. "I missed you." I hugged the little dog tight. What would happen to Huckleberry if I were in prison? I had to solve this not just for myself and my family but for him.

My dad's truck was there.

"I think it's time we go in and face the music and talk to Grandpa." I set the pug on the grass.

He looked up at me and cocked his head one way and then the other. Even when I was in the worst spots, Huckleberry had the power to cheer me up.

I walked to the farmhouse and went through the front door. "Dad?" I called.

There was no answer. I walked to the back of the house to the kitchen. Not surprisingly, I found my father in his collection room. His walker stood ready while he sat on a metal stool among his treasures. In front of him on the workbench, a gun lay in pieces. He polished the cylinders with a gray rag in his hand.

"It's about time you got home," he said, not looking up from his work.

"I'm sorry, Dad. I had a meeting. Did you get my text?" I asked.

"That you were going to Traverse City? Yes. I don't know what business you have there with so much going on back home."

I didn't see any point in telling him about the café people. It would only worry him more that I was planning too many changes for the farm.

"What are you working on?" I asked.

He glanced up. "You have never shown much interest in my collection before."

"Maybe not, but I'm interested now."

He eyed me as if to gauge if I was telling the truth. "I'm cleaning one of my rifles. I hate the idea of someone being in my collection and going through my things. No one had any right to do that. Everything needs to be polished." He picked up a piece of the gun and rubbed it hard with the rag.

"Was anything else missing other than the bullets?"

He shook his head. "No, whoever took those rounds knew what he was looking for and where they were."

"Who would know this?"

"You," he said and cleaned the gun with renewed vigor.

My heart sank. "Not me. I haven't looked at your collection in such a long time."

He scowled. "I just don't know who else would come in here."

"Dad, I didn't steal those bullets, and I didn't kill Crocker."

He sighed. "I know you didn't kill him, but someone did," he said. I noted he didn't say that I didn't take the bullets from the collection. "After I am done here, I'm going back to the theater to make sure all the artifacts I let Stacey borrow for the play are in order and nothing else is missing."

"Did you loan her many items?"

"A few of my reenactor uniforms, some camping paraphernalia, and five guns."

"Five? Why five?" It seemed like an excess number of guns to lend out.

"It's for the scene where Julius Caesar dies."

I wrinkled my nose. "I said this before, but wasn't he stabbed?"

He shot me a look. "In Stacey's interpretation of the play, each member of the senate has a gun and shoots him to death one by one. It's more in keeping with the time period."

"Was each actor assigned a particular gun?" I asked.

He shook his head. "Not that I know of. You will have to ask Stacey."

A worry nibbled at the back of my mind, but I couldn't form it into words yet. There was something particularly important about my father lending Stacey the guns for the play, and I didn't think it had to do solely with someone wanting to frame us. I had the same itchy feeling when I was in the middle of a film's production and I knew in my gut something was off with the manuscript. Adequate made a good movie. It did not make a great movie. In the end, the problem always revealed itself to me. I hoped the same would be true for this problem too.

"Why didn't she just get prop guns instead of borrowing them from you?" I asked.

"Because that would have cost money. Stacey had to pinch pennies any place she could. I offered her the use of my collection. I wanted to help. I have no money to give." Dad set down the cylinder on the worktable and looked me in the eye. "I know I have been in my own world, fussing over this collection of trinkets, most of your life. When your mother died, my collection gave me comfort. Finding just the right pieces and all the history I could about each piece was an obsession of mine. I'm sorry to say it grew worse when you left. There was nothing else for me to think about when you were gone."

"But what about the farm?" I asked in a quiet voice.

"I suppose I should have paid better attention to it. It just got away from me, and the worse it became, the more I didn't want to bother with it. Had you not paid the mortgages on the farm, I would have lost it long ago. My parents would be so disappointed that I let it come to this. The farm is lost. I can't bring it back." He pointed at the walker. "I'm trapped in this house with that metal contraption."

"Dad, I'm here now. We can save the farm together. I know we can do this. We don't need Crocker's money to save the farm. Yes, it would have helped, and yes, bringing the farm back may take a bit longer than I first thought without it, but we can do it. It will just take a little bit more creativity and grit."

He looked at me. "Why now?"

"Wh—what do you mean?"

"Why did you come back now to help with the farm?"

My brow wrinkled. "You asked for my help."

He frowned. "I never thought you would come. I hoped you would... When you left all those years ago, you said you'd come back, but you never did until now."

My heart sank.

"And I certainly didn't think you would sign a contract with that snake Crocker."

I licked my lips. "Chief Randy said you left Crocker a threatening message on his voicemail."

He glared at me. "You bet I did, and I would do it again."

"You have to know how that makes you look like a suspect," I said.

"They haven't arrested me yet." He went back to cleaning his gun.

"Dad, it's serious."

He didn't respond.

I looked around the collection room. "Someone broke in here to steal those bullets. When I find out who did that, I will know who the killer is."

"Do you know how to do that?" He looked up at me.

"No, but I'll figure it out."

"You were always so sure of yourself, just like your grandmother." He went back to cleaning his gun. I wasn't sure he meant that last comment as a compliment, but I chose to take it that way.

After leaving my father alone in the collection room again, I went back outside. Huckleberry followed. When he hit the grass, he pointed his flat nose into the air and barked, then galloped toward the barn.

When I didn't follow, he turned around and barked again.

"I swear if you found another dead body, we're catching the first flight out of here to LA. We can stay in Briar's guest room."

He hopped in place and then ran to the barn. I followed at a much slower pace, fearful of what I might find.

The sliding door was already opened.

My eyes adjusted to the dim light of the barn. Two of the ginger-colored barn cats watched me from the top of a hay bale. Huckleberry was nowhere to be seen. I put my hands on my hips. "Huck, this is no time to play games. I have a lot of work to do." I waited a beat. "Huckleberry, I need you to come out now."

There was no response.

I muttered under my breath. I didn't have the time to play hide-and-seek with the pug. I had a farm to save and a murder to solve. "Huckleberry Bellamy, you'd better come out right now."

There was a whimper, and my frustration melted away to fear. Was he hurt? It was the same whimper he had made when he got a thorn stuck in his paw when we were on a hike on the trails around LA.

"Huckleberry, are you okay?"

The whimper came again from behind the combine that took up a large section of the barn. I hoped he hadn't wedged himself into one of the tight spots in the machine.

I inched around the side of the combine, and a small figure screamed from the floor of the cockpit. "Ahhhh!"

"Ahhhh!" I screamed back.

Chapter Twenty-Two

Y ou scared me to death," Hazel said.

I adjusted my uncomfortable position between the combine and the wall. I stood on the edge of the giant machine. "I scared *you* to death? You scared me. You must have heard me call for Huckleberry. Why didn't you say something?"

"I thought you would go away and not come back here."

"You thought I would leave my dog?" I asked, and that was when I saw that Huckleberry and Hazel weren't alone in the cockpit of the combine. A silver and white cat was curled up on Hazel's lap. It was wound so tightly into a ball, I couldn't make heads or tails of where its head or tail was, but its side thumped away at the fast rhythm of its heartbeat. "Is that one of the barn cats?"

"No," Hazel said as she stroked the back of the frightened animal. "She's my cat—or at least I want her to be. I can take care of her. I really can. Cats are a lot less work than dogs. I can see why Dad wouldn't want me to have a dog, but he can't say no to a cat, can he?"

"Does your father know you have a cat?" I asked.

"No," she said slowly.

"Ah," I said. "Why don't you come out of that combine and talk about it, and if the cat you found is a stray, like I suspect, bring it out so I can make sure it's not hurt."

"It's not an it. It's a her," Hazel protested. "I checked."

"Okay, then bring *her* out too." I stepped off the combine and squeezed myself between the wall and the giant machine so I could get out of her way. When I was out of the tight space, I let myself take a breath. I never enjoyed being in cramped places.

A moment later, Hazel came around the side of the combine, holding the cat. Now that the feline wasn't curled up in a tight fluff ball, I could see she had long, soft white fur, bright blue eyes, and point color on her face. If I didn't know better, I would say she was a Siamese. She meowed loudly. She sounded like a Siamese too. She definitely didn't look like a barn cat.

"She's pretty." I stepped forward and held out my hand to the cat. She sniffed it and dipped her head. I took that to mean I received the all-clear to scratch her between the ears.

"This is Esmeralda," Hazel said.

"You named her?" If she had named her, I knew she was attached.

"Doesn't she look like an Esmeralda to you?" Hazel looked up at me with bright blue eyes. Eyes that weren't too different from the cat's, actually.

"To tell you the truth, she does, but she's in good health and looks like a pure breed. I'm guessing she is someone's beloved pet that got out. I think we should find out who her owner is."

Hazel gasped. "Give her away?"

"Give her *back*," I clarified. "But if we can't find who she belongs to, then…"

"I get to keep her?" Her eyes were hopeful.

"I can't make that call. It's up to your dad."

Her face fell. "It won't be up to my dad. It will be up to my grandma. She will never let me keep her. Grandma hates animals. She says they smell bad and are messy. She was going to take her to the shelter today." Giant tears rolled down her cheeks. "I wasn't going to let her do that, so Esmeralda and I left."

I winced. "So no one knows you're here? You didn't tell your grandmother you were coming here?"

"She won't even notice I left for an hour or two. She's hosting book club. She doesn't pay any attention to what I'm doing then, as long as I'm quiet and stay out of the living room."

"Hazel, I'm going to have to call your grandma and tell her. You can't just run off like that."

"She was going to take Esmeralda away." She dug the toe of her shoe into the dirt.

Huckleberry walked over and smelled Esmeralda's dangling tail. The cat looked down at him and started to purr. I raised my brow. She was the first cat we'd met in Michigan that didn't seem to be annoyed by Huckleberry. The barn cats had made their distaste of the little pug clear by hissing or swiping at him with their paws whenever he got too close.

I hoped I wasn't going to live to regret what I said next, but I didn't think I had any other choice. "If your grandmother doesn't want Esmeralda, the cat can stay here until we find her owner."

Hazel's lower lip trembled.

"I know you want to keep her. But we have to give it an honest try to find her owner first," I said. "What if it was your pet that was lost? Wouldn't you want some kind person to bring her back to you?"

Hazel sighed. "Yes. You're like my dad. He always tells me to put myself in other people's shoes when I'm upset. It can be so annoying. Don't you just want to stay upset sometimes?"

I laughed. "Hazel, I think you and I are a lot alike, which means you must be a problem solver."

"I am."

"Thought so. So let's solve this problem of finding where Esmeralda should be. The first step in doing that is calling your grandmother."

She winced. "Okay, but she's going to be super mad."

"We can handle it." I pulled my cell phone from my pocket and held it out to her. "Call your grandma."

She rolled her eyes but traded the cat for the phone.

The cat cuddled under my chin.

"Oh my, I can see why Hazel wants to keep you," I said.

"Hi, Grandma!"

There was an angry voice on the other end of the line, and Hazel winced.

I took a couple of steps back. "Let's give her some privacy," I said to the animals. I carried Esmeralda outside, and Huckleberry followed at my heels.

Outside the barn, I took in a deep breath and looked down at my pug. "It seems we have taken on another project. Find Esmeralda's home. At this point, why not pile something else on our plate?" I said.

A moment later, Hazel came out of the barn. "She's coming to get me, and just to warn you, she's not happy. She might be thinking all this is your fault."

"And where did she get that idea?" I asked.

She held up her hands. "Not from me."

I eyed her. "Are you hungry?"

"Starving, and I think Esmeralda is too." She scratched the fluffy cat's head.

"Okay, let's get something to eat while we wait."

Inside the farmhouse kitchen, I had Hazel sit on the old metal stool at the counter while I rooted around for something to eat. There wasn't much there. It had been such chaos since I returned to Michigan, I hadn't been able to go to the store for any food. My father had a good stock of microwave meals and cans of soup, but I didn't think either would appeal to an eleven-year-old. They didn't appeal to me, but I had the bag of produce from my restaurant visit, and there were eggs from the chickens.

"How does a veggie omelet sound?" I asked.

"That would be okay, but no cheese. I'm allergic to dairy."

"Then you are in luck," I said as I removed the carton of eggs from the fridge. "I don't have any cheese."

I whipped up the omelet with tomatoes, onions, green pepper, and broccoli. My stomach growled, and it felt good to be cooking again. Back in LA, I had loved to cook for my friends, and this was the kind of meal I'd love to serve customers at Bellamy Farm one day—organic, farm-to-table meals to fill empty bellies.

After handing Hazel her plate, I'd decided to make an omelet for myself too. When I finished, I turned around to find Hazel on the floor watching Esmeralda eat a portion of her omelet from a paper napkin on the floor. "She's really hungry," Hazel said. There was just the slightest hint of worry in her voice.

"Then I'm glad we were able to find something she would like," I said with a smile.

As if she had expected a different reaction, Hazel let out a sigh of relief and ate the rest of her food.

Chapter Twenty-Three

The farmhouse doorbell rang, followed by my father's voice from the second floor. "Someone is here!"

"Doesn't he know you can hear the doorbell too?" Hazel asked.

I shook my head and left the kitchen. At the foot of the steps, I called up to my father. "I'll get it. It's just Mrs. Killian picking up Hazel."

Dad appeared at the top of the steps. "Hazel is here?"

"Just for a quick visit," I said. "She's going back to her grandmother's now."

Dad nodded and disappeared from the landing.

Hazel joined me at the foot of the stairs. "I like your dad. He can be kind of grumpy, but he means well."

I smiled. "I think so too."

The doorbell rang again.

"Oh, you're in trouble. No one keeps Grandma waiting," Hazel said.

On that foreboding note, I walked to the front door and opened it. There was a sixtyish woman standing on the doorstep. She wore glasses and a flowered blouse and pressed trousers. A large beaded bracelet dangled from around her wrist. "Where is my granddaughter?"

I stepped back. "Mrs. Killian, I—"

She pointed her finger at me. "Don't you say a word. How dare you speak to me? You're a killer, and now you have kidnapped a child."

I held up my hands. "Whoa! I didn't do either of those things."

"I know you killed Jefferson Crocker. No one believes the police that it would be one of our own like Sully. It had to be you."

At that moment, Hazel walked into the living room with Esmeralda in her arms. "Shiloh didn't kidnap me, Grandma."

Her grandmother glared at her. "I don't want to hear a word from you either. Wait until I tell your father what you've done. I'm watching you for him out of the kindness of my heart, and you repay me by running off." She opened the front door. "Let's go."

Hazel dropped her head and started walking toward the door.

"No," her grandmother said. "No, you will not be taking that cat with you. It's the start of all this trouble."

"But, Grandma…" A tear rolled down Hazel's freckled cheek.

"No. End of discussion. Put it down."

"Hazel, I'll take good care of her until we find out where she belongs. I promise," I said.

Hazel nodded mutely and set the cat on the ground. Esmeralda meowed so loudly in protest I wondered if they could hear her at Jessa's Place.

"Get in the car," Mrs. Killian said.

With tears in her eyes, Hazel ran out the door.

"Mrs. Killian, I know Hazel should have never left your house without telling you, but she really loves this cat. She made a mistake. She didn't do it to hurt you or to cause any sort of trouble."

She pointed at me. "Stay away from my granddaughter and my son. You hear me?"

"Your son?"

"Yes. I won't let you break his heart again."

I blinked at her. "His heart? I never broke Quinn's heart."

She shook her finger at me. "You did when you made Logan get into that car crash. He and Logan were going to live and work in Cherry Glen forever, and after Logan died, Quinn left." She dropped her hand. "That was your fault. You shouldn't have been so selfish about your dreams and just been a good farmer's wife like you were supposed to be."

I sucked in a breath.

"I will not let you drive him away again. I won't."

Before I could tell her she had the completely wrong idea, she stomped out of the house and slammed the door behind her.

I looked down at the cat who sat at my feet next to Huckleberry like they had been in that pose all their lives. "Well, Esmeralda, I guess you are staying with us."

After Hazel's little visit, I spent the rest of the day organizing the barn and thinking about the investigation. By early evening, I decided it was time to start digging. My intention was to go to the farmers market. Maybe by going and walking around the market, I would spot the woman who knocked me over the morning Crocker died. Kristy said she would try to find out who the woman was, but it wouldn't hurt for me to look too. It was a long shot, but I had to try. I had to clear my father's name for him, but also for me. If he went to prison, there was very little chance we would ever have the father-daughter relationship I wanted. I wanted the closeness that Quinn and Hazel had. When I had seen them together, I realized how different they were from my father and me.

When I arrived at the market, shoppers and vendors chatted as goods and money exchanged hands. I looked around for Kristy, but I didn't see her.

I walked up to a vendor selling homemade cheese and butter.

"Can I help you?" the older woman asked.

"Maybe. I was looking for a young woman with long, dark hair who would have been here very early Saturday morning."

She cocked her head. "You will have to be more specific than that."

"She was running." I paused. "She left right before…" What did I say? Right before the dead body was found? It seemed crass and especially so while standing in front of a cheese booth.

She put her hands on her hips. "I know who you are. You're that girl from California who killed Crocker."

"I didn't kill Crocker, and I'm not from California. I grew up right here in Cherry Glen."

"That doesn't matter if you left. You're no different from the fudgies who come through town."

"I didn't—"

"I can't say I blame you for killing him. If that man had his way, there would be wind turbines all over town, and Cherry Glen wouldn't make one red cent off them. Can you imagine having the giant white eyesores overhead and knowing the only thing they were doing was making a rich man richer? It's a travesty."

"I didn't know the town wouldn't benefit from the wind farm," I said.

She laughed. "You must know nothing about Jefferson Crocker at all then. The only person who benefits from Crocker's deals is him. You would not believe the number of gullible people who fall for his promise of financial rescue."

I felt ill, because I was one of those gullible people.

She held up a wedge of Swiss cheese. "If you aren't going to buy any cheese, I'm going to have to ask you to move along. I need to make a sale."

I walked away without another word. It was like that at each booth I visited. Not a single vendor wanted to answer my questions about the young woman I saw, and each one of them blamed me for Crocker's death.

Quinn's mother was right. I was the prime suspect by public opinion. My father was off the hook because he was a member of the town. When I left Cherry Glen fifteen years ago, I became an outsider.

Chapter Twenty-Four

After Hazel and her grandmother had left, I took photos of Esmeralda with my phone and made up a quick flyer. My dad didn't have a printer, and mine was still buried in a moving box somewhere, so on my way back from the farmers market, I printed two dozen flyers at the local grocery store for ten cents a pop, with Huckleberry whimpering at my feet every time a piece of paper shot out of the machine. Even though he was an LA dog, Huckleberry was low tech. I hoped that Stacey would let me hang one up in the theater.

When it came to Esmeralda, I had to do my due diligence just like I told Hazel we must, but a small part of me—no, a *big* part of me—hoped no one came forward. I had fallen hard for the friendly cat just like Hazel had.

The next morning, I was up so early that my head hurt. Huckleberry and Esmeralda slept at the foot of my bed. The pug was curled up in a ball, and the cat lay over the top of him like a fur rug.

The animals didn't even stir as I slipped out of bed. I went to the window and moved one of the eyelet curtains aside. It was still dark out. I hoped this harebrained idea of mine was worth it.

After the disappointing visit to the farmers market the night before, I had made a phone call. I had called Hedy Strong, using the business card Wes had given me. Much to my surprise, she answered on the first ring, and when I told her I wanted to speak with her about the Cherry Glen Wind Farm, she asked me to meet her in the morning. The only problem was she asked me to meet her at six thirty a.m. at the county park where she was doing her morning bird count. When I asked if there was a better time, she'd said that was the only time and for me to take it or leave it. I took it, of course, but my sleep-deprived head was seriously questioning how wise that decision had been.

I glanced down at the animals. "No, it's okay. Don't strain yourself by waking up." I padded down the hall to the bathroom.

Dawn was just breaking over the farm when I walked to my convertible. The pink and ocher light was breathtaking over the overgrown fields. I could just imagine what it would look like in years to come when those fields were full of lavender and sunflowers. One way or another, I had to save the farm from being lost. I owed Grandma Bellamy that.

The park that Hedy asked me to meet her at was part of the county park system on the edge of Torch Lake. Torch Lake wasn't one of the Great Lakes, but it was still impressive. It was the longest inland lake in the state and was over one hundred feet deep in some spots. I turned on the county road that led to the park. My car bumped from the pavement onto the gravel and dirt parking lot. At this time in the morning, I was surprised at the number of cars in the lot. I checked my phone to make sure I wasn't late. She'd told me to be there at six thirty sharp. I was five minutes early. Was predawn hiking a thing?

Just before I left, I had decided to take Huckleberry with me. I looked down at the little pug, wondering if I had made a mistake by bringing him. "You're going to have to be quiet. I think these birder folks take their sport very seriously. No barks, no yips, no heavy breathing."

He snorted.

I sighed. That was the best answer I was going to get from him.

Remembering Hedy's brisk instructions on the phone, I followed the path marked with the loon, which would lead me to the lakeshore. In the woods between the parking lot and lake, the light was dimmed by the dense cover of trees. Bugs hummed in the tree branches, and bird twittered high above my head. A chipmunk scurried across my path. I tried not to think about all the wild animals that were in the woods. You'd think growing up in Western Michigan, I wouldn't be a scaredy-cat about such things.

Finally, there was a break in the trees, and I could see the sparkling dark blue water of Torch Lake. Because of the lake's different depths, you could see three shades of blue when the light hit it just right. The early morning was the perfect time to see those colors. When I stepped out onto the beach, it was quiet, so I jumped when I saw a cluster of ten people standing on the rocks and sand at the edge of the water. They all held giant cameras or binoculars up to their eyes.

A petite woman at the front of the group and with the largest binoculars of all, which were strapped across her chest in a harness, gave some sort of hand signal. Collectively, the group aimed their lenses up and to the right. There was a gasp, and one person whispered, "A tundra swan. It's my first!"

"Shh," the rest of the birders hissed, even though she had spoken softly.

With their reaction to the woman's comments, I was afraid to approach the group to find out which was Hedy, though if I had to guess, I'd say it was probably the one with the largest pair of binoculars.

On the lake, a group of swans took off into the air. There was a rapid succession of shutter clicks as the flock took flight.

"That was amazing! Hedy, you must have a sixth sense to always know where the birds will land," a large man in a pocketed vest and fisherman's hat said.

"Thank you," the small woman who had made the hand gesture said. "I have been birding on these shores for so long, I know the birds' patterns. I'm lucky they haven't strayed from them much. Let's meet at the next dock. I believe from there you will be able to get another look."

Hedy didn't need to say this twice as the group quickly dispersed, heading in my direction to the parking lot. They blew by me with not so much as a glance. I supposed I wasn't nearly as interesting as the tundra swans.

Hedy started up the path after them. "Ah, you must be Shiloh Bellamy." She looked me up and down. "You're taller than I expected you to be." She glanced at Huckleberry. "You brought your dog."

"He needed a walk."

She frowned. "You are lucky he didn't scare off those swans. You do *not* want a dozen angry birders after you."

When she put it that way, it did sound bad. "He's very well behaved."

Huckleberry looked up at me as if he knew I was fibbing too.

I glanced over my shoulder in the direction the rest of the birders had gone. "Am I keeping you from seeing the swans?"

"They are beautiful birds, but I can take a minute or two. I've seen them dozens of times before, so it's not like they're lifers for me." She paused. "That being said, let's make this quick. I don't want to miss a bird."

"Like I told you on the phone, I'm Shiloh Bellamy from Bellamy Farm—"

She held up her hand.

"Don't you want me to tell you why I'm here?"

"Shh!" She held her finger to her lips and stepped away from the lake and deeper into the woods.

"Are…"

She held up her finger again. "Shh! Listen," she hissed.

There was a slight twittering in the woods. It was a light bird song, repeated three times before going silent.

"Yellow-rumped warbler by its song." She made a mark in her phone.

"You can tell what bird it is from the song?" I asked. She had spoken in a normal volume, so I had taken that as permission to speak.

"Of course I can. Any dedicated birder worth her salt can. I have been studying birds for the last forty years. There is no bird call or song heard in Michigan I can't identify within a few notes."

Since I could barely tell a cardinal from a robin, I was not one to challenge her on that claim.

"Are you—" I started to ask to get back to my original question.

"Shh!" was her response to that.

A little bird with a yellow feather just above the base of its tail hopped on the branch of a nearby oak tree and repeated the song he had sung.

"See, yellow-rumped warbler," she said confidently. "I'm never wrong. It's not a lifer of course, but it's my first one this year, which is surprising."

"Lifer?" I asked.

"Oh. That's birder slang for a bird I was seeing for the first time in my life. Birders keep life lists of birds. I keep several lists. I keep a life list, an annual list, and a region list."

"It sounds complicated."

She looked at me for the first time. "You have no idea. There is so much pressure to see the birds. I'm up at night waiting for dawn so I can go out again. You never know what you will find. This is truly a case of the early birder getting the bird."

There was a twittering above us that sounded different from the warbler's song. Hedy must have heard it too, because she grabbed her binoculars from that intricate-looking chest harness and put them to her eyes. "Knew it. Scarlet tanager. One of the prettiest summer birds. Even though they are bright red, redder that a cardinal even, they are hard to spot since they keep to so high in the trees. You really have to follow the sound to spot them. Would you like to see it?"

"Sure."

She removed her binoculars and held them out to me. "Look straight up."

I held them to my eyes and looked up. At first, all I could see were fuzzy tree limbs. Then I adjusted the lens for my sight. A bright red dot came into view; I zoomed in on that. The bird was completely red except for its black wings. "Wow. She's beautiful."

"That's the male. Like with most birds, the female is not as brightly colored. In fact, the female is a dull yellow. It's the men in the bird world who have to attract the ladies."

I handed the binoculars back to her, and she snapped them back into the harness.

"Now what did you want to talk to me about? If it's not about birds, I can't help you. Birds are all I know and all I care to know."

"I wanted to talk to you about Jefferson Crocker."

"Crocker?" She wrinkled her nose like she smelled something bad. "Why would I want to talk about him?"

"You may not have heard that he died," I said.

At my feet, Huckleberry buried his nose in the fallen leaves on the forest floor.

"Yes, I heard someone shot him. I can't say I blame the person. If anyone had it coming to him, it was Jefferson Crocker. He was the worst kind of man. All he cared about was making money. He didn't care what impact his choices made on the environment and the birds. Like so many, he assumed he would be dead in twenty-some years, so what's in it for him to take care of the earth now?"

"You and he were in a dispute."

"A dispute. I would call it a war. A battle between good and evil. Against short-sightedness and forward thinking. I had spent the last five years of my life fighting that man. Now, I can finally rest. Perhaps I won't even keep an attorney on retainer any longer. Whoever killed him did me a favor."

I shivered at her cold tone. I almost thought if Hedy were the one who had shot Crocker, she would just come right out and say it with a big smile on her face. I couldn't see her hiding it. Which meant I might as well be back at square one.

Chapter Twenty-Five

Huckleberry shook his whole body, rattling his collar as he sniffed the air. I inhaled just as he did, breathing in the scent of lake water and pine trees that mingled with the heady air off the lakeshore. It smelled like a fairy tale in my mind. That was the scent of Western Michigan: water and dirt.

Above, the scarlet tanager sang in the canopy, and other songbirds chimed in with their own special verses.

Hedy lowered her binoculars. "Vireos," she muttered, like I was supposed to know what that meant. "If that's all you want me to talk about, I had better catch up. These are novice birders I'm with today. They have all the gear, but they wouldn't know a red-tailed hawk from a red-shouldered hawk if it really came down to it." Hedy said this like this was a major failing on their birder prowess.

I didn't say I wouldn't have known the difference either.

"I promise not to keep you much longer, but I'm just trying to understand the conflict you had with Crocker. I'm friends with Wesley Sumner. He told me you would be a good person to talk to to better understand Crocker's plan for the wind farm."

"Wesley." She frowned and eyed me. "He's the one who sent you?"

I nodded. "We're old friends."

She pressed her lips together. "Then I suppose you can't be too bad. Wesley would know better than to send someone here who wouldn't take me seriously. I know there are people in town who think I'm a crazy, old, bird-obsessed woman, and maybe I am. Someone had to be to make sure there are birds for years to come." She removed her pack and sat on a fallen log. "All right, I will give you ten more minutes. I can eat my lunch while we talk."

"Your lunch? It's the morning."

"I've been up since four, and I go to bed at as soon as the sun sets every night. Well, when I'm not doing owl walks, I do."

"Owl walks?" I asked.

"Walks at night to look for owls." She shook her head like I was the densest person she'd ever met.

"Oh right," I said and sat on a tree stump a few feet away from her.

Hedy removed a thermos and a peanut butter and jelly sandwich wrapped in a dish towel. She spread the dish towel on her lap, opened the thermos, and set it by her feet. Every move she made was practiced and confident. I had a feeling Hedy not only took birding very seriously, but she took herself very seriously too.

I was quiet while she got settled. There was a ritual aspect as to how she set out her lunch. While she organized her meal, I oscillated between fears she'd tell me to leave or she'd quiz me about my hawk knowledge. I didn't know which might be worse.

Finally, she looked up. "What do you want to know?"

"I was the one who found Crocker dead at the farmers market. Because of that, the police think I might have something to do with the murder."

She took a big bite out of her sandwich and chewed while she considered what I said. "Because you have the best motive."

Huckleberry appeared at her side and looked forlorn.

Hedy peered at her sandwich, then at the pug, and then back again. Without a word, she broke off a piece and held it out to Huckleberry. Delicately, he took it from her hand and gobbled it up.

I stared at her. "How would you know if I have a motive?"

"You're Sully Bellamy's girl, aren't you? You've come back to our little town to save your farm."

How did she know this about me?

"Don't look so surprised. Cherry Glen is a town of three thousand residents. Half of them are related in some way. We all know one another's business, and until Crocker got himself killed, you coming back home was the biggest news the town had heard in years."

I nodded. I had been away in the big city for too long and sometimes forgot how things worked around here—and not just the gossip. "What's my motive?" I asked, expecting her to mention my contract with Crocker. Everyone else in Cherry Glen knew about it. I expected Hedy did too.

She took a bite out of her sandwich. Watching her eat with such determination made my stomach growl. All I had that day so far was cold coffee that had been left in the coffee maker from the day before. At my feet, Huckleberry licked at the top of his mouth where the peanut butter from her sandwich had gotten stuck. It was hard to be a pug sometimes.

"The wind farm." She was matter-of-fact.

I blinked. "The wind farm?"

She laughed. "Either you're a great actress or really don't know. I can't believe you don't know. The wind farm is supposed to go right through Bellamy Farm. I think twenty turbines will be up over several fields."

I almost fell off my stump and righted myself at the last second. "What? I mean my cousin told me Crocker wanted to use our farm for his wind farm, but I thought there might be a turbine or two. Not twenty!"

"Your farm is the best place to collect wind power. It's also one of the main routes the birds travel to the lake because they can ride the updrafts that propel them forward. I have been fighting Crocker from putting the turbines there in particular for five years. There are other places where they could go that would be less loss of life, but he was the type of guy who wanted the best. Bellamy Farm is the best."

My mind raced. Would Crocker have sabotaged my efforts so he could have his wind farm? If everyone's opinion of him was true, the resounding answer to that was yes.

"So you have the perfect motive to want him dead," she went on between bites of her sandwich. "He was appealing to the town council to see if your father could be forced to sell. In my mind, that gives you motive. Your father's not well. Crocker's pestering of him caused him stress. You would have reason to remove Crocker not just to save the farm but to help your father."

"I didn't kill anyone."

She wiped at her mouth with the back of her hand. "We don't really know that."

"*I* know that."

She shrugged and went back to eating her sandwich. For someone who thought I might be a killer, she was quite calm about sitting alone in the middle of a forest with me.

"Maybe Crocker really did want to build the wind farm to save the planet," I said, trying to find something positive for this man so many people detested.

"Crocker was scum. I'll be the first to fight for an environmental cause, and I know from first glance that wind power is a no-brainer, but you have to be careful where those farms go. We are a main highway for so many warblers, including that yellow-rumped that we just saw. Studies have to be done. I even took him to court so that the government could force him to pay for a study on the bird migration over his proposed wind farm."

"Did he pay for the study?" I asked.

"Yes. He had no choice, and the findings were conclusive. The migration patterns of six species of birds, including endangered and threatened species, were documented over three years. We followed their migration patterns during fall and spring migration every year, and each year, they took the same paths right over your farm. The findings should have been significant enough to stop the wind farm. Songbird populations across the country are declining. That's mostly due to the loss of habitat, but we can't be interfering with migration either. Thousands of birds are killed in wind turbines each year. They nest in certain places and raise their young, and the routes they take must be protected."

When I was a child, I remembered great flocks of ducks and songbirds flying high overhead at the farm. I used to lie on my back on a straw bale and watch them flutter by.

Having gotten the peanut butter off the roof of his mouth, Huckleberry was at Hedy's side to rest his head on her knee as if he sensed her sadness. He was a very empathic pug.

"Why is the wind farm still a possibility then?" I asked.

She patted his head. "The judge threw out the findings. He said a reliable environmental source said the study the lawsuit forced Crocker to pay for was corrupted and couldn't be used because the results had been tampered with."

"Who tampered with them?"

"No one knows, and the judge isn't talking either." She scowled.

"Why not do another study then?" I asked.

"Crocker's attorneys argued that he had already paid for the study once and should not be forced to pay for it a second time." She wrinkled her nose in disgust. "If you're the one who did him in, I thank you."

"It wasn't me."

She folded up the dish towel, tucked it back into her bag, and took a swig from her thermos. She then wiped her mouth with her sleeve and put the thermos back in her bag. "You say that, but you can't prove it." She stood up and put her daypack back on. "Break's over. It's time to get back to the group."

"How do I find where Crocker wanted to put the turbines exactly? Maybe if I know where he'd planned to put them, I will be able to figure out why he was killed." I didn't say it, but it would give me more suspects; if I was a suspect because turbines were being built on my land, so was every other farmer with the same problem in the area.

She looked at me for a long moment. "Go to the town planning office. Crocker would have to file a plan there. He'd been working on this a long time, so there would have been several plans on file. I heard rumors the council would have voted on his plans again tonight, and it was likely to pass since he had the council between a rock and a hard place. I'm glad it won't come to that." She shook her head. "In any case, the town planning office should have the latest copies of the plans. They are public record, so they will be legally obligated to show them to you whether they want to or not."

My, but she sure knew a lot about this legal stuff. I stood up. "What else should I do?"

She turned as if she was about to march deeper into the woods without answering, but at the last second, she looked over her shoulder. "You do what's best for you, but if it were me, I would find out who killed him. I wouldn't take a back seat to anything. If it were my freedom on the line, I'd fight back." With that, she left.

It wasn't until she disappeared into the trees that I realized I had forgotten to ask her if she had ever been to Bellamy Farm before…and perhaps stolen bullets from my father's collection while she was at it.

Chapter Twenty-Six

Huckleberry and I stood alone in the forest for a moment while I pushed down the panic attack that was rising in my chest. It had been a long time since I'd had a real attack. When I first moved to LA, they had been a common occurrence; I had still grappled with losing Logan and Grandma Bellamy so close together. But then I started taking care of my health and seeing a counselor. I thought I had beaten the panic attacks. I supposed I shouldn't be surprised that being accused of murder would bring my anxiety back to the surface. I counted myself lucky I hadn't had a full-out attack earlier.

I sat back down on a stump along the path and took a couple of deep breaths. I closed my eyes. I tried to just focus on the sounds around me. The scarlet tanager that Hedy pointed out sang high above in the canopy, and there was a soft hum of wind through the trees and the buzzing of insects. Behind it all, I could just make out the faintest sound of the lake lapping up against the shoreline. Slowly, I felt better, but I did feel an underlying hum of nerves. I doubted that feeling was going to go away until I had a better grasp on this situation.

Huckleberry put his head on my lap, and the weight of it brought me comfort.

Nothing was solved, but I felt mildly better after my slow breathing session. I stood up and retraced my steps along the path to my car. To my surprise, all the cars that had been in the lot when I arrived were gone. They must have been Hedy's novice birders.

There was an SUV idling beside my convertible.

"Shiloh Bellamy and her faithful pug. I would have never taken you for a nature hiker." Wes laughed as if this were the funniest joke he'd ever heard.

"Hey, Wes. What are you up to this morning?"

"Oh, just making my rounds about the park. All in a day's work. Did you go down to the lake?"

I nodded.

"Isn't it gorgeous in the early morning light? This is my favorite part of the day before the park fills up with visitors." He chuckled. "Without the visitors, I wouldn't have my job, but at the same time, they can really disturb the natural order of things here in the park. What are you doing up so early?"

"I had a meeting with Hedy Strong about the wind farm, like you suggested." I leaned on my car for support. I was still a little wobbly from my panic attack and didn't want to show Wes any signs of weakness.

"Oh, and how did that go?" he asked.

I frowned. "I don't know. I think I'm even more confused by it all."

He leaned farther out of his car window and hung his arm outside the SUV. "I'm sure the police will sort it all out in the end. Why don't you just relax about it?"

Relax? "I can't. There's too much at stake, not just for me but for all of Bellamy Farm."

He shook his head. "All right. I see your mind is made up, and if you're anything like the Shiloh I remember, there is no hope of me talking you out of your plans. Did Hedy say anything that helped at all? There had to be something."

"There was one thing. She said the government forced Crocker to pay for a study on the effect the wind farm would have on migrating birds."

He nodded. "I remember that. It was all Hedy could talk about for months. She was thrilled and really thought she was going to win out in the end. I never heard the findings."

"The findings were that Crocker's proposed wind turbine field was directly in the migration path of many birds, including some endangered species."

"That should have ended it then." He wrinkled his brow. "Why has the debate continued at all?"

"An environmental source said the results of the test weren't valid, and a judge agreed with the source, throwing them out."

"Who was the source?"

I shrugged. "Hedy doesn't know. I have a feeling she would have told me if she knew. She'd also have whoever it was tarred and feather and dragged through the streets of Cherry Glen."

Wes winced. "That sounds about right."

"Would you have any idea who might do that?" I asked.

He shook his head. "Everyone who is green-minded and involved agreed the wind farm shouldn't be in Cherry Glen. It wasn't someone from the area. Perhaps an outside source? Like an expert that Crocker hired."

I nodded. Crocker had hired a lawyer to protect him. Who was to say he didn't hire environmentalists too? I remembered my initial thought about the wind farm being a positive one. Maybe other people saw the wind farm as a good thing, despite the bird issue.

After I left the park, I went straight to the town planning office like Hedy suggested. As soon as Huckleberry and I reached the front door of town hall, my shoulders sagged. It was still early morning, and the office didn't open until nine. There was a giant "closed" sign hanging on the inside of the door.

"Now what, Huck?" I asked.

"It seems every time I see you, you are talking to your dog. Are you sure he doesn't talk back?"

I looked up to see Baker Loyal smiling at me. I flushed. "He hasn't answered in English at least."

"I don't know if I'm relieved or disappointed by this. Is there something I can help you with?"

"Actually, maybe. I was hoping to get into the town planning office. To look up some records."

He raised his brow. "Records for what?"

I licked my lips. "I just want to take look at the property lines of my farm." I smiled. "Maybe since it's your office, I can take a look."

He shook his head. "I wish I could, but I can't let you in the building yet, I'm afraid. Town policy. As the town planner, it is important I set a good example. We open at nine. It's not that long from now."

"I can come by later."

"Tell you what," he said. "Let me take you to coffee and make it up to you."

I eyed him. "You want to make it up to me that I arrived at town hall too early?"

He shrugged. "I'm a nice guy."

"That's so nice of you to ask, but the only place to get coffee around here is Jessa's Place, and…" I couldn't tell him I didn't want to go to Jessa's Place because I was the talk of the town over the murder.

"Jessa's is nice," he said, not seeming to have noticed my discomfort. "But our general store in town serves coffee too. If you ask me, it's a lot better than Jessa's." He laughed. "By the look on your face, I would guess you're debating whether or not I'm an ax murderer."

"Sorry. I lived in LA for a very long time. After living alone in a big city, maybe some of my defenses are up."

"I'm sure you got asked out on coffee dates all the time in LA."

My face turned red. *Okay…* So, he was asking me on a date now?

"Listen, I'm going to the general store for a cup of coffee regardless of whether you come or not. I just thought you would want to pick my brain since I'm the town planner. I have heard that you are quite interested in the wind farm." He turned to walk away.

When he did, I realized my mistake. He was right. I couldn't let this opportunity go by, but I sure as heck wasn't considering this a date. There was something about Baker that put me on edge. I picked up Huckleberry and hurried after him. "Baker!"

He turned around with a wide smile.

Chapter Twenty-Seven

S orry about that," I said, "You caught me off guard. I just moved back to Cherry Glen, and I would be lying if I didn't say I was experiencing a little bit of culture shock."

"I can imagine. I actually grew up in Chicago, so when I moved here, it was a bit startling."

"I thought you were Mayor Loyal's son. Hasn't he always lived here?"

"He has. He and my mom got divorced when I was a kid. I lived with my mom and stepdad in the Windy City. I came up here for parts of the summer, and that was it. When I finished grad school, I decided to move to Traverse City to be close to the lake. I love any water sports."

"Couldn't you have done that in Chicago too?"

"I could, but I was just over the city congestion. Traverse City is more my speed."

"I can understand that, but Traverse City is still a little bit away from Cherry Glen. How'd you end up here?"

"I was working for the city of Traverse City as a city planner and got laid off when a new mayor came into office. My dad told me about the opening here, and here I am. That was three years ago. Honestly, I hadn't expected to be here this long, but there are some exciting things happening in Cherry Glen. I think we are just on the verge of really bringing the town back. It's exciting to have such a pivotal role in that. I wouldn't have as much authority in a larger town as I do here in Cherry Glen."

I nodded and set Huckleberry on the sidewalk just as we approached the general store. It was a brick building with multipaned windows that looked in at large displays of cherries and Michigan-made products.

Baker held the door open for Huckleberry and me. "After you."

I stepped inside. A stuffed teddy bear sat on the table just inside the door.

"Cherry?" the bear asked in its mechanical voice and held up a basket that had pieces of cherry licorice in it.

I stared at it. "I can't believe that bear is still here. It was here when I was a child."

"Not everything has changed in Cherry Glen since you left, Shiloh, and that's how we like it." The gravelly voice that said this belonged to a rail-thin, white-haired man with a tie-dyed bandanna wrapped around his head. He wore a Grateful Dead T-shirt and a smile.

"Norman?" I yelped and then stopped myself from saying that I thought he was dead. Norman Perch had been old when I was in grade school. Now, he must have been on the other side of ancient, but he didn't look any different than he had when I was child.

He came around the counter and gave me a big hug. "It's good to see you. You're the talk of the town. And Jessa was right; you cleaned up nice while in LA."

I blushed.

Baker raised his eyebrows at me.

"What will you have?" Norman asked. "I know Baker's order already. He comes in here every day. My best customer."

The counter to the right of the door had been an old soda fountain counter. Now it was a coffee bar. As far as I could tell, that was the only difference from fifteen years ago. I looked at the menu on the black chalkboard behind the counter. There were so many good choices, and all of them had calories. Lots of calories. "I'll just have an iced coffee with skim milk."

"I'll do the same thing," Baker said.

Norman eyed him. "You usually get a French vanilla latte with extra whipped cream."

"I'm turning over a new leaf. It's always good to try something new, isn't it, Shiloh?" he asked.

My brows knit together.

"With no flavor," Norman muttered. "What's the point?" He turned his back to us and started putting ice in plastic cups.

Baker led me to one of the wrought iron tables in front of the bar. Huckleberry toddled along behind me. When I sat, he laid his head on my foot. I thought the early start to meet Hedy had worn out the pooch.

"Your cousin has done an amazing job with the theater. It really is the backbone of bringing Cherry Glen back to its former glory. This was a vibrant farming town up through the 1960s. After that, with farming subsidies and people moving away to the cities for work, it fell on some hard times."

I nodded. "When I was a child, it was small and run-down. So many young people fled to the cities. The only businesses that seemed to be able to hang on were the general store—I think mostly because Norman was too stubborn to let it go—and Jessa's Place, because farmers still had to have a place to eat." As I spoke, I realized I was one of those young people from town who'd fled for one of the big cities. "What brought about the change? It seems Cherry Glen has really turned a corner."

He grinned. "Living in the country is more desirable now. People want to get back to basics and have more land to raise their kids. Also, people seem to want to know where their food is coming from. The farm-to-table movement has been huge for Michigan farms and farms all over the country."

I had read about this too, which was why I thought Bellamy Farm could make a profit, eventually, by becoming an organic farm.

"Beer touring has helped too," he said.

"Beer touring?"

He nodded. "It's a very popular vacation nowadays, and Fields Brewing Company has put Cherry Glen on the map. They bought the old granary and turned it completely around. People come all over to tour, eat in the restaurant, and visit their tasting room."

I thought the cherry towers the brewery made probably helped too.

He laughed. "I'm sorry I've been talking so much. As you can see, I'm really excited about the changes happening around here. But tell me about you. What brought you back to town?"

"My father needs help on the farm."

He nodded. "Bellamy Farm is a beautiful piece of land. I was out there a few months back." He paused. "It didn't look like farming was going on. A lot of the property had gone wild."

"We will bring it back," I said with more confidence than I felt.

He shook his head. "It can't be easy coming home."

"There you are." Norman set the iced coffees in front of us. "Two flavorless iced coffees." He walked back to the counter and set a bowl of whipped cream on the floor for Huckleberry. The pug looked at me. I gave a slight nod, and he buried his face in it.

"Thank you, Norman," I called after him.

He waved his hand without turning around.

Returning to my conversation with Baker, I said, "I don't think coming home is easy for anyone."

"But it's even less easy coming back to a small town. The people of Cherry Glen didn't exactly welcome me with open arms, even though I'm the mayor's son." He reached across the table and put his hand over mine. "If you need help, that's what I'm here for. My office can give you suggestions and make sure you start everything off on the right foot. I know you were headed to the office to see your property lines, but we can do so much more for you than that."

"That's very kind of you," I said and started to move my hand when the door opened. Quinn walked in. He wore cargo pants and a fire department T-shirt. I couldn't help but notice how his shirt fit him perfectly. He moved with the grace of an athlete. It didn't matter how much I worked out, I never moved like that. In fact, one of my spin instructors told me not to stand up on the stationary bike for fear I might fall off.

He spotted Baker and me sitting across from each other, and then his gaze fell to our hands on the table. As if I had been burned, I removed my hand and let it fall to my lap.

Quinn turned to the counter. "Norman, can you give me six coffees for the department, and one large French vanilla cappuccino with extra foam for the boss. You know he likes his fancy drinks."

Norman laughed. "You got it."

Quinn turned and leaned against the counter as he waited for the coffee. His jaw was tight.

Across from me, Baker tensed up. I looked from him to Quinn and back again, completely clueless as to what was going on.

"Hey, Quinn." I waved, hoping to break up the incredibly awkward stare down.

"You know him?" Baker asked.

I frowned. "Sure. He's my neighbor at the farm." I didn't add that I had basically known Quinn Killian all my life. I didn't see how that could be relevant.

Baker shook his head. "Oh, that's right." He pressed his lips together.

Quinn walked over to us. "This seems like an unlikely duo."

"And why do you say that, Quinny?" Baker asked.

Quinn scowled at him. Logan had called him that once when we were in high school, and Quinn had pushed him into Kristy's family pool for it.

"How's everything at the fire department?" Baker asked. "I plan to stop by next week and have a look around. We need to make sure everything is up to code."

"You're the town planner, Baker. Not a fire inspector."

"Even so, it's important that I know everything is happening properly. Cherry Glen is on the brink of a renaissance, and every aspect of it must be ready."

Quinn curled his fists and looked at me. "What are you doing here?"

I blinked. I was taken about by the abruptness of his question. What was *I* doing here? Why did he care?

Baker answered for me. "Shiloh and I were just grabbing a cup of coffee and getting to know each other. We had a lovely conversation going until you showed up."

I wouldn't say that was true. Baker had done most of the talking.

"Quinn!" Norman called. "Coffee is up."

"Thanks," Quinn called over his shoulder. "See you two around," he said, a scowl fixed on his face before he walked back to the counter. What was that about?

Baker looked at his expensive watch. I knew it was expensive because it was the same brand the lead actor on my last sitcom wore, and he was strictly a designer only man. "I'm so sorry to cut this short, Shiloh, but I have to get back to the office. I know it's still early, but I have to finish some paperwork before the day starts. My life is meetings, meetings, meetings. It was nice chatting with you. Let's do it over dinner next time."

Over *dinner*? I wasn't sure how I felt about that.

He stood up, and I did too. He leaned forward like he was going to kiss me on the cheek. I took a big step back, and he settled for a pat on the arm with a bright smile. "We'll talk soon, Shiloh."

I nodded. I couldn't think of anything to say.

Baker walked up to the counter and laid a ten on the counter. "That should cover both of us." He held his iced coffee up to Norman. "Thank for the coffee, Norm."

The general store owner grunted in response while he handed Baker his receipt.

Quinn picked up the two cardboard carriers of coffee, balancing them precariously in his hands. "See you, Norman." He wouldn't look at me. "Later, Shi."

He pushed the store door open with his back and backed out of the store.

I picked up my own coffee.

"Looks to me like you have some man trouble, Shiloh," Norman said as he cleaned the tips of the espresso machine with a damp white cloth.

Man trouble? Me? That was laughable. Norman couldn't have been more wrong, but there was something going on between Quinn and Baker. And I refused to be put in the middle of it.

I hurried to the door. "Come on, Huckleberry."

The pug licked the last drop of whipped cream from the bowl and toddled after me.

Chapter Twenty-Eight

Q uinn!" I called outside the general store as I picked up
Huckleberry.

He was halfway up the sidewalk. To my relief, he stopped and
waited for me to catch up.

Holding Huckleberry, I ran up to him. "What was that all
about?"

He balanced the two cardboard coffee cup holders in his hands.
"What do you mean?"

"You and Baker. You guys were shooting daggers at each other."

"I think that's a bit overdramatic." He started walking again.

Huckleberry grew heavy in my arms. I set him on the sidewalk,
pulled his leash out of my pocket, and snapped it on his collar. The
little dog began to walk beside me.

"I don't think I'm being overdramatic at all. It's clear that the
two of you don't like each other," I said.

Quinn eyed me. "I hate to be the one to break it to you, but
that's not unusual. Not everyone likes everyone else. That's just
life." He eyed me. "Anyway, it seems you like him enough for the
both of us."

I jerked back. "What is that supposed to mean?"

"Nothing," he said.

I shook my head. "I don't have time for this."

"You had time enough for a date."

"It wasn't a date."

He snorted. "I bet if we ask Baker that question, he will have a different answer."

"You're being impossible. You haven't changed a bit in fifteen years!"

"And you are a completely different person," he shot back.

I narrowed my eyes at him. "What does that mean?"

"Logan wouldn't even recognize you today. You've changed so much."

I felt like I had been donkey kicked in the stomach.

"You think you can just come back to Cherry Glen and pick up where you left off by saving your father and saving the farm. I've got news for you: Logan is still dead."

Tears gathered in my eyes. "I know that." My voice was barely above a whisper.

"You should remember that before you go on dates with other men."

I stared at him. "Logan died fifteen years ago. Do you think he would want me to spend the rest of my life alone?"

"No," he said. "But you shouldn't be with someone like that, someone Logan wouldn't have liked."

"Who should I be with?"

He glared at me and then dropped his shoulders. "Sorry I ruined your date."

"It wasn't a date!" My face turned red. Why was I shouting, and why did I feel like I had to explain myself to Quinn Killian? He wasn't even my friend. He had been Logan's friend, and clearly if I even looked at another man, he saw it as some kind of betrayal of Logan. I took a breath. "I'll say it for the last time. I only agreed to go to coffee with him because he told me he was the town planner. I thought he would be able to tell me something about Crocker and the wind farm. Since the farm was to be in town, I would think the town planner would have to be involved with the plans."

"And did he?" Quinn asked.

"Not really, but he just started to get to that part of the conversation, and then you showed up."

"So it's my fault you didn't learn anything."

"No." I sighed. "I'm not blaming you; I'm just telling you what happened." I shook my head. My brain was already jumbled with everything that had happened since I came back to Cherry Glen. I couldn't get in the middle of whatever guy issues Quinn and Baker had with each other. It wasn't my business and not my problem. This conversation was pointless.

"I have to go." I picked up Huckleberry and hustled down the street.

"Shiloh, be careful!" Quinn called after me.

I turned the corner without looking back, wondering why he felt like he had to give me that warning.

I walked to the theater. Huckleberry followed me around the building and in through the front door of the theater. We had just crossed the threshold when a high-pitched voice said, "I'm not going to work with a murderess."

Minnie was in the building.

"She's the only one I have," Stacey told Minnie as Huckleberry and I stood close to the front door, debating whether to make a run for it. Truth was, I didn't know what the pug was thinking, but I was definitely tempted to bolt.

"I don't care," Minnie said back. "I can't even be in the same room with her."

Stacey folded her arms. "Well, you already are, because she's here."

Ack, I had been spotted. So much for my plan to flee. I joined them by the ticket booth. Huckleberry walked behind me.

"Hi," I said when I reached them. It was the best I could come up with after what I'd heard. I thought it was a pretty warm greeting considering Minnie's comments.

"I'm glad you're on time. I was just telling Minnie how things will work on opening night. The sales need to go like clockwork. We only have one chance to make a good first impression."

"Are you helping with the ticket booth too, Minnie? How can you do that if you're in the play?"

"I'm not in the play," Minnie said like that was a ridiculous idea. "As part of the Women's League for the Betterment of Cherry Glen, I'm running concessions."

"The Women's League for the Betterment of Cherry Glen?"

"Yes, we just call it the Women's League for short. At least most of the members do. I much prefer if people call it by its full name." She sniffed. "People just don't have the patience for it." She said this like it was a character flaw on their part.

"It sounds like a great organization."

Minnie studied me as if assessing if I were lying.

"Cherry Glen is a wonderful town," I went on. "I'm happy to come home and see how much it has changed and improved."

She sniffed again. "Thank you, but this doesn't mean I don't think you are a murderer."

I dropped my head.

Minnie didn't seem to notice and said, "I will have to work with you if you're at the ticket booth. Stay out of my way."

"Noted," I said.

Huckleberry gave a quiet bark as if he agreed. I leaned over and patted his head. I appreciated his backup.

"Now that we got that settled," Stacey said. "I want to go over how money will be handled by both of you."

"Settled?" Minnie shrieked. "Things are most definitely not settled. They aren't settled at all." She pointed her finger at me. "Kathy Killian is a good friend of mine. She told me you had Hazel at your farm when she should have been with her grand-mother." She folded her arms as if that were all she needed to rest her case.

Ah, yet another reason for Quinn's mother to have a low opin-ion of me.

"Minnie," Stacey snapped. "That's enough. The play opens tomorrow night. There is no time left to make any changes. You will work with my cousin. I'm not asking you to like it. The Women's League committed to this project. Do you want the group to look bad by backing out?"

"I suppose you don't give me any choice," Minnie said.

"I don't," my cousin agreed. "Now, can we start?"

"Yes," I said. I was eager to learn what I needed to know and then get out of there and as far away from Minnie as possible. It didn't feel like I was in any danger when I was around her, but it wasn't comfortable to be around someone who disliked me so strongly.

All business now, Stacey went over the ticket system, how to collect money, where the receipts should go, and also where to find the extra supplies of concessions, or in my case, tickets.

"Like I told you before, Shiloh, opening night is sold out. Most people booked online, so they will only have to scan the barcode they received via email. However, it is possible they will want to buy a ticket for another night, so you need to be prepared."

I nodded.

"I don't need to hear this part," Minnie said. "Before creating the Women's League for the Betterment of Cherry Glen, I ran the local boosters club for the high school for forty years and was at every home football and basketball game. I don't need to be taught how to run a concessions booth." Minnie sniffed.

Stacey pressed her lips together and then said, "I have no doubt you will do a great job, Minnie."

The older woman puffed out her chest just a little. I believed that was just the sort of praise she was looking for. "Very good." She picked up her handbag from the ticket counter. "I'll be here tomorrow afternoon to make sure everything is set up for the show." She marched to the theater's front door.

Stacey shook her head. "I wish I could say that I could replace Minnie, but the truth is, she *is* the queen of the concessions. I can't have any mistakes this first weekend of the show, so I will put up with her for now." She glanced at me. "Are you ready?"

"I think so. It seems straightforward from what I can tell."

She nodded. "Good. I want you here at no later than five tomorrow. The show starts at seven. You don't need to be here quite as early as Minnie, since you don't have much setup." She started across the chipped wood floor to the grand staircase that led into the theater itself.

"Stace," I said and hurried after her.

Behind me, Huckleberry's toenails made a *click, click, click* sound on the floor.

She glanced over her shoulder. "If you want to talk to me, you will have to come to rehearsal. I'm already running behind. I hope they are already in process like I asked." She made her way up the steps. I followed at a quick pace.

I looked behind me to see Huckleberry staring bewildered up at the large red-carpeted steps. He hopped on the first one, paused, and then went onto the next. His progress to the theater would be slow.

"Stacey," I said as I walked behind her. "Can you tell me about the guns that were being used for the play?"

She eyed me. "Not this again. I'm tired of talking about those guns." She reached the landing and headed to the left theater door.

"Stacey, it's important. How many guns did you borrow from my dad?"

With her hand on the handle of the door, she turned and looked at me. Then she sighed. "Five for the senate members who will murder Caesar."

"Do you still plan to carry on the scene in the same way? Shooting Caesar instead of stabbing him?"

She tightened her grip on the door handle. "Why should I change my play? Just because someone stole one of the guns and used it wrongly does not mean I have to change my play. In order to set the play in the time period I want, this is the best, most dramatic way."

I frowned. I wanted to tell her that making changes after Crocker's tragic death would not compromise the play, but I thought better of it. When Stacey made up her mind, there was no way to change it.

"And were the individual guns assigned to any particular actor?"

She frowned. "No."

"So the gun that was stolen could have been used by any of the actors playing a role in the senate?"

"Yes." She scowled at me. "Do you have a point?"

"I—I don't know. It just seems significant." As I said this, Huckleberry crested the final step and lay splayed on the landing like he had just climbed Mount Everest.

"When you figure it out, let me know. I have a play to direct." She opened the door and went inside. I caught the door with my hand before it could slam closed after her.

Inside the theater, I saw seven actors on the stage. Six of them stood around the mayor as Julius Caesar. My father as the sooth-sayer stood in the wings.

The mayor held his arms out to hold them back. "'And men are flesh and blood, and apprehensive. Yet in the number I do know but one that unassailable holds on his rank, unshaked of motion; and that I am he let me a little show it, even in this: that I was constant Cimber should be banished and constant do remain to keep him so.'"

The other men quickly said their brief lines, and the guns went off in a cloud of smoke. "'Et tu, Brute? Then fall, Caesar!'" The mayor collapsed to the floor.

There was silence. No one on the stage or in the theater moved for several seconds. When the smoke cleared, it was impossible to know who shot which gun. It could have been any of them.

"'People and senators, be not affrighted. Fly not; stand still. Ambition's debt is paid,'" the actor playing Brutus recited.

"Cut!" Stacey called as she made her way down the aisle. "I need you all to do that scene again so I can fix the staging. It was all off. Two of you were standing in front of Caesar. We can't have that. The audience has to be able to see his death scene."

The mayor stood up and dusted himself off. "I think I did a

great death scene. Yes, I need the audience to see it and fully appreciate my tragic end."

I stepped out of the theater, and my brain whirled. I knew I had learned something important today. What exactly, I could not be sure.

Chapter Twenty-Nine

❧

T he town planning office was in the municipal building with the mayor's office, the police station, and fire department. I wasn't thrilled with the idea of seeing Baker again. However, it was the only way I was going to find out where the wind farm would be.

I walked through the main door with Huckleberry at my heels, and cheerful Connie Baskins was at her post at the receptionist's desk.

"Are my eyes deceiving me?" Connie asked. "It's Shiloh Bellamy! I thought I wouldn't see you here ever again after the chief brought you in. Should I call the chief for you?"

"No!" I said a little too loudly. I cleared my throat. "I mean, no thank you. I'm actually here to look up some farm records in the town planning office."

"Baker Loyal, our town planner, isn't here right now, but his clerk is and should be able to help you. What are you interested in?" She leaned forward as if ready to gather the latest news.

I hesitated. "I just wanted to look at the property boundaries for my family farm."

"Oh." She settled back in her seat, and I got the impression

FARM TO TROUBLE 217

she didn't think that was nearly as interesting as she had hoped it would be.

"Where's the planning office?"

"It's in the basement. You can take the elevator there." She pointed to an elevator that had an old-fashioned gated door. It appeared to have been there since the turn of the twentieth century.

"Are there stairs?" I asked.

She cocked her head. "Of course. They are just through the metal door there. When you get to the basement, just go straight, and you will run into the planning office. You can't miss it."

I thanked her and headed for the stairwell.

"Oh wait. Is your little dog going with you?" she called after me.

I glanced down at Huckleberry. I was just so used to taking him everywhere I went, I hadn't even thought about leaving him at home. "Is that all right?"

She shrugged. "I don't think we have a rule against it."

I nodded, picked up Huckleberry, and went to the stairwell. I followed Connie's instructions and, at the bottom of the stairs, immediately found the planning office. There was a glass door that led into the office. Inside, the air smelled of old books and paper. A young man who looked like he was just out of college sat at a desk, typing away. He looked up at me from his computer screen. "May I help you?"

"I'm Shiloh Bellamy from Bellamy Farm. I was wondering if I could see some town plans."

He stood up. "Wow, really? Hardly anyone comes in here and asks me to do that. What do you need?" He was eager to assist.

"I need to see some new construction plans."

"Oh." His mouth fell open. "Are you the one who was supposed to have killed Jefferson Crocker?"

I scowled at him. "I didn't kill him."

He held up his hands. "Sorry, I didn't mean to cause any offense."

I rolled my eyes. Like it wasn't offensive to tell someone you thought they were a killer.

He blinked a few times from behind his glasses. "You have a dog with you."

I looked down at Huckleberry in my arms. "Is that a problem?"

"Not for me. I love dogs, but if he has an accident, you're responsible for cleaning it up. I don't do poo."

It was a good policy.

"Huckleberry is very well-trained in that regard," I said.

"So what town plans do you need?"

"I'd like to see Crocker's plans for the Cherry Glen Wind Farm. I was told he would have had to file them here in order for them to be presented to the town council."

He snapped his fingers. "He sure would. We have four versions of the plans. The first three were voted down by the council. The fourth, the latest version, is being voted on tonight."

"They are still going through with the vote even though Crocker is dead?"

He nodded. "Town staff just got an updated version of the agenda about an hour ago, and it's still on there."

"Can anyone attend a town council meeting?" I asked.

"Sure. It's open to the public." He said this like the answer was obvious.

"Can I see those plans?"

"Which ones?"

"How about the first and the last to start."

"You got it."

Behind the clerk's desk was compact shelving like I had seen at my university library when I was in college. The clerk turned the crank, and shelves began to move apart. He disappeared down one of the aisles the opened shelves had created.

Huckleberry strained in my arms. I knew he wanted to go check out the shelves. "No," I whispered to him.

A moment later, the clerk returned with two large rolls of paper.

Using one of the rolls as a pointer, he said, "We can lay these out on the table for you to take a closer look."

I nodded, removed Huckleberry's leash from my pocket, and clipped it on his collar before setting him on the floor. I wasn't going to let him get lost in those shelves behind the desk.

"Which do you want to start with?"

"The oldest one."

He nodded and rolled out one of the papers on the long table. I stared at the aerial view of my farm and the farms around it. There were site markers where the turbines would go. There was one right next to the farmhouse and barn. That surprised me. The property was labeled "S. Bellamy." I wasn't sure if that was for Sully, my father, or for me. The next farm over was labeled "St. Bellamy." I knew that had to have meant my cousin Stacey.

Looking at the plans, I could see why my father was so against it. There wasn't a piece of our two-hundred acres that wasn't touched by the wind farm. It was either a turbine or a small support building. Stacey's farm wasn't nearly as peppered with turbines.

I took a photo of it the best I could with my phone. "Can I see the newest plan?" I asked.

He nodded, rolled up the original plans, and smoothed the new ones across the table. Immediately, I noted the difference.

The name over Stacey's farm was no longer "St. Bellamy." It was Crocker.

I stared at the paper. I had to be seeing things. I blinked, and the name remained the same.

"Is this right?" I asked the clerk at the desk. I showed him the name on the paper. "On the previous sheet, this was owned by Stacey Bellamy, my cousin. When did this change?"

"I can look that up for you." He walked back to his computer and sat down. He tapped on the keyboard for a few minutes. "Here we go. It says it was sold to Jefferson Crocker at the end of February for $2.5 million. All cash by the looks of it."

I stared at him. This did not compute for me. Stacey was still living in the farmhouse on her family land. "Can you look up when Stacey Bellamy purchased the theater?"

He tapped away. "She bought it for four hundred thousand dollars," he said. "Looks like she's put twice that money into it, working on renovations."

Stacey claimed I was the one ruining Bellamy Farm, and she had already sold half of it to Crocker. She was a hypocrite. And now I knew how my cousin could afford to buy the theater. But did my father know? And if he did, why didn't he tell me?

I needed evidence of this latest development, so I took another photo of the paper that lay across the table. "Does your computer say who the land will go to now that Crocker is dead?"

He shook his head. "There is no survivorship deed or transfer upon death on record. So that must be listed in his will." He eyed me. "If you think you or someone you know is eligible to inherit, be patient. An estate as big as Jefferson Crocker's is bound to be in probate court for a long while. The minimum is six months, but I would guess over a year for an estate of his size. A lot of people will come out of the woodwork and challenge the will when there is so much money involved."

I tucked my phone into the pocket of my jeans. "Thank you. This had been so helpful."

"No problem. It was fun to do a little bit of a treasure hunt. Typically, Thursdays are slow. Who am I kidding? Every day is slow around here."

I left the planning office wondering how I was going to bring this up to my cousin. She must have some sort of explanation. In some ways, I didn't blame her for doing it. Acting and theater were her passion, not farming. It was her land to do with what she wanted, but I couldn't help wondering why was she still living on her old farm and acting like it was hers. Was it to keep the peace with my father, or was it a more secret and nefarious reason? I had no idea what that secret and nefarious reason would be though.

I was so preoccupied, I didn't see the other person in the stairwell leading back upstairs to Connie's post, but Huckleberry barked.

"I can't believe they let you bring a dog into the building," Baker Loyal said with a charming smile. "Connie must be getting soft upstairs."

"I did ask her if it was all right for Huckleberry to come with me."

He smiled. "Find what you needed in the town dungeon?"

"The dungeon?"

"Just a little joke of mine. That's what I call the basement of town hall. What I wouldn't give to work in a place with some windows. Learn anything interesting?"

I had, but I didn't want to tell him about it until I had a chance to speak with my cousin. "The property lines are right where I'd expected them to be," I said. I did not add that the owners had changed. "Your clerk was a great help."

"Good, I'm glad to hear that." He paused. "Would you be available for dinner some time?"

I stared at him.

He held up his hand. "I can tell you're not keen on the idea. Pretend I never asked."

Briar's voice was in my head, urging me to move on with my life. I knew she was right. Going on one date with Baker didn't mean I had to marry him, but it might just mean I was willing to start over in Cherry Glen.

"No," I said quickly. "It's not that. I think I would like that."

He grinned. "You do?"

I blushed. "It's just… I just moved back here, and everything has gone topsy-turvy with the murder and everything," I rambled. "Can I take a rain check until this mess is over?"

He gave me a slow smile. "Of course, Shiloh. It will give me something to look forward to."

I smiled, but I knew my face was still bright red. I needed to change the subject. "Do you go to the town council meetings?"

He raised his brow. "Typically, I do. There have been a lot of town planning changes in Cherry Glen of late, so usually I'm expected to be there to present the town's opinion on the votes that are going to be taken."

"Are you going tonight?" I asked.

"Yes."

"I'm going too. I want to hear what the town decides about Crocker's plan for the wind farm. It will directly impact my farm and my livelihood."

He smiled. "I'll see you then. It'll be our second unofficial date." He winked and continued down the stairs.

I watched as he disappeared through the door I'd just come through. I tried not to read too much into his last statement and failed.

Chapter Thirty

M y head spun as I drove back to the farm. Did I confront my father with what I learned about his niece? Did he know? I knew he and Stacey were both at the theater, and this evening was the dress rehearsal. Given the timing, I decided I would talk to Stacey before talking to my dad about it. She should be the one to tell him. I just didn't know when I would have a chance to speak to her in private about it. I wasn't sure I could wait until the end of opening weekend.

When I parked my car, Huckleberry was eager to get out. I thought he was starting to like farm life. As soon as I let him out of the car, he ran around in circles. I laughed. Esmeralda must have heard the commotion, because she came running out of the barn. The two orange barn cats, which I had decided to name Peanut and Butter, came out after her at a much slower pace.

There was so much to do on the farm, and I wondered if all the work would be worth it. I supposed it was still possible for Cherry Glen to vote in favor of Crocker's plans. What would that mean for the farm? What would that mean for my father and me living on the farm? I didn't have any answers.

I suspected the person who would have had answers was my

Grandma Bellamy. In her no-nonsense way, she always knew what to say to get her point across, and she could be brash at times, but she was rarely wrong.

I looked down at the cluster of animals that had now been joined by my father's five chickens. For a brief moment, I felt like the farm version of the Pied Piper. "You guys want to go on a little adventure?" I asked.

Huckleberry and Esmeralda seemed to be game. The other cats and the chickens showed no interest at all. I headed around the barn. My destination was a half mile away at the very edge of where my farm met Stacey's, or at least what I had thought was Stacey's farm.

Just shy of the property line on my side was Grandma Bellamy's cabin. My grandmother had asked that her cabin be built here because she could be right in the middle of her two sons and therefore never more than a ten-minute walk from either of her granddaughters.

The small building was tucked in a clearing in a wooded part of the farm that was the dividing line between the two farms.

The grass around the structure was as high as my knees. I was glad I wore jeans. It was hard to say how many ticks would be in that grass. I looked down at Huckleberry and Esmeralda. Huckleberry stared at the grass uncertainly.

I picked him up and draped him on my shoulder as I waded through the sea of grass toward the cabin. Behind me, Esmeralda jumped over the tall blades of grass as if they were hurdles. She meowed happily as she made her way to the building as if she were telling each blade of grass how she felt about it while she jumped.

She might not wear an identification collar, but I'd be getting her a flea-and-tick collar soon enough, even if she wound up going home to her rightful owner.

I reached the front door and set Huckleberry on the large, jagged rock where Grandma Bellamy would clean mud from her boots before entering her house. I tried the door and was surprised to find it unlocked. The door opened inward.

The inside of my grandmother's cabin was a time capsule. Grandma Bellamy's teacup was still in the center of the table. Her reading glasses, which she refused to wear anywhere outside her own home, lay beside the teacup like she had just set them down.

But there were clues that she hadn't just stepped away. Everything was covered with a layer of dust. It had been fifteen years since she passed. The dust proved it.

Huckleberry stood next to me on the door's threshold as if he sensed my hesitation. Esmeralda didn't have the same qualms and walked right inside. In a way, I was grateful to the cat for doing that. I might have stood on my grandmother's old doorstep all day and night if she hadn't made the first move.

I stepped inside, and the idea I'd had on the roof of the barn solidified—that I could live in the cabin. Here I could have my own space and still take care of the farm and my father. It seemed like the best of both worlds.

I sighed and walked through the one-bedroom house. Every step I took kicked up dust, and I sneezed.

The Siamese ran ahead of us into the bedroom. Over the bed was a circa 1970s daisy-patterned sheet in bright colors dulled by dust. Esmeralda catapulted her body onto the bed. When she landed, a huge cloud of dust ballooned up around her, and she sneezed.

Huckleberry and I sneezed too. I waved the dust away from my face. "Yeesh, Esmeralda. We are all going to have hay fever after being in here."

When the dust cleared, I saw there was a blue envelope tucked into the mirror above her dresser. In my grandmother's curvy hand, which I recognized immediately from the hundreds of letters and cards I had received from her in my lifetime, my name was written. Shiloh. That was all it said. Shiloh.

Personally, I didn't know any other Shilohs, and I doubted my grandmother had either. This card, note, or whatever it was was most certainly intended for me.

Did this mean no one had been in here since Grandma Bellamy died? After her death, I had been too heartbroken to go inside her cabin, then Logan died, and I fled this town where I had lost the two people I'd loved most in the world.

I knew I hadn't been back inside my grandmother's home, but I was surprised Stacey hadn't poked her nose around at all. She was Grandma Bellamy's granddaughter too. If my father had seen it there, why hadn't he mailed it to me in California or at least told me it existed? I would have loved to have my grandmother's words of comfort, especially right after she died.

I missed my mother, of course, but she died when I was so young; my grandmother's death was the more painful of the two. I didn't know if I missed my mother the person so much as I longed for the experience of having a mother who could have raised me. My life would have been so different if she'd lived.

Carefully, I removed the envelope from the mirror. I had to tug a bit since it had been there so long. An impression of the envelope was left on the mirror's glass. With shaking hands, I turned it over. It was sealed, which meant only my grandmother knew what could be found inside it.

Huckleberry whimpered at my feet. Esmeralda paced back and forth on the bed. It seemed after the initial shock, she enjoyed making clouds of dust float into the air.

I sat on the edge of her bed and was surrounded by another cloud of dust. All three of us sneezed again. As careful as possible so as not to tear it, I opened the envelope.

Dearest Shiloh, my grandmother wrote. *If you are reading this, I am gone. I wrote this letter on the day of your high school graduation, and if you're reading it now, that means I remembered to put it in a place where you'd find it before my end. Kudos to me for a job well done. I love you, my dear, and you already know that, so let's get to the heart of this matter.*

I have always been good with money. When your grandfather and I operated Bellamy Farm for all those years, I was always the one who was in charge of the accounts. Your grandfather—God bless him— was an exceptional farmer. He knew when to plant and when to harvest by simply watching the weather. But he was not that good with money. He always wanted the next gadget or solution. He didn't like to figure out things on his own. He would have bought every farmer toy in the book if I had let him. One of us had to have a good hold on the purse strings. That person was me.

Because of that, I have been able to save some money from the budget. I socked away quite a bit. I never sold any of the land. That's not an option for Bellamy Farm.

I paused my reading as I read that last line over. How would my grandmother feel if she knew my cousin sold half the farm to invest in the Michigan Street Theater? I continued to read.

I need you to remember that. The farm needs to stay together. It is the legacy that your grandfather and I left. And those before us.

I stared at the letter. That was a lot of pressure to keep the farm together. So many of the old family farms in the area had been sold. I thought of what Wes Sumner had said when we were outside Jessa's Place just a few days ago.

I chose not to tell your father about the money because he's like his father in so many ways. That comes to money too. Sully is a good man, but he would use the money to buy more baubles and trinkets for his collection. That's not what the money should be used for. You may be wondering why I'm telling you and not Stacey. She is my granddaughter too, and I love you both equally. But Stacey has different dreams than what this farm can offer her. You are the one who will come back and work the land.

I fled after she died and after Logan died. I fled so quickly that I didn't even come in this room to find this letter. Grandma Bellamy may not have known I hadn't stayed, but she had known that if I did leave, I would come back. I continued reading.

And if you are reading this letter, you did. Again, kudos for me for being right. I love it when I'm spot-on like this with my predictions.

Stacey may say that she wants to help around the farm, but her heart is not in it. Soon, she will find something else that suits her fancy more.

I thought about Stacey's theater again.

When this letter was written, Grandma Bellamy would not have known Stacey would return to Cherry Glen. I wondered if I should tell my older cousin about this. If my grandmother had known, would she have picked her above me? It seemed she was right in her prediction that Stacey would become bored with farming though. Shaking my head, I continued reading.

So I have saved this money and hidden it for you for when the farm needs it most. I am trusting you to use it for the right purpose. To save this place that your grandfather and I loved so well. The money can be found beneath the surface in the heart of the farm. Just toe-tap and you will know what I mean. I trust you will know where that is. I love you, dear girl. I know you have grown up wise and strong. I wish great happiness to you and Logan.

My breath caught on that line.

I'm so happy you are sharing your life with a good man like him. You're lucky to find a person as good as your grandfather.

All my love, Grandma.

I stared at the letter and read it beginning to end a second time. I might be wrong, but it seemed to me that my grandmother was sending me a real-life treasure hunt. I read the instructions again. "The money can be found beneath the surface in the heart of the farm." What on earth did that mean? Where was the heart of the farm? I had never heard my grandmother mention such a place before.

My heart hurt at her mention of Logan. He died just a year after she did—the two events that unraveled my life's plan. Well, at least my plan up to that point.

I closed my eyes and willed away the tears that threatened to overtake me. I had to get to the heart of the letter. The money. My grandmother hid money on the farm?

If I didn't know what the heart of the farm was, how could I find the money? And how much money were we talking about? Was it really enough to save the farm? That would cost hundreds of thousands of dollars. How could she have saved that much from a working farm that seemed like it was always just scraping by?

I held the letter in my hand and looked down at the dog and cat that were now sitting at my feet and looking up at me with quizzical expressions on their faces.

"Guys," I said. "It looks to me like we have yet another mystery on our hands."

Esmeralda began licking her right forepaw. Clearly, she was not impressed.

Chapter Thirty-One

On shaky legs, I left my grandmother's cabin. Her letter was tucked in the back pocket of my jeans. I hadn't been in the cabin since Grandma Bellamy died, but the note still being there undisturbed must mean my father hadn't been in there either. Perhaps I was more like my father than I thought. It was clear we both preferred to run from our emotions rather than face them head-on.

Tears rolled down my face as I walked back home. Why hadn't my grandmother just told me where the stash of money was? Why leave just a clue? What was the heart of the farm anyway?

I wiped my eyes and increased my pace. Both Huckleberry and Esmeralda had to run to catch up with me. Grandma Bellamy wouldn't want me to cry. She left me that letter because she wanted me to save the farm. She knew someday it would need saving, and I would be the one to do it. I couldn't let her down. I couldn't let myself down. And this money might be exactly what I needed to succeed—murder investigation or no murder investigation.

I broke into a run. Huckleberry barked as he and the cat ran after me. When I reached the old barn, I pushed the door open with a great heave and yanked the push mower out. "It's time to get back to work."

The cat and dog stared at me and then hurried out of my way. I marched the mower back to the edge of the yard where I had stopped when the police chief arrived and got to work.

I don't know how long it took me to mow the lawn. An hour, two? But I didn't stop there. I hurried back into the barn and pulled out a wheelbarrow and shovel. One by one, I started digging up the dead plants in front of the house and tossing them into the barrel. They would make for the start of a good compost pile when I could make an area for it. The hard work kept my hands busy as I went over again in my head who the killer might be. Part of me was still disappointed that Crocker's wife had such a good alibi. She would have been a stellar suspect.

But I had others. Hedy Strong remained a good suspect. She certainly hated Crocker and his wind farm that threatened her beloved birds. Then there was the woman who ran away from me at the farmers market right before I found the body. She could have been fleeing the scene. I still needed to find her. Lastly, I could not count out my cousin Stacey. She sold her half of Bellamy Farm to Crocker. It was her right to sell it, but why didn't she tell anyone? Did anyone else know? Would she kill to keep that secret?

I was digging out a stubborn bush that had seen better days when my father's truck came down the driveway. I stopped working. My legs wobbled, and my arms felt like jelly. I had to lean heavily on the shovel to stand upright. I was going to be sore in the morning and probably the rest of the weekend.

Dad climbed out of the truck and reached up to pull out his walker. Even in my precarious state, I wanted to offer him help, but I knew he would never take it. He pushed the walker through the freshly cut grass and stopped a few feet from me.

"You've been busy."

My mouth felt dry. "Just working out some of my frustrations."

"You are so much like your grandmother," he said. "I can see it when you tighten your jaw like that."

"I'll take that as a compliment." I almost told my father about the note I found in Grandma Bellamy's cabin but stopped myself. "I miss her."

"I do too," he said, squinting into the sun. "I've made mistakes with you; I know that. I suppose after your mother died, I just buried myself in my collection. I should have cared for you and this farm. Instead, I spent money on things I didn't need." He adjusted his hold on the walker. "If it hadn't been for my mother, I don't know what kind of childhood you might have had. She raised you more than I ever did."

I wiped sweat from my brow. "Dad, it's all right."

"No." He shook his head. "It's not all right. Let me say my piece. I was barely able to keep the farm up when your grandmother was alive. After she died and you left, it only got worse. You would ask me how things were, and I lied to you. I knew things were bad but not how bad. You've spent so much of your money on saving this place, and I've let it go to ruin. I buried my head in the sand and my life in my collection. If I had been wise enough to look up, I would have seen I had dishonored my mother's memory."

"I didn't mind helping you pay the bills." I wiped sweat from my brow.

"I know, and that only makes me feel worse about it. You came here with a plan to rescue the farm from the mess I made of it, and I have fought you every step of the way. I owe you an apology."

Tears welled up in my eyes. "I owe you an apology too. I shouldn't have left after Logan died. That wasn't fair to you."

"If you had stayed, I don't know what your life would have

been. You needed to go. I know that." A tear rolled down his weathered cheek. "I'm just grateful you came back. Quinn reminded me that you were just trying to do what you thought was best for the farm."

"Quinn? Quinn told you that?"

"He did. He has a lot of respect for you. He thinks you can save the farm too."

I opened and closed my mouth. "When did he tell you this?" I asked.

"A few hours ago. He popped into play rehearsal, and we talked there."

It must have been after we had the awful fight outside the general store. Why would he go to my father then?

My father cleared his throat. "Anyway, I'm an old man. It might take me some time to change my ways. Be patient with me."

I dropped my shovel on the ground and walked over to my dad. Stepping around the walker, I gave him a hug. "I think we both have to change something." I let him go. "As long as Chief Randy doesn't throw one of us in lockup, we'll get through this."

Dad laughed.

"I'm looking forward to your acting debut in the play." I smiled through my tears.

He seemed relieved to change the subject. "I am too. It's the first time I have felt alive in a very long time. I have Stacey to thank for that. If she hadn't asked to use my collection for the play, I might have never left the house."

I thought of Stacey differently when he said that and knew I owed her my thanks.

"She got me to come to rehearsal, and then next thing I knew, I was cast in the play. At first, I agreed because it was the best way to keep an eye on my possessions. Then I got into the part so much I didn't even notice when someone stole one of the guns."

"I'll find out who took your gun," I said.

"How?" he asked.

Before I could answer, my cell phone buzzed in my pocket. I assumed it was a text from Briar asking me to come back to LA. It wasn't. It was my timer going off, telling me the town council meeting started in forty minutes. That gave me just enough time to clean up.

"I'm going to start finding out what happened by going to the town council meeting tonight."

"Not without me," he said with a smile that looked a lot like his mother's.

Chapter Thirty-Two

D ad, Huckleberry, and I rode back to town in my convertible with the top down. The wind blew through what was left of my father's hair. He looked quite pleased with himself, as did the pug on his lap.

"I can see why you like a car like this. It's nice to sit in sunshine. It's hard to believe in a few months it will be dark by this time in the evening," Dad said.

I smiled at him. "It may not be the most practical car for Michigan when winter comes. Maybe I should sell it and get something more suitable."

"No, if you do that, I won't get to ride in it again. At my age, I will take all the simple joys I can find, even if it's just sitting in a car with the sun on my head. You can use my truck in the winter."

I glanced at him. "Thanks, Dad."

He nodded as if that was the end of the conversation.

I let out a breath. Something had shifted between us for the better. I was hopeful we could be a real family again after all. Making amends with my cousin would be the last piece of the puzzle, but that would have to wait until after the town council meeting.

It was taking all my courage to go to this meeting when I knew the whole town was gossiping about me. I also knew I was already on thin ice with Mayor Loyal and Chief Randy. I had to convince them both my father and I were innocent.

I dropped Dad and Huckleberry at the front door of the town hall. After I parked the car, I walked around to the front of the building. I expected Connie to be waiting at the door, ready to ask questions. Now that I had seen her skills at work on more than one occasion, I could see why she'd held her job at the front desk so long. Not much got by her when she was present.

When I opened the door, Connie wasn't there. Instead, dozens of people stood outside a room that had its double doors wide open. The detective in me surmised this must be the location of the meeting.

I looked at my cell phone. I was ten minutes early for the meeting, but it was already standing room only.

Weaving around the crowd and earning some dirty looks in the process, I wriggled my way to the door where I was able to peek into the room.

The meeting was in the old conference room of the building. It was a large room close to the size of the bottom floor of the farmhouse, but still not large enough for the number of people who squeezed themselves inside. Considering that the fire department was also in this building, I was surprised no one had complained yet over what was a clear fire code violation.

Minnie and a group of women were in one corner of the large room. I guessed it was the gathering of the Women's League for the Betterment of Cherry Glen. I ducked my head, hoping she wouldn't see me. This really wasn't the place to be called out as a murderer.

I spotted Shannon at the front of the room, sitting on the riser next to the mayor. The two of them chatted happily. There were four other men and women on the risers who I guessed comprised the rest of the council. Baker leaned against the wall nearby as if waiting to be called forward.

I was surprised Shannon was here. She had told me she didn't want to pursue the wind farm. Had she changed her mind?

People shifted uncomfortably next to me as the minutes ticked by. After what seemed like forever, the mayor stood. "I call this meeting of the Cherry Glen town council to order."

The crowd quieted down, and the mayor smiled as if he was pleased by their reaction to his calling the meeting to order.

I scanned the room for Dad and Huckleberry but didn't see them anywhere. I glanced behind me into the overflow crowd in the lobby. I didn't see them there either.

The mayor cleared his throat. "We have a number of items on the agenda tonight, but I think most of you are here about our decision over the Cherry Glen Wind Farm. We will address that first."

A murmur ran through the room, and it sounded like the buzzing of bees.

He gestured to his son. "Baker, our town planner, will outline what the proposal is."

Baker pushed himself off the wall and stepped up onto the riser. "Thank you, Mr. Mayor. The proposal is for a wind farm in Cherry Glen. It would be located on the Bellamy Farm. Sully Bellamy refused to sell his land, and the Crocker Company requested we pass an ordinance that forces him to do so. That's what the council is voting on tonight."

My stomach tightened. I was about to learn the fate of my farm. The very notion of which was ludicrous! Why hadn't my father told me that we—our family's legacy—was in so much trouble? This wasn't about just putting up turbines; it was about usurping our very heritage. If I'd known that was what this meeting was about, I could have tried to stop it. Surely, I would've been granted the opportunity to speak, to do something.

The press of people—of these circumstances—crowded in with the weight of a dozen combines, and I felt my chest tightening, my hands going cold. The panic was escalating.

"Bird killer!" There was a shout from the middle of the room. Even though I couldn't see her because she was so small, I recognized the voice as Hedy's.

I stood there in a state of denial and concentrated on breathing my next breath.

"Ms. Strong," the mayor said. "There is no reason for outbursts like that."

I thought I might have an outburst of my own! Wasn't there some due process? I was the owner of the land on paper and paid the taxes. Shouldn't I have been formally approached about these things? If my father had so much as breathed a whisper of these happenings, I'd never even have given Crocker the time of day. He must've had quite the laugh over his good fortune and my stupidity.

"I think you, Ms. Strong, and many in the town"—he glanced in my direction—"will be very happy with the news that we are about to hear." He nodded to Shannon. "Do you wish to tell them, Mrs. Crocker?"

Shannon didn't stand but said in a clear loud voice, "I have inherited the Crocker Company, and I have canceled the project. Neither the town nor the Bellamy family need worry about it any longer."

A cheer rang up in the crowded room while others shouted out questions, asking Shannon why she decided to cancel the project. She ignored all of them. I made no sound as relief flooded my body.

As the council moved on to the next agenda item, I wrestled my way out of the room. I needed some space as the full enormity of all this hit me. I walked straight out of the building and stood on the sidewalk, breathing in the humid summer evening air. The sun was just beginning to lower itself in the western sky. It would be another two hours before it completely set.

The door behind me opened, and Shannon Crocker came out. I noticed she was wearing one of the dresses I had seen in the boutique in Traverse City. Apparently, the shopping trip had been a success.

I was about to say hello to her when she pointed at the telephone pole a few feet away. "Oh my God! Fluffy!"

I stared at her. "Fluffy?"

Fluffy seemed like such a provincial name for Esmeralda, but I didn't say so.

She ripped the paper from the pole. "I've been looking all over for this cat. I thought it was somewhere in Jefferson's mansion, just hiding from me." She stared at the paper. "Your name is on here. You're the one who found the cat."

"I didn't. Hazel Killian did. She's the police chief's granddaughter. I told her I would spread the word about the cat because she looked like she was someone's pet."

"She was. She was Jefferson's cat, and he doted on her like he had never doted on me even when we were together." She scowled at the paper.

"You don't want the cat?" I asked.

"No, I don't want the cat. I'm allergic. That's why it was a full day before I realized the cat was missing. I was planning to take her to the shelter."

My heart sank at the very idea of Esmeralda in a shelter. "You don't have to do that. I can keep her, or I know Hazel Killian would if her dad allows it. Either way, she has a good home with one of us."

"Really? You'd take her? That would be a relief. There're so many things I need to tie up since Jefferson died and would like to have this off my plate."

"Consider it off," I said happily. "Es—Fluffy is at my farm right now."

She smiled. "You know, you aren't so bad, and you should know I tore up the contract you had with my husband. You don't have to worry about that any longer."

I stared at her. "You're going to let me out of the contract?"

"I sure am. He never gave you any money, and I don't want the land for the wind farm. The whole idea is moot. Besides, the contract did say if either party was unable to continue with the agreement, it would be null and void. Consider it done."

I stared at her with tears gathering in my eyes. I was speechless. Completely speechless.

She narrowed her eyes. "Are you crying?"

"No, I'm not." I forced back the tears. "Thank you. I can't thank you enough for what you've done. It's a great relief to me, and it will be to my father too."

I still needed money to save the farm, but I would find another way to get it. The more I could distance myself and the farm from Crocker and his murder, the better.

"It's nice to know I've made someone happy." She smoothed

the front of her dress. "I plan to do more of that. It actually feels sort of nice." She walked away.

I watched her leave with a bewildered expression on my face.

Dad and Huckleberry came out the front door of the town hall. "Land sakes, there is not enough room in there to breathe." Dad struggled with the door, his walker, and the pug leash.

I hurried over to him, held the door, and unraveled Huckleberry's leash from his walker. "Dad, you should have waited for me outside."

People were starting to trickle out of the town hall. I didn't know if the meeting was over or they had only been there to see how the wind farm issue would pan out.

"If I did that, I would have never gotten a seat. The place was packed."

"I know. I stayed just long enough for the vote about the wind farm."

"Or non-vote," Dad said. "I'm very happy with the outcome."

"Dad, why didn't you tell me it was going to come to this? Why didn't you tell me we could have completely lost the farm?"

He sighed and shuffled along the sidewalk behind his walker. "I was afraid you wouldn't come back. I pushed away your ideas for so long, I didn't think you would forgive that. And if it was a lost cause, why would you come back from California at all? You had built a good life for yourself there. If we lost the farm, I had nothing to offer you here."

"Dad, you're here. That's enough. For years, you told me everything was fine and it was all right for me to stay away. I know you thought you were being kind, but if you needed me, I would have come running."

He wouldn't look at me. "I know that, but after Logan died, it felt selfish to ask you to come back and face painful memories."

I stepped aside as a group of townsfolk walked by. "I shouldn't have stayed away for so long. I know that now."

He reached out and squeezed my hand. "Then we both learned something."

Chapter Thirty-Three

I asked my dad to wait with Huckleberry in front of the building so I could pull the car around.

I felt like a thousand pounds had been lifted off my shoulders. The farm would not be lost. Dad and I were on the path to a better relationship. Sure, I was still a murder suspect, but if the farm could be saved, maybe, just maybe, I had hope of staying out of prison too.

I couldn't wait to tell Hazel the good news about Esmeralda. I guessed her grandmother would not see this as welcome news.

When my convertible came into view, I saw someone leaning against the driver side door. Quinn Killian waited to talk to me.

"Hey," I said, folding my arms.

"Hey to you too." He smiled sheepishly.

"Can I help you with something?" I asked with a frown.

"I need to talk to you."

"What about?" I asked, but I guessed he had heard about the cat situation from his mother by now.

"I just finished my shift at the station and saw your car. I thought this would be a good time to talk to you."

"About Esmeralda?" I asked.

"Hazel told me that's what she named the cat. She's been so worried about her."

"You can tell her there's good news." I went on to fill him in on what Shannon had said about the cat.

"What are the odds that Esmeralda would have been Crocker's cat?" He shook his head. "Hazel will be relieved. I'll be sure to tell her."

I smiled. "Can she keep the cat?"

He sighed. "Let's leave Esmeralda with you for the time being. My mother is a little hot under the collar about the whole thing."

"Oh, I know."

"That's actually what I wanted to talk to you about."

I winced. *Here comes the reprimand.*

"I want to apologize for how my mother treated you. Hazel told me what happened. She heard some of the stuff Mom said about Logan." He didn't look at me. "It's probably my fault my mother feels the way she does about it."

"It probably is," I said quietly.

"That's fair." His Adam's apple bobbed up and down. "I could say I was out of my head with grief, or I was drunk, to make an excuse for the way I behaved at Logan's funeral, but I won't. You loved him, and he loved you very much. He would have been ashamed by the way I treated you that day. I'm sorry. I'm sorry it's taken me this long to apologize." He licked his lips. "I always wondered what I would say to you about the funeral when I saw you again. I knew from the moment you drove up to Sully's farmhouse that I should have cleared the air with you, but I couldn't bring myself to do it. I thought pretending it never happened was better, but I realized that was like pretending Logan never lived. I can't do that, and I don't want to."

I swallowed hard. "Thank you. My father said you talked to him about me too."

He nodded. "I hope I didn't overstep, but every time I saw the tension between the two of you, it broke my heart. I don't want Hazel and me to end up like that someday."

His words stung, but I understood what he meant. I cleared my throat. "You didn't overstep, and thank you for doing it. I know there's a lot of things Dad and I have to work on, but we will get there."

"And what about us?" he asked.

I played with my car keys in my hand. "I do accept your apology, but we will have to wait and see."

He met my gaze. "Okay."

"I meant what I said about Hazel coming to the farm. She's a great kid." I moved toward the car. "My dad is waiting in front of the hall to be picked up."

He stepped back. "Hazel is a great kid, but she was in the wrong too. She shouldn't have run away from my parents' house like that. She lost her iPad for a month for it." He rubbed the back of his head. "It's a hard juggling act. Because of my work schedule, my mother is with Hazel just as much as I am. I can understand that Hazel balks at how strict my mother is, but her grandmother does love her. Things would have been different if Hazel's mother were still here."

I didn't know what to say to that.

He looked at me. "I know my mother doesn't like the idea of Hazel spending any time with you. Just know, no matter what her opinion is, I make the decisions as to who my daughter can be friends with. She's not had an easy transition to Cherry Glen. You're the first person she's excited to have met. I don't take that lightly." He walked to his truck, climbed in, and drove away.

I stared at his taillights until they disappeared around the corner of the building.

I drove my car to the front of the town hall where I had left my father and Huckleberry. Connie Baskins was standing next to my father and holding on to Huckleberry's leash. The pug pulled her in my direction.

I got out of the car. Huckleberry ran with all his might and yanked the leash from Connie's hands. "Why, I never. Ms. Bellamy, you need to teach your dog some manners. All I was doing was holding on to his leash to keep him out of traffic."

I bent over, and Huckleberry jumped into my arms. "Thanks for watching out for him, Connie." I glanced at my father. "Dad, are you ready to go?"

"Sure am." He moved double time on his walker toward the car.

"Sully, you need to be careful on this uneven pavement," Connie said. She hurried over to the car and opened the passenger door for him. "Let me help you in."

"I got it," Dad muttered. And then said something under his breath about an "insufferable woman." I guessed my father wasn't a fan of Connie Baskins. "Let's go, Shiloh. I have to get over to the dress rehearsal for the play. Stacey will not like it if I'm late. They already started, but I needed to be at this meeting. The farm hung in the balance."

Connie smiled at my father. "It's so nice to see you out and about, Sully."

My father grunted. I raised my eyebrow as I folded up his walker and set it in the back seat with Huckleberry. I could be wrong, but it seemed to me that Connie might have a little crush on my father.

Townspeople were coming out of the town hall now in larger numbers. The sidewalk grew crowded.

"Sully," a deep voice called just as soon as Dad was settled into the convertible. Chief Randy sidled up to the car.

"Hello, Chief," Dad said as he buckled his seat belt.

The police chief tipped his hat to him.

My father stiffened.

The chief rocked back on his heels. "The play will have to wait. Come over to the station now." He cleared his throat as if he were uncomfortable. "Sully, we are friends, and as a courtesy, I don't want to arrest you right here in front of all these people."

"Arrest me!" my father bellowed. His face turned bright red. "You can't arrest me!"

People on the sidewalk stopped and stared.

"Let's talk about it at the station," the chief said.

"No," Dad said. "Shiloh, take me to the theater for rehearsal."

I stood a few feet away from Chief Randy on the sidewalk and looked from one back to the other.

"Shiloh," my father snapped.

Two police officers appeared at the chief's side, and one removed his handcuffs from his belt.

"Sully," the chief said. "Don't make this harder than it has to be."

I stepped forward. "Why are you arresting him now? What's changed?"

The chief glanced at me, and I thought he wasn't going to answer until he said, "We have witnesses who saw Sully and his truck in the vicinity of the farmers market at the time of the murder."

I gasped. "That's not possible. Dad, don't say another word. Let me contact my lawyer."

"You have a lawyer?" he asked.

"Yes. I'll call him. Don't answer another question until he arrives."

The officer with the handcuffs stepped forward.

"Don't touch him." I held out my hand. "You're not going to take a man on a walker away in handcuffs."

"Shiloh," the chief began.

"At least let me help him into the building," I said. "Please don't make more of a scene."

The chief nodded. "If you walk him into the police station, that would be all right."

"Don't worry, Shiloh," Connie said. "I will stay here with your dog."

"Thank you."

Connie glared at the chief. "I know Sully is innocent!"

Maybe it was good that Connie had a crush on my father.

Chapter Thirty-Four

C hief Randy and his officers went back inside the police station. I was relieved they didn't wait and watch for me to guide Dad into the building. We had attracted enough attention from the townspeople leaving the meeting already. Had they arrested my father in the middle of the sidewalk, tongues would have been wagging for days. I removed Dad's walker from the back seat of my car and unfolded it. Carefully, I helped him out of the car, and we shuffled toward the door. I put my head close to his once we were back inside the town hall. "Dad, why were you at the farmers market?" I asked.

He wouldn't look at me.

"You have to tell me. It's important." I guided him to the elevator.

"I may have hurt my back, but there is nothing wrong with my ears. When Crocker was at the farm, I heard him ask you to meet him at the farmers market, and you said it again the next morning. Once you left, I trailed you in my truck and hoped I might be able to intervene and talk some sense into him before your meeting."

"Oh, Dad…"

"But when I got there," Dad said. "Crocker wasn't around. I just drove around the market for a little bit, and he never showed. I didn't know he was already dead. I finally left because I didn't want you to catch me there." He paused. "I didn't kill him."

"I know that," I said as the interior door to the police station opened.

When it did, I found the chief and his two officers waiting. They were ready to take my dad away.

"You can't come any farther, Shiloh," the chief said. He put a hand on my father's arm. Dad let him. I could see on his face that some of the fight had gone out him. That was the worst part of all.

"Dad, remember, don't answer any questions," I said. "I'll call the attorney."

He nodded, and the officers guided him away.

"We'll take good care of him, Shiloh," the chief said and shuffled after them.

I stepped outside and called Leif Jansen. He said he would be there as soon as possible.

After the call, I thanked Connie for watching Huckleberry and let the little dog out of the car.

"Is your father all right?" Connie asked. "He's such a good man. I can't believe the police chief thinks Sully could kill a man. Do you want me to wait with you?"

"No, you should go home, Connie."

"I feel like I should do something," she said as she nervously fluffed her hair.

"My dad has a sweet tooth. Maybe make him a treat for when he can come home?"

She smiled. "That's a great idea. I will go do that right now."

I let out a sigh of relief when she disappeared around the corner of the building. Most of the townsfolk had left by that time, and I wore a crease in the sidewalk in front of the hall while waiting for the lawyer to arrive. I hated the idea of my father in custody.

Forty minutes later, a late-model luxury car pulled up into the spot next to my convertible. A tall, bookish-looking man got out of the car. He wore wire-rimmed glasses, jeans, and a polo shirt. He wasn't what I expected, but I knew not all attorneys dressed like Briar, who always looked like she was ready for a high-powered meeting, even on the weekends.

"Shiloh?" he asked and extended his hand. "I'm Leif Jansen."

I shook it. "Thanks for coming."

"Tell me what happened," he said in a no-nonsense way.

I quickly gave him a summary.

He nodded. "All right." He made his way to the door, and I followed. He spun around. "Where are you going?"

"With you to see my dad."

He shook his head. "You can't. It's best that you don't come in too."

"But—"

He held up his hand. "You're not an attorney. The police won't let you in the interrogation room. I will call you as soon as I leave the building."

"As soon as you leave the building with my father," I said.

"I cannot guarantee the police will let Sully leave at this time."

My heart sank as I watched Leif go into the building without me. The urgency to solve this murder had just been heightened tenfold by my father's arrest. It was time I confronted my cousin about her dealings with Crocker. I didn't care if she was getting ready for opening night or not.

I left my car parked on the street and walked down the block to the theater. I walked around the side of the building to an industrial metal door. It was unlocked, and I held it open for Huckleberry.

He shuffled inside. We found ourselves in a long, narrow hallway, but it was clearly not a place for the viewing public. The lights were bare bulbs overhead, and the floor creaked as Huckleberry and I walked over the old wooden boards.

"We have to get this rigging right," I heard Stacey say. I scooped up Huckleberry and followed the sound of my cousin's voice. She stood with a stagehand next to a rope and pulley system. She wore a pioneer dress, and with her hands on her hips, she looked like a schoolmarm disappointed with her student. "The rigging has to move with ease." She tugged on the ropes. "Fix it."

"What are you working on?" I asked as I stepped closer.

She dusted off her hands and eyed me. "The fly system is giving us fits."

"Fly…like a bug?" I asked.

She gave me a withering look. "No, it's the theatrical rigging that raises and lowers the scene." She glared at the stagehand. "I thought we had it under control."

The younger man ducked his head and concentrated on the ropes in front of him.

She glanced back to me "Where's Uncle Sully? He's missed half of dress rehearsal."

"About that, can I talk to you in private?"

She scowled but followed me to a corner of backstage. I told her Dad was under arrest.

"That's the most ridiculous thing I've ever heard. It's insane to think he would kill anyone. You're more likely to be the killer."

"Thanks," I muttered.

"Stacey," a voice said, and Wes appeared. "The cast wants to know what you want to go over next."

I stared at Wes. "What are you doing here?"

"I'm in the play," he said.

"You are?" I asked.

"Just the understudy."

"You're the understudy for what part?" I asked.

"All of them," he said.

"*All* of them?"

Stacey put her hands on her hips. "He's exaggerating. Wes is the understudy for all the male parts, and I am for all the female parts. Of course, with Shannon out of the play, I will be playing the role of Calpurnia."

"I lucked out," Wes said. "All the guys are still in it, so I get all the perks of being in the play without actually having to do it."

"You should have been knocking on wood. Shiloh just told me some very upsetting news. My uncle might not be here opening night. You will have to fill in for the soothsayer."

Wes swallowed. "Really?"

"I hope you learned the lines." She glared at him.

He swallowed.

I bet Wes hadn't bothered to learn any of the lines in the play.

"Stacey," I said. "I need to talk to you about another matter."

She scowled at me. "What other bad news do you have?"

"I know you—"

My answer was cut off by my cell phone ringing. It was Leif. "I have to take this."

"And we need to get back to rehearsal," my cousin said.

I frowned at her as I put my phone to my ear. Wasn't she even concerned that her elderly uncle was under arrest?

I answered the call.

"Sully has been officially charged with Jefferson Crocker's murder."

"How is that possible?" I pressed her hand against her cheek in horror.

"The evidence. Crocker was killed with his gun. He had a motive over not wanting Crocker investing in the farm. He left a threatening voicemail before he died, and he was seen at the scene of the crime by at least five people."

I gasped. When he put it that way, it seemed there was no hope of clearing my father's name.

"I think the judge will let your father go home on house arrest starting tomorrow because of his advanced age," Leif went on as if it were business as usual. "Unfortunately, I couldn't make that happen tonight."

"What should I do?" I asked.

"Go home, Shiloh," the attorney said. "Let me take care of all this. I'll call as soon as I know more."

"But—"

"Do not get involved in this. Do not get it in your head you can help," he said. "You will only make it worse for your father if you do."

Fat chance on me following that order.

Chapter Thirty-Five

I tried to talk to Stacey again before leaving the theater, but she avoided me with the skill of a professional dodgeball player. I finally gave up for the moment, but I would not rest until Stacey answered some questions.

It was so strange to go back to the farmhouse without my father and know he wouldn't be spending the night there at all. Wandering the Bellamy property as darkness slowly fell, I knew I had to do all I could to help him. Leif would do his part, but I had to find the real killer. I could not have my father spending his golden years in prison. Going over the investigation at the kitchen table, I realized there was a vital lead I hadn't fully pursued, and it was time to finally get some answers. Since I had never heard back from Kristy on the strange woman at the farmers market, I texted her to meet up the next morning. I needed answers, and Kristy was out of time.

As the first light of Friday morning crested Bellamy Farm, I headed back to the farmers market. Kristy was helping install a new booth in the lot that morning, and I would not leave until I finally found out about the woman who knocked me over the day of the murder.

Throughout the summer, the farmers market was two days a week: Wednesday and Saturday. So when I went to the old high school parking lot early Friday morning, I wasn't expecting to run into the normal hustle and bustle. Huckleberry happily walked on his leash just ahead of me, stopping every so often to take in all the interesting smells the farmers market had to offer. I wished I could be as happy. I was on edge over my father's arrest. I could hardly sleep the night before. I kept thinking of him being trapped in jail.

The booths were there because many of them stayed up for the whole season, their wares stored away behind locked compartments or cleaned from the shelves. Walking among the empty displays, I would have never known the upset that happened at the market just days ago. Minnie's honey stand was still missing, but other than that, everything was back to normal.

I stopped at a wildflower booth that had its sales window shaped like a sunflower. Huckleberry smelled the petals of the wooden flower that he could reach, which admittedly weren't many. I loved how creative the booths were. I began to daydream about what my booth would look like when, if all went well, I had one here next summer.

There were so many things I wanted to do with the farm. Maybe not all of them would be possible right away with Crocker's money off the table, but I knew if I worked hard enough, they would come together in due time. Then there was Grandma Bellamy's…I guess I had to call it *treasure*. Maybe that would be the key to all my plans, but I still didn't have the faintest idea what the heart of the farm was.

I wanted to plant wildflowers to attract bees to pollinate the fruit trees and fields. The cherry grove needed to be brought back to life, and so much more had to be done. Baby steps. I just needed to take it one step a time. As much as I wanted a booth at the farmers market, I knew I was a long way off from earning it. That wasn't why I was at the empty market that morning. Kristy knew the woman who nearly ran me over the morning I found Crocker's body. I just had to convince her to tell me who it was. It was time I put this murder investigation to rest.

As it turned out, I wouldn't need to ask. Ahead of me, a dark-haired woman walked through the market with a clipboard and a pencil. She stopped at each booth, walked around it, and made a note on the paper in front of her.

I stared at her. It was the woman. It was the woman who knocked into Huckleberry and me that first day at the market. She was the one I was looking for. I couldn't believe my luck!

She saw me, and her eyes went wide. Without a word, she ran off.

"Hey!" I called after her.

The woman kept running.

I scooped up Huckleberry and went after her, but she was too fast, and she wasn't running while trying to hold on to a pug.

Kristy must have heard the commotion, because she stepped out of the trailer that was her office, stepped into the woman's path, and stopped her. The younger woman clung to Kristy's arms.

"What's going on here?" Kristy wanted to know.

"I saw her in the market, and she ran away from me," I said, out of breath.

"Mercedes?" Kristy asked.

I stared at Kristy. "You know her?"

"Of course I do. This is my cousin, Mercedes Garcia. Mercedes, why'd you run away from Shiloh?"

"Because she chased me."

I set Huckleberry onto the blacktop. "I didn't chase you. You took off before I started after you." I looked from Mercedes to Kristy and back again. "She was the person who ran away from the honey booth just before I found Crocker's body."

Kristy frowned but didn't seem the least bit surprised by this revelation.

"Did you know?" I asked Kristy.

Kristy sighed. "We didn't want to get involved. Mercedes is here on a work visa. We hope she can stay here permanently. We have six more months to get all her papers in order to apply for permanent resident status, or she will have to go back. She's a bright girl. She wants to go to college here."

"What about a student visa?" I asked.

"She could apply for one, but that's not the reason she came into the country. It's likely if she wanted a student visa, she would have to leave the country and apply for reentry. It's a scary risk to take. There is a chance she won't be approved again. The fact that she got a work visa at all is some kind of miracle."

I nodded. "Mercedes, can you please tell me what you know?"

"I didn't kill anyone," Mercedes said.

"Tell Shiloh what happened," Kristy said softly.

"I can't," she said.

"You have to," I said. "My father was arrested last night for the murder."

"What?" Kristy asked.

"He was arrested last night." I turned to her cousin. "Please, Mercedes. You have to help my dad if you can."

"I—I saw the man shoot him from a pickup truck, but he was not old."

"What man?" I asked.

Mercedes's face fell.

"Mercedes, you have to tell us," Kristy said.

She looked pained as she stared intently at her cousin. "It was your friend Wes."

Kristy and I gasped.

"I think he saw me, so I have been hiding." She grabbed Kristy's hand. "I have been so afraid."

"You should have gone straight to the police," I said.

"I know, but like I told you, I was scared. I am afraid of Wes, but I have other reasons too." She took a breath. "I'm in this country on a work permit. If I'm involved with a crime, even just as a witness, they can send me back to Mexico. I'm not in this country illegally. I know that's what many people think. I have my papers." She took a breath. "But I know people who are here legally can also be sent away if the government finds you to be a nuisance."

Kristy rubbed her cousin's arm. "We can understand that, but we have to talk to the police. We won't let them send you away. We have to tell the truth."

"We have to tell the police," I said.

Kristy nodded. "You make the call."

I nodded. Tears came to my eyes knowing that my father was just minutes away from being set free.

Then Kristy turned back to Mercedes. "Are you sure it was Wes? Was there anyone else? Was there anyone else around right before the shooting?"

"It was him." Mercedes hung her head as if she were somehow responsible for Wes's sin.

"I'll make the call," I said. I started to step away.

Kristy patted her cousin on her arm and spoke softly to her in Spanish. Mercedes nodded and went inside the trailer.

I had the phone poised in my hand, ready to call the chief.

"Can we talk a second?" Kristy asked.

"Kristy, my dad is in prison." Why wasn't she getting my sense of urgency here?

"Please don't blame Mercedes for not talking sooner. Things with immigration are tense, and of course she would be nervous."

I nodded, knowing this. My heart softened just a tad. "It's so complicated," I said, beginning to fully understand Mercedes's hesitation about coming forward as a witness.

"It is. Much more complicated than when my parents came here over forty years ago. They still might not have been welcomed with opened arms, but I think farmers realized they needed their help. The climate has changed literally and politically." She rested her hand on her stomach. "My prayer is by the time these two little ones are adults, things will be different. There's no easy answer to any of it. That's the most frustrating thing. Everyone should be judged on individual merit or individual reasons for being here. The system is just too overwhelmed for that. That's how we are where we are today."

I nodded.

"That being said, the killer must be caught. Go ahead and make the call."

I nodded and lifted the phone to my ear. Dad was going to be free.

Chapter Thirty-Six

E very townsperson in Cherry Glen was talking about Wes's arrest, and they wanted me to share my part in the story. I went from Cherry Glen's most wanted in the court of public opinion to a sought-after celebrity. Jessa's Place was not safe for me right now, and I planned to avoid it for the next few days if not the next few weeks. I was as reluctant in my new role as I had been in the last. No matter what he had done, Wes had been my friend. Rumors, I knew from personal experience, did more harm than good.

Even so, having my father released from jail was a relief, and I took him straight home. He said he wanted to take a nap in his own bed before the play that night. When I said he didn't have to act considering the last twenty-four hours he had had, he replied, "The show must go on."

After Dad was settled, I paced around, knowing I should try to figure out what my grandmother meant about the heart of the farm, but I was still distracted by the murder.

My nightmare was over. Dad was in the clear. I was in the clear too. I should have felt relieved. But I didn't. Something about the murder still bothered me. One of those things was: I didn't know why Wes had committed the crime.

I removed my phone from my pocket again and texted Quinn. "Can I ask you a favor?"

The text came back immediately. "Of course."

That was all I needed to hear.

A half hour later, I was parking my convertible behind town hall for the second time in less than twenty-four hours. This time, I didn't plan on going through the front door. I told Huckleberry to stay in the car. The top was down, and I knew he would enjoy the nap in the afternoon sunshine.

I found Quinn by the back door of the hall, right where he'd promised he would be.

He smiled at me. "I could get in so much trouble for this."

I looked up at him. "Then why are you doing it?"

"Hazel would want me to."

I nodded.

He opened the door with his passkey, and we went inside. We were already in what I had come to think of as "the linoleum portion" of the old building.

"This way to the jail cell."

"The jail cell?" I asked.

He smiled. "There is only one in Cherry Glen. We don't have much crime around here."

At least the town hadn't had much crime until recently.

Quinn used his passkey again, and we entered a room with a jail cell in one corner. Wes was in the cell, sitting on a cot. He stared down at his folded hands.

"Can I get some water?" Wes asked. He blinked when he saw it was Quinn and me. "Shi, what are you doing here?" He stood up and came to the cell's bars.

"I needed to talk to you."

He hung his head. "I'm sorry, Shi."

"Did you kill Jefferson Crocker?" I asked. I had to hear his answer, straight from the source.

"I did! But it's not my fault."

I stared at him. He'd pulled the trigger. How could it not be his fault?

He must have seen the doubt on my face, because he said, "It's not my fault because I didn't know the gun was loaded. Yes, I took the gun from the theater, but it was only to threaten Crocker. I never planned to kill him. I would never point a loaded gun at someone." He said this like pointing an unloaded gun at someone was okay.

"Wes, why did you threaten him?" I asked.

Wes walked across his cell and sat on the cot.

"Shi, we don't have much time," Quinn said.

I nodded so he'd know I had heard him, but all my concentration was on Wes. "Wes, tell me."

He jumped off the cot. "Because he was double-crossing me. I did so much for him and his wind farm, putting my own reputation on the line, and he owed me."

An idea dawned on me. "You were the one who convinced the court to throw out the bird report on the wind farm. Hedy said it was someone with environmental connections."

"I did." He sat on the cot again.

"But you acted like you didn't know the report was tampered with when I told you what Hedy said about it." I shook my head. Of course he would lie. He was a murderer.

"And Crocker offered to pay me handsomely for discrediting the report." He looked up at me with tears in his eyes. "You have to understand. I'm a park ranger. I make very little money, and my wife is a teacher. Her contract wasn't renewed for next year due to budget cuts. I have two kids who are just a few short years away from college. I needed the money."

"But what about the birds you claimed to have loved? What about the environment you promised to protect?" I asked.

He didn't answer me.

"Geez, man," Quinn said. "There were other ways you could have approached Crocker without a gun, or you could have at least gotten out of your truck and faced him like a man."

"Like I told you, I didn't know the gun was loaded!" Wes exclaimed. "I just wanted to scare him, to show him I meant business."

I frowned when Quinn mentioned the truck. Something had bothered me from the moment Chief Randy said that Crocker had been shot from above. "If you shot him from the truck, how did the gun end up under the honey booth?"

Quinn's face flashed red. "I was so shocked and horrified over what I'd done, I threw the gun from the truck. It slid under the booth. I thought about retrieving it, but I didn't want to be caught standing over the dead body."

Like I had been, I thought.

"Did you tell the police that?" I asked.

"Yes, but they don't care, Shiloh. I killed a man. No matter what happens, I have to live with that the rest of my life."

"There is still the problem of how the bullets got into the gun," I said.

"I don't know. I didn't put them there. In every rehearsal, the guns have been empty."

My mind reeled. Wes was my friend, but could I say I really knew him at all after all this time? Could I really trust what he said was true?

I thought back to the rehearsal, to the scene when the senate shot the mayor in the role of Julius Caesar. My senses had tingled when I watched it the day before. Because it was impossible in the smoke from the blanks to know who shot which gun.

Quinn put a hand on my arm. "Shiloh, we've got to go."

I nodded and turned to leave.

"Shi!" Wes called out to me.

I faced him again.

"I'm sorry." His voice was low. "You were always a good friend to me, and I'm sorry I put you and your father through this. Sully was always good to me when we were kids."

I nodded. I couldn't think of a word to say.

When Quinn and I were outside the police station again, Quinn said, "The murder is solved. You should be proud of yourself. You were a big help bringing it to the end."

"I don't think it's the real end," I said. "Wes said he didn't know the gun was loaded. Someone loaded that gun with the intent to kill Crocker or someone else. I'm thinking it was someone else. Wes didn't plan to confront Crocker. He was desperate."

"Don't you know Wes would say anything to make himself look better?"

"I don't think he's lying."

"Like he wasn't lying to you for days after the murder?" Quinn folded his arms. "He framed you and your father for murder, Shiloh. You need to remember that you were just moments away from being arrested yourself, and your ill father spent a night in jail because of him."

"I know but…"

He sighed. "I thought bringing you here would end it, and we could move on."

"Move on to what?" I asked.

He ignored my questions and asked, "Why aren't you ready to let this go?"

"Let it go?" I asked. I felt annoyance rising in me.

"Yes. That's why I let you inside to speak with Wes in the first place. I thought it would convince you the police got their man."

"Yes, Wes killed Crocker, but…"

Quinn folded his arms. "Nothing changes the fact that he's the one responsible for Crocker's death."

I stared at him. "You're right, but there's more going on here. That gun was supposed to be used in the play. The play where Julius Caesar is killed. You see where I'm going with this?"

"The mayor," Quinn said, his eyes going wide.

"Right. If we know who might want to kill him—the mayor—then we can find the person who started this chain reaction that led to Crocker's death."

"What are you going to do now?"

"I'm going to go to the theater. I need to be there in a half hour to get the box office ready for opening night anyway. Maybe I can steal away a minute and speak to the mayor before the performance. My dad should be there by now. He planned to drive himself."

"After what he's been through? He's a lot tougher than me."

"Than me too," I said.

"Be careful, Shiloh. I don't want anything to happen to you." He broke eye contact. "Hazel has grown very fond of you."

As much as I liked Hazel, I was disappointed that was his only reason.

Chapter Thirty-Seven

"Friends, Romans, countrymen, lend me your ears. I come to bury Caesar, not to praise him. The evil that men do lives after them; the good is oft interred with their bones. So let it be with Caesar—'"

"Cut!" Stacey shouted. She was dressed in her petticoats and bustle dress for her part as Calpurnia. "Cut! Say it with a little more feeling. This is the big eulogy of the play. You have to give it everything you have. This is your big moment. Don't waste it on a half-hearted speech. You are beseeching the people to have sympathy for Caesar and to remember all he has done for them."

The shoulders of the actor playing Mark Antony sagged. "I thought I was doing that."

"Not very well." Stacey tapped her script. "The performance is in three hours. We all have to be on point."

On the stage, Mayor Loyal as Julius Caesar lay in a wooden coffin. He sat up. "Can we take a break? I need to visit the little boy's room."

Stacey threw up her hands. "Fine. Take ten minutes, everyone. Just ten minutes. It's not like opening night is tonight. It does not hurt to go over your lines a few more times."

The cast scrambled from the stage like mice fleeing the light before Stacey could change her mind. My father in his costume shuffled off with the rest of them. My cousin dropped her script on the table in the corner of the stage and sat on a chair. "You're late."

"Do you have eyes in the back of your head?"

She stood up and turned around. "No, but I can hear. There was a distinct sound of dog toenails on the floor."

I looked down at Huckleberry. He wasn't great when it came to being an undercover sidekick.

"It doesn't matter. The play seems to be coming apart at the seams. I'm hoping the old adage is true that a bad dress rehearsal makes for a great opening night. I don't know what I will do if this fails. I put so much into it."

"Even your half of Bellamy Farm," I said. It might not be the best time to bring up her selling her half of the farm to Crocker, but I was tired of playing games with her or anyone else in Cherry Glen.

She stared at me. "How did you know that?"

"I went down to the town planning office to see why Crocker had such an interest in Bellamy Farm. That's where I learned that your portion of Bellamy Farm belongs to Crocker."

She folded her arms across her chest. "What are you going to do about it? Are you going to tell Uncle Sully? And break his heart?"

"How would it be me breaking his heart? I'm not the one who sold the farm."

"It was mine to sell. I inherited it from my father." Her mouth drew into a stubborn line, but her hands fidgeted. "Look, I was going to tell you. I even followed you out to the orchard once when I knew Uncle Sully was here rehearsing. But when I saw you, I realized I didn't owe you that conversation." Her eyes narrowed at me.

I remembered the menacing shadow in the cherry orchard, the twig breaking beneath someone's rushing feet. That was Stacey?

"But don't you think Dad deserves that conversation? You should tell him."

Dad shuffled onto the stage. "No one needs to tell me. I heard everything." He stared at Stacey as if seeing her for the very first time.

Stacey paled. "I'm sorry, Uncle."

He shook his head. "It was yours to sell."

I stared at him. "You are going to let her off the hook? Just like that?"

He frowned. "I did a lot of thinking when I was in jail last night, and I came to the conclusion that I need to change some things. I have been holding on to the farm too tightly but not making it any better. You two are the new generation. If you want to sell it, sell it. If you want to make it into something new, you can do that too." He cleared his throat as if he might cry. "I don't want to risk the time I have left with either of you fighting over the farm."

I bit my lip. There was so much I wanted to say about him giving Stacey a pass, and I knew this dispute with my cousin wasn't over. Huckleberry sat on my foot as if to tell me I had his full support. At that moment, my phone chimed with an incoming text, and Stacey narrowed her eyes.

"Turn that thing off and leave it backstage. I don't want any distractions while you're running the ticket booth."

I grumbled and dropped it on a table behind the curtain before I excused myself and walked away.

I found Mayor Loyal in the dressing room in the back of the theater, reading over the script.

I knocked on the doorframe.

He looked up from the script, and our eyes met in the mirror. "Ah, Miss Bellamy, it's nice to see you here. You must be most relieved that the killer has been arrested. Sorry for that mess of thinking you did it." He shrugged. "And then your father. You have to admit the evidence against him was damning. I hope Sully will understand."

I bit my lip to hold back a smart retort and took one small step inside the room. Huckleberry remained outside the room. "I know the police have arrested Wes, who shot Crocker, but I don't know if they got their culprit yet."

"What? What do you mean? The culprit, as you put it, is sitting in jail right now. Chief Randy assures me the streets of Cherry Glen are safe again."

"That may not be the complete truth." I told him what Wes told me and my theory that he was the intended victim for the person who put bullets into the gun.

The mayor laughed. "Oh, you have quite an imagination, don't you, Shiloh? Too much time in LA, playing at movies. Why would anyone want to hurt me? I'm the town mayor."

"Someone put real bullets in that gun knowing it would be used against you on stage. That's a conspiracy to murder."

"Conspiracy to murder." He laughed. "You *have* been in California too long," he said again. "Things like that might happen in the big city, but not in Cherry Glen. Wes Sumner killed Jefferson Crocker. Everyone knows that."

"But he didn't put the bullets in the gun," I argued. "I believe he was telling the truth in this case."

"Because killers always tell the truth," the mayor said with a chuckle. "I would not have thought someone from the big city would be so naïve."

"I'm just trying to tell you that you might be in danger."

He laughed again and picked up his script, signaling the conversation was over.

"I should get back to the ticket booth," I said.

"That's a good place for you, Shiloh. Stick to ticket sales, and leave the detective work to the police." He waved me away.

I was fuming when I stomped out of the dressing room. Huckleberry hurried after me. Here I was, trying to protect the mayor and tell him he was in danger, and he belittled me.

Just outside the room, I heard feet moving backstage. I stood in the dark for a moment. Had someone been eavesdropping on my conversation with the mayor? It could have just as easily been a stagehand who was in a hurry to get back to work before Stacey yelled at him. Shaking my head, I went to the box office.

Minnie waited for me outside the ticket booth. "Finally." She put her hands on her hips. "Where have you been? I thought I was going to have to run the concessions stand and the ticket booth all by myself."

"I'm here." I wasn't in the mood to argue with Minnie.

She sniffed. "Well then, I'll get back to my snacks."

What about an apology? I wondered. Minnie had accused me of murder on more than one occasion, but I seriously doubted I would ever hear an "I'm sorry" from her.

Huckleberry waddled into the booth and curled up on the pillow I had brought him to sleep on during the performance.

There was a line of people outside the theater ready to come in for the show. Stacey's opening night was going to be a great success.

And I wondered if it was just the cover the real murderer needed to make a clean getaway.

Chapter Thirty-Eight

T hree hours later, the show ended without a hitch, and the only murder was Caesar's on stage. I watched from the back of the theater, leaning against the wall. The crowd clapped, and Stacey came out for another bow. She beamed at the audience, placing her hands together and bowing twice more. She mouthed "thank you." She had a lot to be proud of; the play was wonderful. It had, in fact, been a great opening night after a bad dress rehearsal.

She went backstage, and the curtain came down. The audience stood, and I slipped out of the theater to get back to the box office to man my post and answer any stray theater questions as patrons left. To my surprise, I found Quinn and Hazel waiting for me. Hazel sat on the floor petting Huckleberry.

"I didn't know you two were going to the play."

Quinn raised an eyebrow. "I texted you before the show letting you know we were coming."

I checked my back pocket absently before remembering, "Oh shoot, I left my phone backstage. I must have missed it. How did you like it?"

"I had to watch it for school. We were supposed to do one cultural event over the summer, so this counts," Hazel said. "But it was okay. I wish I didn't have to write a report on it though. I hate writing."

I gathered up the brochures about upcoming performances and stacked them neatly on the counter before turning back to Hazel. "Maybe you don't like to write because you haven't found the story you want to tell just yet."

She looked at me. "Nope. It's just not my thing."

Quinn shrugged. "My daughter is brutally honest. She got that from her mother."

"It's kind of refreshing. Not many people say what they think. I think that's becoming even more apparent to me since I came back to Cherry Glen. It seems like everyone in this town had lied to me a time or two."

"Myself included?" he asked.

"I don't know yet."

He threw back his head and laughed. "You have the brutally honest thing going too."

I gave him a small smile. "Maybe I have a new goal to be refreshing."

"Are you going to the after-party?" Quinn asked. "Stacey invited us."

"I haven't decided. It's been a crazy few days. I might just want to go home, but I do want to support my dad on his big night. He did great."

Hazel stood up. "You should just come. They are having cherry cake."

I smiled. "I guess you two have talked me into it."

"Great! You can help me pick out the people I need to talk to for my paper."

"You will probably want to start with Stacey since she was the director and producer. She'd be my first choice."

"Thanks," Hazel said. "Also, can I come over tomorrow to see Esmeralda?"

"Sure." I glanced at Quinn. "If it's okay with your dad."

Quinn smiled. "We both will be over. I want to meet this special cat."

"Yay!" Hazel pumped her fist in the air.

The play's audience was filling the lobby, and a line was forming in front of the box office for questions and upcoming performance times. "I'd better get back to this. I'll see you at Jessa's Place." At least the after-party was being held at a place I knew and loved.

Hazel waved, and they left.

After answering what felt like a million questions and waving to Stacey and Dad as they ushered the last of the patrons out and gave me the keys to lock up the front doors, I went into the theater to grab my cell phone from backstage.

The auditorium was eerie now that the theater had emptied out. I grabbed my cell off the table backstage and maneuvered around the props still scattered about, thinking about how quickly Stacey and my dad had rushed out to join the cast party. My phone beeped with a text message from Quinn, interrupting my thoughts. "Everyone is at Jessa's. We're waiting for you."

I texted back that I was on my way and smiled. Even after the time I'd had in Cherry Glen, an evening celebrating with friends did sound good.

I took a step onto the stage and pulled up short when I saw two men standing there in the empty theater. The mayor and his son.

"Ah, Shiloh, I'm glad you're here," Baker said, spotting me, the single stage light left on casting his charming smile into a menacing leer.

I brushed my hair out of my face. "What are you doing here? I thought everyone was at the party."

Baker smiled. "We were waiting for you, right, Dad?"

That was when I noticed that the mayor was sweating profusely in the spotlight.

"What's going on?" I looked from one man to the other.

"Well, I was catching up with Dad after the show, and he told me you're not completely convinced that Wes was solely responsible for Crocker's death. In fact, he told me you think Dad was the intended victim for that bullet. So when we saw you sneak back here alone, we figured it might be time for a chat."

My fingers felt cold under Baker's stare and the mayor's frantic gaze. "I don't see how that's any of your concern, Baker." I started toward the steps.

"Shiloh!" Baker called.

I turned around and saw he now had a gun in his hand and was pointing it at his father.

"I think you want to stay for this, since you were able to unravel most of it already." Baker grinned, and my stomach plummeted in fear. I tried to think of an escape route—how could I save the mayor and get out of here unscathed?

"Baker," the mayor said. "Let her go. You meant for me to get the bullet."

Baker glared at his father. "You planned to narc to the town council about me. You were snooping for more evidence to ruin me. What choice did I have?" He glanced back at me. "Dear old Dad had become suspicious when I was buying a new home and so many new suits. He knew what I made as town planner, and it wasn't much. You see, for me, it was hard to adjust to this small-town lifestyle after making a good income in the city. I had to find another way to make some money. I offered my services to Jefferson Crocker to help convince the town council that his improvements were a good idea. He readily agreed."

"You took bribes," I said, hoping to keep Baker talking as I searched for a way out. That was when I noticed the fly system that Stacey had been worried about just in my line of sight back-stage. I inched slowly toward it as Baker retrained his eyes on his shaking father.

"I like to call it 'compensation for a job well done.' This town has come back from the brink because of Crocker and me. My father and the rest of the town should have been grateful. Instead, they looked at every new business with suspicion. I found it tire-some. I worked hard for this ungrateful place and deserved some-thing more, since gratitude was difficult to come by."

I glanced up and noted the large cabin setting dangling above where Baker stood.

"What are you going to do?" I prompted, praying Baker wouldn't notice as I ran my eyes along the rope holding the cabin aloft, finally tracing to the corresponding fly system brake.

"Since you and Dad are the ones who know my story, I'm sorry to say I have to get rid of you."

My eyes flew back to Baker, who was slowly turning in my direction. Get rid of us? That sounded bad, like really bad.

"When you came to town, I thought maybe Cherry Glen wouldn't be so bad after all. I liked you, Shiloh. I really did," Baker said.

My heart thundered in my chest, and I inched toward the rope in the fly system. *If I could just reach the rope.* It was just two feet from me now.

"It gives me no pleasure to kill you too. But I can't risk going to jail. I can't." He leveled the gun at me.

Not taking an extra second to consider whether or not it would work, I leaped over to the fly system and yanked the brake free as a shot rang out, pinging against the rising counterweight. With a mighty crash, the cabin fell from the rafters and on top of Baker, flinging the gun from his hand. I rushed over and kicked it off the stage.

"Baker! Are you all right?" the mayor said and kneeled by Baker, who was pinned to the ground by the scenery.

"Get away from me," Baker snarled. "If you had loved me, you wouldn't have threatened to report me to the council and gotten us into this mess!"

The mayor fell back like he had been shot.

Epilogue

After Baker was arrested, the mayor and his son were the talk of the town. For once, it wasn't me, or worse, my father as the main topic of conversation, and I was grateful. Baker was charged with attempted murder, and Wes was charged with manslaughter. It was still murder but a lesser charge. In any case, they both would be in prison for a long while. The mayor didn't fare much better. After it was discovered he knew about his son taking bribes but hadn't come forward yet, the town council asked him to step down.

A few days after the mayor announced his resignation, I tried to put my rocky return to Cherry Glen behind me. I threw myself into work on the farm. I got the riding mower working, cleaned out the barn, and finished mending the front fence. I was exhausted, but it was a good kind of tired. The kind of tired you get from a job well done.

However, I was so exhausted that anything that interrupted my sleep was unwelcome, so when a noise scared me awake and made me sit straight up in bed, I was less than cheerful about it.

I was even more upset because I had been awakened from a dream about my grandmother. In the dream, I asked Grandma

Bellamy for her forgiveness for leaving the farm. "You expected me to stay, marry Logan, and take care of everything. I'm so sorry I let you down." Tears rolled down my face.

"You didn't let me down. I always knew in my heart you would leave someday. I thought both you and Logan would go. I'm sorry it didn't happen for you that way, but I always knew you would come back." I felt her hand on my face and was just about to ask her where her treasure might be hidden.

I sat up in bed, wondering what woke me, when I heard a truck rumble up the driveway. The sun was just dawning outside.

Huckleberry and Esmeralda slept on the foot of my bed undisturbed by the noise. "What can it be now?" I asked them.

I went to the window and saw Quinn's truck parked in front of the barn.

"What on earth?" I grabbed my robe and shoved my feet into an old pair of tennis shoes before hurrying down the stairs.

Huckleberry and Esmeralda followed me all the way out the front door. There was a chill in the early morning air, and I wrapped my robe more tightly around me. "Quinn, what are you doing here? Is Hazel okay?"

He was in his fireman's uniform and looked exhausted. "Yes, she's fine. She's at my mom's. I was just about to go get her. My shift just ended."

I relaxed. "Oh, then why…"

"I came here because I wanted to tell you something. It's been eating away at me ever since you moved back."

Huckleberry sat on my feet like he was guarding me from what Quinn was about to say, and Esmeralda sat at my side. "Okay," I murmured.

"That night that Logan died—"

I waved my hand. "We already talked about all that. You already apologized for what happened at the funeral."

"It's not that." He took a breath. "That night that Logan died. He was going to Traverse City to get you because he had decided he would go to California with you. He didn't want you to give up on your dreams, and he didn't want to be away from you either. He was happy. He wanted to marry you and be with you, even if that meant leaving everything he knew behind."

"H—how do you know this?"

He looked at me. "Because he came to me after your fight and told me his plan. I tried to talk him out of it. I told you weren't worth that. I said this because I was selfish and didn't want him to leave Cherry Glen. He said you were worth everything and he was going. I have never seen him so determined or so happy."

A knot tightened in my stomach. "I—I don't know what to say."

"You don't have to say anything, but now you know the truth about how much Logan loved you. It's important you know that."

"Thank you," I murmured. My mind was racing as I tried to process what he had said.

He walked back to his truck and opened the door. "Can Hazel come over this afternoon? She's dying to see Esmeralda again."

"Yes, I would like that," I said.

He nodded and drove away.

The sun was rising now. The sky was pink, yellow, and orange over the tall grass and soybean fields. Huckleberry spotted a cricket and leaped after it. Esmeralda followed suit. I was glad to be home.

SHILOH'S
Quick Farm Tips

Want a raised bed for your garden? A quick and easy way to create one is with cinder blocks. With twenty standard-sized blocks, you can make a sixteen-inch-high rectangle. The blocks can be bought at any hardware or home improvement store for a dollar or less each. Even better, there are no power tools or tools of any kind required. You are literally stacking blocks like you did as a toddler. Remember to be careful. Each block does weigh around thirty pounds, and you may need help.

After the rectangle is constructed, fill the garden bed with grass clippings or compost from your yard. Egg shells and coffee grounds from your kitchen are great additions. Do this a few weeks before adding topsoil so that the grass can soak up the moisture from the ground underneath and begin to decompose. Then you will have a strong basis for a healthy garden. In addition, you can add in peat and cow manure to enrich the top soil. If you are hoping for an organic garden, always check the packages for names of chemicals that might be present.

Some edible plants that do well in raised beds are herbs, lettuce, tomatoes, blueberries, carrots, and onions. If you are looking to plant a flower garden, perennials like Shasta daisies, black-eyed Susans, and coneflowers are good choices too.

The benefit of raised beds is drainage. Most plants do better in soil that is well drained rather than overly damp. The elevation of a raised bed allows the garden to drain more easily, producing healthier plants and many times a higher yield of vegetables.

Happy farming & gardening!
Shiloh Bellamy

Acknowledgments

W hen I met my fiancé, he told me, "I own a farm. I want to make it into something better. All organic. A place safe for the birds, bees, and wild animals." My reaction was shock. I never in my life had any plans to have a farm or be a farmer, but in that moment, I realized if I wanted to be with this man, the farm was something I would have to accept. Even though I have written about hundreds of farms in my Amish mysteries over the years, I had never actually worked on one before. The most I knew about it was from books and friends who grew up on farms. All agreed it was hard work. For a girl from the suburbs who had things like city sewer and water and a Target within two miles from my home, it was more than a little bit overwhelming.

The more I worked on the farm, the more I realized that I could write a book about my experience, and that's how *Farm to Trouble* came to be.

First, I want to thank my fiancé, David Seymour, for introducing me to a whole new world. Yes, the farm is hard work, but I wouldn't trade it. I've learned so much about myself and about us through caring for it. And as always, I thank him for his loving support of me while I wrote this book—over the holidays, no less—and every book I write. He is also the kindest and funniest man I have ever met. I am blessed.

Thanks, too, to my agent, Nicole Resciniti. When I pitched the farm idea to her, she immediately asked for a proposal. I'm grateful she embraces my ideas and lets me try new things… Not all ideas are good.

Special thanks to friend and super birder Sarah Preston, who helped me be in the know about all things birds.

Thank you also to friends Delia, Mariellyn, and Kimra, who helped with moral support and/or feedback on the book. And to my canine nephew, Pedro, who inspired Huckleberry.

Gratitude to Sourcebooks for buying this series, especially to my editors, Anna Michels, MJ Johnston, and Jenna Jankowski.

Finally, thank you to God in Heaven, who has blessed my farm both in life and in fiction.

About the Author

Amanda Flower, a *USA Today* bestselling and Agatha Award–winning author of over thirty cozy mystery novels, started her writing career in elementary school when she read a story she wrote to her sixth grade class and had the class in stitches with her description of being stuck on the top of a Ferris wheel. She knew at that moment she'd found her calling of making people laugh with her words. In addition to being an author, Amanda is a former librarian with fifteen years' experience and owns a small farm in Northeast Ohio with her fiancé.